PARKWAY VILLAGE DEC 0 2 2006
BPV

Discarded
Memphis Public Library

84

"If you want me to stop I will," he whispered.

"And if I do not stop you?" she asked, her voice so low that he barely heard her.

"Then I will kiss you again," he breathed, his body afire with the very idea of what would follow. "But stay, and I'll not warrant that I will want to stop myself."

She sighed and lifted her lips to his. "Then kiss me again," she said.

He groaned and caught her lips with his. She gasped then, and hoped he never ceased what he did. Her heart raced, her skin burned. In all her life she'd never felt so alive.

My Lady's Temptation

Denise Hampton

AVON BOOKS
An Imprint of HarperCollins*Publishers*

This is a work of fiction. Names, characters, places, and incidents are products of the author's imagination or are used fictitiously and are not to be construed as real. Any resemblance to actual events, locales, organizations, or persons, living or dead, is entirely coincidental.

AVON BOOKS
An Imprint of HarperCollins*Publishers*
10 East 53rd Street
New York, New York 10022-5299

Copyright © 2002 by Denise Lindow
ISBN: 0-7394-2310-X

All rights reserved. No part of this book may be used or reproduced in any manner whatsoever without written permission, except in the case of brief quotations embodied in critical articles and reviews. For information address Avon Books, an Imprint of HarperCollins Publishers.

Avon Trademark Reg. U.S. Pat. Off. and in Other Countries, Marca Registrada, Hecho en U.S.A.
HarperCollins ® is a registered trademark of HarperCollins Publishers Inc.

Printed in the U.S.A.

Chapter 1

With the skirts of her workaday gowns lifted to her knees, Elianne du Hommet ran, her soldier-escort panting at her heels. Beneath awnings raised against the day's unusual heat, the startled merchants of Knabwell left off their haggling to stare after the sheriff's grown daughter. Chickens squawked and flapped out of her way. Stubble-fed geese, an autumn delicacy, hissed from their wicker carriers.

Elianne's chaperone collided with an unfortunate housewife, spilling the contents of the hapless woman's basket.

"The lord sheriff's business," he shouted to the townswoman, then sprinted after his charge.

As Elianne and her companion flew out onto the higher of Knabwell's two cobbled thoroughfares, the soldier shot a look toward the city's southern gate. "Jesu save us! That's Haydon's party," he cried. "Hurry! Our lord sheriff wants you at the priory before they arrive."

Elianne threw a glance over her shoulder. Not three dozen yards behind her rode a knight upon a dappled steed. He was a big man, broad-shouldered and tall. Beneath his green surcoat, which named him Lord Haydon's man, his mail gleamed like silver. With his helmet off, the knight's hair glinted gold in the sun. His gaze was turned up toward the castle her sire ruled. There was a forceful, forward bend to his body as he sat upon his horse, as if he were eager to reach his destination, or for battle.

At the knight's side rode a dumpling of a woman dressed in sturdy green. Although the broad brim of her straw hat hid her face, there was something in the woman's posture that named her Lady Haydon and no other.

Hat!

Elianne clapped her hands to her bare head and staggered to a halt, leaving her chaperone to lope on alone toward the priory. Oh Lord, not only was her hair uncovered but she wore it in a single tail, instead of decent plaits. She was no married woman and without dowry never would be, but four and twenty was too old to go about with her hair exposed like some virgin bride.

Groaning, Elianne looked at her stained hands; she'd been draining the apple press when her father's messenger had arrived. No matter how tragic the deaths of Lord Haydon and his daughters, or how panicked her father had been since that event, she couldn't meet the grieving widow bearing the marks of the chores that made up her daily life.

Annoyance flared. Acceding without thought to her father's whims had become a bad habit. She shot another glance over her shoulder at Haydon's approaching party. What had she been thinking? She had no more place greeting Haydon's party than there was point to her existence.

"I'm going back," she shouted to her escort.

My father is dead.

Rage churned in Josce FitzBaldwin's belly. He leaned forward in his saddle. His father wasn't just dead. Baldwin of Haydon had been murdered by bandits not worthy to lick his boots. That fact would cost someone his life.

Josce turned his gaze to Knabwell's castle. Set atop a great knob of rock near the city's center, its native limestone walls glared down upon all that lay below it. Towers bulged at every corner, each one wearing a conical cap tiled in dark and gleaming slate. It was there in yon pile of stones that Josce would find the man ultimately at fault for his father's death: Reiner du Hommet, sheriff of this shire.

Josce's mouth tightened. It didn't matter that killing a royal servant meant his own death as well as the damnation of his immortal soul. To satisfy Josce's grief Reiner du Hommet would either capture those murdering thieves and deliver them to him, or the sheriff's blood would flow.

Beside him, Lady Haydon's mare stumbled on the rutted street. Josce's stepmother made a quiet, startled sound and clutched more tightly at her reins. No great rider was Beatrice of Haydon.

Afternoon light streamed through the open weave of his stepmother's hat brim, revealing the dark rings beneath her eyes. Her linen riding attire, damp against this autumn day's unusual heat, hung from her shoulders. She had dropped a stone, maybe two, in weight since receiving news of her husband's and daughters' deaths less than a week ago. Grief had aged her, making her look a full score older than her six and thirty years.

Aye, the only thing keeping Beatrice upright in the saddle was the same need for vengeance that Josce possessed. So great was Beatrice's ambition to avenge her daughters' deaths that she'd set aside her customary dislike for her husband's bastard son to solicit Josce's sword to her cause, begging him to aid her in wreaking her revenge. Josce had gladly given her his vow. For Lady Beatrice, for Clarice and Adelaide and for the love Baldwin had showered on his only son, Josce would be her conduit of retribution.

Treasuring his vow, Josce straightened in his saddle only to catch sight of the most amazing woman racing along the curving lane ahead of him. Jesus God, but she towered a full head over the soldier who accompanied her. Josce was taller than most men he knew, yet she might well be able to look him in the eye.

Not that she wasn't womanly. Her faded blue gowns clung to the slim line of her body, revealing nicely rounded breasts, a narrow waist and lush hips. Her hair, caught in a single curling tail the color of dark honey, bounced from side to side with her every step, not so much as a head scarf to shield it from the world. Not married, then. No surprise that, as tall as she was. Save for a rich dowry, not many men, common or noble, would accept a mate bigger than himself.

The woman abruptly stopped, her hands at her head. As her escort loped on ahead of her, she threw a glance in Josce's direction. He strained to make out her features, wondering if she had a face to match her body, only to relax in disappointment. The distance was too great to offer detail.

Her companion turned to rejoin her and an argument ensued, the woman shaking her head at whatever her escort suggested. Rather than heed her refusal, the soldier grabbed her by the arm, then pulled her along with him until she ran once more. That one so crude might manhandle her named the woman of no consequence. This startled Josce, for there was something of command in her bearing. He watched them round the corner onto a nearby lane, disappearing behind a row of narrow two- and three-storey homes, regretting that he could no longer see her.

"Tell me again this is no mistake. Tell me my babies are truly gone," said his stepmother from her horse beside him, her gaze locked upon some distant spot as she spoke.

That she didn't look at Josce was a reminder that theirs was but a temporary truce. Once Beatrice had what she craved, she'd no doubt reclaim her previous distaste for him. Josce didn't begrudge Beatrice her dislike. To his stepmother his existence was living proof of her greatest failure, Josce being the boy-child she'd been unable to produce for her noble husband.

Beside him, Beatrice drew a shaken breath. "Tell me, for I fight and fight and still cannot make sense of it. How could my daughters leave Haydon two weeks ago in the company of their sire and six of our strongest men only to be slaughtered by some ragged band of thieves?" With each word, her voice tightened, a sign of her battle to govern what ached in her.

"Tell me," she continued, her voice dropping to a pained breath, "that their deaths aren't my fault for wanting my darlings schooled with the same nuns who tutored me." Her eyes squeezed shut. She pressed a fist to her lips. "Why didn't I send them to the convent in Haydon's shire where Emma was raised?" she muttered around her fingers.

Her words stirred Josce's guilt. It wasn't Lady Beatrice's fault that their kin had perished but his own. Why hadn't *he* insisted on accompanying his sire to Knabwell instead of letting his father shoo him off to spend time with friends at a companion's newly acquired manor? Damn him, but he'd been too eager to go, making his friends more precious to him than his own family. As pain stirred, rage rose to consume it.

"Nay, you cannot fault yourself, my lady," Josce commanded her, and himself as well. "All blame belongs to the sheriff. Is he not guardian of the peace here? Yet under his watchful eye your good lord and husband has been murdered, along with two sweet innocents."

His words brought Lady Haydon more upright in her saddle even as she swayed unsteadily. What he could see of her profile might have been carved from stone as she stared ahead of her.

"Aye, it's the sheriff at fault and he who will be held accountable on this very day. There is Baker's Walk." She pointed to the same lane down which the tall woman had turned. "We follow it, then bear east onto Priory Lane, which takes us to the convent's gate."

"The priory? Nay, we go to the castle, to the sheriff's seat." Vengeance howled within him. Josce wanted no delays before he skewered du Hommet, first with his questions, then, later, as vengeance dictated, with his sword.

"Why, when the sheriff already awaits us at the priory?" his stepmother retorted, shooting him a sidelong glance and almost looking at him in the process. "Thus did I command in the messages our man carried to both him and Prioress Gertha this morn."

Josce bit back his desire to scream in frustration. God take him, but he couldn't draw his sword on hallowed ground! What if the sheriff refused to set aside all else to capture the thieves? It was intolerable to think the opportunity to vent what ached in him might arise while his own hands were tied.

"Madam, I thought we went to confront him." Josce did his best to gentle his voice and failed. "How can we do so when we meet at the prioress's office?"

Her laugh was knife-edged. "At the prioress's office! That's not where we'll meet him." As Beatrice spoke, she tilted her head to look directly into his face, peering up at him from beneath her hat's wide brim.

Breath rushed from Josce's lungs as he looked upon her countenance for the first time since they'd broken camp this morn. Her skin was ashen, her eyes clouded, as if she struggled to hold her focus. Her smile was naught but the baring of her teeth.

"We go to the icehouse in their orchard," she said.

Josce stared at her, unnerved. An icehouse would be a cold enough place in which to store bodies whilst they waited on a proper burial. God help him, Beatrice meant to look upon the corpses of their loved ones. He wasn't at all certain she could survive that encounter. "They'll expect us to come to the office," Josce warned, hoping to dissuade her.

Her smile widened, the twist of her lips ugly. It was madness and nothing less he saw in the depths of her gaze. "The portress will tell Mother Gertha where I've gone. She'll come to me bringing the sheriff with her." Beatrice's eyes narrowed. "I want to see his face as I stand beside my cold darlings. I want to hear his excuses when he faces the result of his incompetence. I want him to kneel before me and beg my pardon so I might refuse it!" Her voice rose with every word until she fair shrieked.

Behind them, Haydon's men muttered. Haydon's master-at-arms, Nick of Kent, drew his horse a little forward to send a concerned look at his lord's son. Nick's worry was no less than what Josce already felt. With a lift of his hand Josce signaled that the men should halt. Nick's sigh of relief was audible.

"What are you doing?" Lady Beatrice snapped, a hint of helplessness in her voice. Rightly so. She might be Haydon's lady, but command of her husband's soldiers fell to Josce.

Reaching across the gap between their horses, Josce took her reins, drawing both their mounts to a halt. "Stopping," he replied. "We go no farther until you reconsider this plan of yours, my lady."

"Reconsider?" So violently did the word leave her lips that she again swayed in her saddle.

"Aye, for the sake of your two surviving daughters. You took my oath to serve as your avenger. Let me do as you begged me. You're not strong enough for this. Leave visiting our loved ones for a later moment."

"Upstart!" Beatrice spat the word at him. "You've no right to refuse me anything."

"My right or not," Josce told her, "these men take commands from me. If I tell them to retreat from Knabwell with you, they'll do it."

"Nay, you cannot deny me this," Beatrice cried, then caught her breath. A new slyness took light in her eyes. "Spite me, and I'll exclude you from his burial."

Josce glared at her. Damn her, but she could do it, she could keep him from attending his father's interment. Josce was no heir, but a bastard. With Baldwin gone, Beatrice had the right to refuse Josce any further contact with all things Haydon, including his two surviving half sisters. In her present state she might well do it, no matter that she knew Baldwin of Haydon had been the last of Josce's direct family; his mother and maternal grandparents had passed long ago.

Because of the love his sire had ever showered on him Josce couldn't lose the chance for this final farewell. Even as he despised himself for letting her manipulate him this way he had no choice. Eyes narrowed and jaw tight, he bowed his head. "I am at your command, my lady."

"Not good enough. I want your vow that you'll not stop me in this," she demanded.

"I so vow." Resentment burned in every word.

"Nay, that still isn't enough to bind you, is it?" Beatrice eyed him, unsatisfied, then smiled, the lift of her lips cunning. "You're too clever by half. You'll abandon me at the priory's gate, going to Mother Gertha's office yourself to stop me. I want your holy oath. Vow that you'll not leave my side whilst we're within the priory's walls. Vow, as well, that you'll allow no one else, not these men, not the nuns, to stop me. I will reach the icehouse."

Josce's breath seared from his lungs as her trap closed around him. What choice had he? He lay his hand upon his sword's hilt and gave her what she wanted.

Chapter 2

Down Baker's Walk Elianne and her escort flew. Tall, narrow homes lined this lane, the shutters on their shop windows lifted to reveal the men within working dough and forming loaves. The air around their homes was thick with the yeasty scent of baking.

The street forked, Elianne and her escort veering to the right onto Priory Lane. A clutch of yearling piglets, autumn hams come October, squealed and scattered before them. Here merchants' houses gave way to tiny thatched-roofed cottages, the homes the nuns life-leased to their pensioners. Each house claimed a wee vegetable plot, each plot ending at the priory's perimeter, a tall stretch of wall built from the same stone as the castle Elianne's father ruled. Ivy, still lush and green although it was now early September, tumbled over the top of the wall. In the distance a few treetops could be seen, the occasional red flash speaking of apples in the nuns' orchard, which was the fount of the priory's income.

At a full two storeys tall, pretty carvings trimming the triple arches of its windows, the priory's guest house loomed at the lane's end. Here, Elianne's gasping chaperone fell away to wait beneath its eaves until the time for her return to Coneytrop, her home. The sheriff was ever cautious with his daughter's person when she was away from their estate, and had been since she'd come into her monthly cycles, but Elianne needed no guarding within this women's realm.

Elianne slowed as she neared the priory's great, arched gateway, the portal that connected God's world to man's. As it was on most days, one of the thick oaken doors was thrown wide. Two sisters, clad all in black as befitted their order, stood in the opening.

Of the pair, only the portress belonged here. Mathilde, a plump, cheery woman who loved her duty as greeter, smiled when she saw Elianne. Not so the convent's subprioress, who no doubt waited for the convent's auspicious visitor.

Disapproval clung to every harsh fold of Sister Nilda's face. "You're panting," she said as Elianne stopped before them, "when we taught you no well-bred woman runs." Nilda's French was the clipped and precise tongue spoken by England's upper class.

Elianne's jaw tightened. Their dislike was mutual, formed during the time she'd been a student here. It was hard enough to be the sheriff's burdensome third daughter, a dowry-less, useless woman with no hope of husband, children or career, without tolerating Nilda's venom. "If you must know, I was commanded to haste by my sire," she snapped.

"But of course," Sister Mathilde said, defending a child she liked against a despised superior. "Elianne would run for no other reason."

Nilda's mouth only curled as she looked askance at Elianne's shabby attire and loosened hair. "Your sire may rot for all I care. You won't come anywhere near our exalted and bereaved visitor dressed as you are. Go home and change your gowns."

"You have no right to send me away," Elianne retorted.

Nilda glared up at the sheriff's daughter. "Forward bitch! You'll not speak so to me."

"Sister Subprioress!" the portress gasped, hands at her cheeks.

The subprioress spoke over her lesser-ranking sister. "By our lady, what airs you adopt when all the city knows how degraded your sire's estate has become. So indebted is he that he foully disparaged your sisters, selling them into marriages with peasants for coins." Vicious lights came to life in Nilda's gaze. "But he couldn't rid himself of you, could he? Even a peasant has more sense than to purchase an ill-mannered giant like you. Well, we don't want you either. When our Lord finally yanks Reiner du Hommet's sinful soul from his overbearing body, don't bother begging sanctuary here. I'll see you never get a place, not even as a lay sister."

"I'd rather starve than beg for a crust of bread from you," Elianne retorted, her vehemence hiding the very real fear that starvation after her father's death was exactly the fate awaiting her.

Nilda's mouth opened for a retort, only to be interrupted by the jingle of harness rings and huff of tired horses. Rumbling, wordless echoes of men's voices reached around the guest house's corner to the gateway, announcing the arrival of Lord Haydon's party. The anger drained from Nilda's face.

"They come!" she cried with more excitement than was due so unhappy an advent. Dismissing Elianne without a glance, she bent to slap dust motes from her habit's skirts.

At last free to pass, Elianne started into the gateway, only to have the portress grab her by the arm and pull her a few feet away from Nilda and the gate. "Sister, I need to reach my father," Elianne protested.

Mathilde waved aside her protest. "You'll do your sire's repute no favors should Lady Haydon see you dashing. Instead, wait and follow Sister Nilda and the lady to your father."

Elianne sighed. Despite the tongue-lashing she knew her father would give her for failing him, Mathilde was right. Sprinting like a servant before the lady would only further upset her sire.

"As for what Sister Pride over there said," Mathilde continued at a whisper, the angry jerk of her head indicating Nilda, "don't you give it a moment's thought. She'll be in enough trouble when Mother Gertha learns she came here to greet Lady Haydon after being commanded otherwise. And, if your father truly leaves you destitute, there are enough of us who want you to sway Mother Gertha on your behalf."

Even as the weight of Elianne's future eased a little with Mathilde's assurance, there was still no guarantee Gertha would take on an impoverished mouth when her house failed. At least Nilda would get what she deserved. The corners of Elianne's mouth lifted in sour amusement. Nilda, an earl's daughter with the pride to match that rank, didn't realize that those she dismissed as inferior, which was everyone, returned the favor.

"There she is," Nilda cried as Lady Haydon appeared around the corner of the guest house.

The noblewoman looked far smaller afoot. Her gait was stilted, as if she walked on sharp stones. There was no seeing her face, not with her head bowed and her hat yet on her head.

Following her like a shadow came the big knight. If his noble mistress looked smaller afoot, he looked even larger. Elianne gawked. Good Lord, but he must stand a half head taller than she when there weren't many men her better. Then appreciation stirred. Aye, and he was handsome as well. Above strong cheekbones his brows peaked over eyes neither too narrow nor too wide. Shaved to a thin line, his golden beard clung to his jaw, lifting at his mouth to outline his lips. His sleeveless surcoat clung to his broad shoulders and powerful chest, but he moved without the heaviness that usually afflicted big men. His hands were bare; he'd stripped off his gloves, tucking them into the belt of his surcoat to reveal well-made hands and fingers seemingly too fine for a warrior.

If he had flaws at all it was the slight hook of his nose and the harsh lines bracketing his mouth. Those lines touched Elianne's heart, for it was grief she saw etched into his flesh. He'd cared for his murdered employer, and she liked him for it.

"Lady Haydon, you poor, dear widow. Pray come find your heart's ease in your childhood home," Sister Nilda called, her voice a strained falsetto as she delivered this greeting in the pretense of compassion.

When there was no reaction from Lady Haydon, Nilda started out onto the cobbled apron before the convent's door, her arms wide in the promise of an embrace. Nilda pivoted as she met her guest, dropping her arm across the widow's shoulders. The lady jerked weakly to the side, as if to elude this embrace. When Nilda clung to her, she stopped, stock-still. Her knight halted behind her, a questioning look upon his face.

"Remove your arm," the noblewoman demanded, her voice hoarse and low.

Rather than accede, Nilda caught her free hand

into the noblewoman's sleeve as if to confirm her ownership of this august visitor. "Nay, don't resist me, not when I can see how worn you are. Let me be your escort now, daughter," she crooned.

Daughter? Outraged astonishment brought Elianne's fists to her hips. Only Mother Gertha had the right to use that title.

"Sir Josce," Lady Haydon said, addressing her escort without so much as lifting her head, "remember your vow. Remove this woman from my presence by whatever means necessary." It was a brittle, cold command.

Elianne's eyes widened. Mathilde gasped. The lady had just given her knight permission to slay Nilda!

Breath gusted from Nilda. She snatched back her arm with such violence that she stumbled on the uneven cobbles and dropped like a stone. She hit the apron's hard surface with enough force that her teeth clacked.

Free again, the lady walked on toward the gate, looking neither right nor left. Sir Josce's face darkened in concern as he followed his lady. Elianne watched him in growing admiration. Not once had the knight's hand moved toward his sword despite his lady's command.

In the courtyard Nilda clambered to her feet, her expression torn between confusion and wounded pride. Pride won. She started after the departing symbol of her prestige. Instantly, Sir Josce shifted to block Nilda's advance, then shifted again when she tried to dart past him.

Elianne smiled, liking him even more. Here was a good knight, indeed. Sir Josce would keep his lady's command but do so without harming a nun.

Beside Elianne, Mathilde loosed a heartsore sigh as Lady Haydon neared them. "Oh, Beatrice. Can your grief truly be so deep?" the portress whispered in sad question.

As if pricked to it by Mathilde's pained tone, Lady Haydon's head turned in their direction. Elianne stared, shocked. The lady's face was ashen. Her dark eyes seemed empty, even soulless.

"Dear Lord, but she's the dead afoot," Mathilde cried in quiet horror, grasping Elianne's arm in a frantic grip.

The lady made her aching way past them and into the nuns' compound. Sir Josce followed, only to stop at the center of the gate and turn to face the women behind him. He positioned his body to block the opening.

Hissing in frustration, Nilda halted at arm's reach from him, fair hopping from foot to foot as she sought a way around him that didn't include either making physical contact or stooping like an old woman to dart beneath one of his arms. The first was unthinkable to Nilda, while the other was wholly beneath her dignity.

Sir Josce glanced at Mathilde, then shifted his gaze onto Elianne. His eyes were a wondrous shade of blue. He watched her, his look intense.

A new and strange sensation came to life deep

in Elianne's belly. It swiftly grew into discomfort as he continued to stare. Men never looked at her the way they did other women. She and her sire shared the same square chin, forceful thrust of nose and straight brows. While Elianne thought this combination of features gave her father a certain rugged handsomeness, they robbed her of her femininity, especially against her unusual height. Indeed, among the royal soldiers her sire commanded many referred to their lord sheriff's unwed daughter as his cock-less son.

"Help me," he said a moment later, his constant gaze making it seem as if he spoke only to her. His voice was a deep rumble. "Lady Haydon is not herself just now and what she intends may harm her more than her soul can bear. Go to your lady prioress. Tell her to come to the icehouse. Warn her at the same time," he went on, his voice deepening in emphasis, "that no men must accompany her as she comes to join my lady."

Not herself. Josce bit back a harsh laugh. Jesu, but that was an understatement. Why, right before his eyes Beatrice descended into complete madness, for in no other state would his stepmother command him to attack a holy sister. Almost holding his breath, he waited for the tall woman's response.

No great beauty she, not with her broad face and wide jaw. But her nose was straight and true, neither overly long nor too snub, and her brows were delicate slashes above the most astonishing clear green eyes. Caught in its casual tail, her hair tumbled around her, that honey-touched silken wealth fair begging for a man's hand, his hand, to straighten it.

Nay, no beauty, but handsome, indeed. Swift of foot as well, and that was what Josce needed. She must once more lift her heels so the sheriff, if the man was here as Beatrice believed, would stay away from the icehouse. Thank God, Beatrice hadn't thought to stop his tongue the way she'd bound his hands and tied him to her side.

Before him, the pompous nun loosed an odd little cry. She ducked low and shot beneath his blocking arm, shoving aside as she went. "Beatrice!" she shouted, trotting stiffly after Lady Haydon. "Wait. You cannot enter our house with a man as your escort. Stop! Wait for me!"

Damn him! He'd thought her too prideful to stoop to such a maneuver. Whirling, Josce lifted his heels to once more put himself between his stepmother and the nun she wished to avoid.

Warned to it by the jingling of his mail, the sister's pace quickened until she scurried. She wasn't fast enough. Keeping his gait an easy jog, Josce swiftly came abreast of her.

"Stay away from me!" the nun shrieked and shied to one side, cowering against the convent's church, a simple stone building with mossy wooden shingles for a roof. Josce passed her without a glance, steadily closing the distance between himself and Lady Haydon.

"Where do you think you're going?" the sister threw after him. "You don't belong within our walls. Get you hence!"

An instant later the plump nun streaked past Josce, her veil flying and skirts lifted. She veered toward the buildings at the far end of the compound. Relief warred with Josce's worry. She hadn't seemed as bright as the tall woman. Would she remember to warn her prioress that it must be only women who came for Lady Beatrice?

"Mathilde, what are you doing?" Sister Arrogance called after the speeding nun, new shock in her voice. "Elianne," she shrieked, new viciousness in her tone. "Come back here!"

Josce shot a glance over his shoulder. The tall woman was sprinting toward him, her skirts lifted. Elianne. Josce tried her name on his tongue and liked it. It suited her. So, she meant to bear him company on this trek to the icehouse. It wasn't just relief that stirred in him at this thought. He slowed so she might join him.

"Hussy! Forward hoyden!" the pompous nun shouted. "Get away from him, or I'll tell your sire. See if I don't!"

Completely undaunted by the nun's threats this Elianne came to jog alongside him. So, Elianne was neither nun nor novice, not if the prideful sister needed to report her behavior to a father. A merchant's daughter, then?

She met his pace, step for step. Josce's brows

quirked. By the standards of his courtly upbringing he should have been disgusted by her bold behavior and movements. Instead, he found this sharing of strides oddly intimate.

Elianne sent him a tiny smile. A brief burst of desire flashed in him. She owned just the sort of mouth he liked, lush lips that invited kissing. Awareness of her grew, seeping past his cloak of grief, then through skin and bone until desire stirred. Startled, Josce yanked his attention off Elianne and put it back where it belonged, upon his stepmother.

"I've sent Sister Mathilde to the prioress as you commanded. Know that Mother Gertha will come at all haste to the icehouse," Elianne told him, her tone reassuring, her French more natural than he expected. "But, even if Mother Gertha isn't in time to meet your lady at the icehouse, you—she won't be alone. Look behind us and see for yourself."

Josce did as she bid. Three silent sisters, brooms in hand, entered the courtyard from the church door. Their faces creased in concern, their skirts whispered across the courtyard's hard-packed earthen surface as they followed. Josce almost sighed. Aye, the more sisters the better. When they realized what Beatrice intended they'd find a way to protect her from herself.

"For that I thank you," he replied to Elianne as, ahead of them, Lady Beatrice led them down the side of a tall, two-storey building. This was surely the chapter house, the place where the nuns did their communal business. If the aching roll of Beatrice's hips said she'd spent too long in the saddle for one unaccustomed to riding, that pain didn't seem to dim her determination, and she obviously knew how to find what she wanted. Dear God, he wasn't ready to confront what Beatrice meant to see. Then again, perhaps what she wanted didn't exist.

"The icehouse," he began, only to find himself incapable of speaking of his sire as a dead man. "Is what Lady Haydon expects truly there?"

That it took Elianne no more than an instant to decipher his cryptic question said much of her intelligence. Her answer came by way of a somber nod. At the same time, compassion took light in her green eyes as pity softened her fine mouth. She cared that he ached, and, stranger though she was to Josce, she offered what little consolation she could.

That she might try to comfort him only increased that sense of intimacy Josce felt between them. With it came the certainty that in her arms he might forget that he was now a man without kin or family. Vengeance's needs howled in protest to such thinking. It wasn't a woman's arms he needed but the blood of thieves staining his sword, or the sheriff's. Only then would what ached in him be satisfied.

Chapter 3

"Lady Haydon's message promised arrival before noon. It's now an hour past that time. Where are they?" Sheriff Reiner du Hommet demanded of no one in particular.

Adelm of Nottingham, captain of the sheriff's guard, eyed his employer. A thick gray beard covered half of Reiner's face. Beneath craggy brows his hazel eyes were narrowed, while his forelock, white with age, straggled out from beneath his brown cap to cross his broad forehead. His new scarlet gown glowed in the room's dim light.

It took but a few strides for the sheriff to reach Adelm, the son he'd sired but still refused to acknowledge. But then, this wasn't much of a chamber any more than this was much of a priory. Driven to it by decades of poor management and a greedy king, the priory was well upon its way to failure. The only treasures it owned were the golden communion cup and the deeds between the priory and its tenants.

Reiner once more stalked past Prioress Gertha, who sat in her chair of state. Behind that massive seat, the nun attending Gertha lifted her head from her meek stance. Sister Amabella, the priory's cellaress, shot a swift glance toward Adelm. So brief was this look that Adelm barely had time to register Amabella's impatience before she once more lowered her gaze to her folded hands.

As he had so often done these past years, he wondered why no one recognized Amabella was his dam. Sculpted by twenty-nine years of enforced holiness and an austere diet, her features were as angular as Adelm's. Their black brows owned the same curve, their eyes were the same dark color. Hidden beneath her wimple was silver hair the same shade as his, both of them having gone to gray before their twenty-eighth year.

With a growl of frustration, Reiner stopped at the room's center and turned to face the prioress. "God's blood," he bellowed, "but I've had enough of this waiting. Even Elianne is late. I say keep your guest for yourself. I'm leaving."

Reiner's obscenity brought tiny Prioress Gertha to her feet. For this day, no evidence of business cluttered the table before her. Rather there was a ewer and wooden bowl for washing, and a tray of cold foods to offer their honored and grieving visitor.

Gertha's face was the picture of calm as she

tucked her hands into the sleeves of her habit. "Pray guard your tongue in my presence, my lord sheriff," she warned Adelm's father, her gentle tone that of tutor to student. "Remember that this is God's house and find peace within yourself."

Adelm's mouth tightened into a hidden smile. Until only months ago England had lain under papal interdict, all her churches and holy houses closed to her inhabitants as the pope sought to bring King John to heel. Instead, a defiant John claimed both the overlordship and the income from all England's monasteries. For the past six years Adelm had served in Reiner's stead as this priory's royal administrator, stripping what little profit the house generated for his monarch. That was long enough for Adelm to have learned that Gertha's mask of serenity concealed a near hatred for her sheriff.

Reiner only huffed angrily. "I'll speak as I please, where I please," he snarled.

Adelm straightened with a start, his arms opening. God help him, but Reiner was purposefully goading Gertha, a woman he despised for being his legal equal and his superior by birthright. Didn't Reiner realize that with interdict now lifted Gertha was at last free to make good on her threat and close the convent's doors on him? If that happened both Adelm and his father would lose access to Amabella, and, through her, seven years' worth of stolen wealth.

Gertha's face stiffened. She turned her back on

her king's sheriff to look at Amabella. "Sister Cellaress, where is Sister Subprioress? She should be here to greet Lady Beatrice." That Gertha's tone was devoid of all emotion meant she raged.

"I haven't seen Sister Nilda since prime service this morn, Mother," Amabella replied, revealing no surprise that her prioress would ignore the sheriff or ask so inane a question of her. Nor was there any rancor in her voice as she spoke of her chief tormentor. Nilda was only the most vocal of the gently born women here, all of them snubbing Amabella, a merchant's daughter. Eight years ago their order's mother house had forced Amabella onto the priory in the hopes that her monetary skills, learned at her merchant father's knee, could bring this house out of destitution. She might have succeeded, if not for John and interdict.

Reiner wheeled again toward his son. This time, he made no effort to hide what drove him. Panic was writ plain upon his face.

Adelm's dismay tightened into disgust. He'd risked his life to reap ill-gotten wealth for his debt-ridden father, and what did he get in return? A sire who became a weak brick in the wall of silence they needed to save them. Reiner feared the murdered nobleman's kin would pry into Lord Haydon's death, revealing Reiner's part in that event.

Gathered outside the prioress's office, the nuns awaiting Haydon's arrival cried out, their voices shrill, not welcoming. Reiner whirled toward the door, reaching for a sword he didn't wear. Startled, Adelm did the same.

Footsteps pounded up the exterior stair, then the door shrieked open, slamming against the wall behind it. Sister Portress exploded into her better's office, her wimple askew and her chubby face red from exertion. "Mother!" she shouted, then her mouth quivered and tears leapt to her eyes. "Oh Mother, our Beatrice is quite mad. Elianne follows her to the icehouse to do what she can, but says you must come quickly."

Gertha's face whitened. Without a word she hurried toward the doorway. Aye, but not even the madness of a beloved patron could stir her pace to anything faster than a long stride. Yet panting, Sister Mathilde trotted after her out of the office.

Uncertainty marked Amabella's face as she glanced between her son and former lover. Reiner suffered no such lack of confidence. His expression flattened in new cunning. "If the lady's mad, then we'd best go find a way to control her. That way, there'll be no questions asked over how her kin died. Come, both of you," he commanded, lumbering toward the doorway.

Horror nailed Adelm's feet to the floor. Not even to save his own life would he enter the icehouse where those two little ladies now waited upon their final rest. As had happened all too often since their deaths the sensation of their warm and childish blood spilling onto his hands returned. Adelm gagged and rubbed his fingers against the body of his gown. If he weren't convinced that God was a fantasy created by man to shield monks who enjoyed futtering children, Adelm would have been certain he faced hell for murdering those sweet lasses. Even he thought he deserved nothing less for what he'd done.

"My presence would be inappropriate," Adelm called after his father. "I'll wait here for you and the lady's return." The words burned as they exited his mouth, each one revealing a vulnerability his father could exploit.

Reiner whirled on his son, his face alive with surprise and a little fear. "What? But—" he began in protest.

"Adelm is right, my lord sheriff," Amabella interrupted, her voice as deep and rich as expensive silk. "He has neither the rank nor status to take part in such an event."

She came around the table's corner to stand beside her son, her head reaching only as high as Adelm's chin. "You, however, must go, ready as the king's representative to take custody of the widow if she truly is mad."

Adelm eyed his mother in surprise as she dismissed Reiner. In the seven years of their acquaintanceship fewer than five of their meetings had been private, and none of those had lasted beyond a few moments. The closest thing they had had to a truly personal conversation had been Amabella's repeated, whispered promises that Adelm would achieve what he so desired, to be lifted into the ranks of the gentry who scorned them both for their births.

Reiner grunted. If he didn't like his former lover's commanding tone, neither did he dare resent Amabella. Without her and her London family his scheme to enrich himself and his son would have failed.

It was Amabella who smuggled their stolen items first into the convent's cellars, then to her uncle in London. There, and for a hefty fee, the old merchant disposed of them, sending the profits back as letters of credit to be redeemed by Reiner and Adelm at some later time. These notes resided in Amabella's cellar, in a chest closed by two locks. Reiner held one key and Adelm the other, this arrangement forged after long and violent negotiation between them.

In the end Reiner's desire to protect himself from Lady Haydon overwhelmed his pride. "Stay then," he snarled and stepped outside the door. The dull thud of his footfalls marked his departure down the exterior stairway.

Only when silence again owned this chamber did Amabella look up into her son's face. "Do something about his panic," she whispered harshly. "Left unchecked, he'll destroy all of us."

Adelm didn't need his mother to tell him Reiner was capable of betrayal. "By his own doing are we well shielded from him. He doesn't dare speak and you won't die, if that's what you fear."

His mother loosed a bitter little laugh. "Fear death? Nay, not me. Mother Church doesn't kill those she claims to own, but she can be very creative when it comes to punishments." Then, Amabella shot another furious glance in the direction Reiner had gone. "I deserve such a fate if he betrays me a second time. Why did I ever think I could control that thickheaded jackass?"

Surprise stirred again in Adelm. "A second betrayal? Reiner said you aided us for love's sake." He didn't add that Reiner had intimated it was love of him, not Adelm, that made Amabella do so. Adelm couldn't add that he prayed the opposite was true, that his mother worked for his advancement because she had some fondness for her long-lost son.

"Love sake!" Amabella spat out in angry astonishment. "Give me a knife and a moment alone with that bitch's son and he'll bleed to death. It's because of him, and my sire, that I'm trapped in this prison." The lift of her hand indicated the prioress's office as hatred's fire took light in her dark eyes. "Your sire seduced me, promising marriage when all he ever wanted was my rich dowry. After you took root in my womb and my sire disowned me, throwing me from my home, Reiner abandoned me. I'd have died if not for my mother and her brother."

She caught herself, the fire in her gaze dying back to seething embers. "My father, may he rot in hell, meant for me to die. He wanted to wipe me and my bloodline off the earth's face. Would that I could hear his howl as I now defy him and raise you into the gentry, making of you a landed knight before my favored brother's get even comes of marriageable age."

Disappointment had been so often Adelm's companion in life that he barely acknowledged its arrival now. So, it wasn't for any love of him that his mother offered her aid. He eyed his dam for a quiet moment. Her idea of vengeance seemed no vengeance at all to him. Moreover, it was a futile hope now that Lord Haydon was dead.

"Your brother's children will be full grown before I can make use of the wealth hidden in your cellar," he told her.

"On the contrary," his mother replied, her voice tight and harsh. "You'll use it and quickly, before anyone connects me to a nobleman's death."

Bitterness stirred atop Adelm's disappointment. Years of thefts and the death of two innocents, all for naught. "Better burn those letters, then. If I came into wealth now there'd be questions I couldn't answer. After all, I'm but a sheriff's captain, barely higher in rank than a soldier and paid accordingly." Aye, and captain Adelm remained, all the while coveting the position of deputy. Reiner steadfastly refused him the promotion, saying custom dictated that only landed knights became deputies.

"What? Burn them now when you can have all

you want through my uncle? Aye, but to do it we must move swiftly. My worm of a brother writes that the old man finally begins to ail." Amabella's lips twisted upward into the pretense of a smile. "I'll send the notes, instructing my brother to use them to purchase an estate in my uncle's name. Meanwhile, my uncle can craft a new will that makes you heir for that property. When he passes, which will surely be soon, you'll have your estate with no one to question how you came into it."

Adelm loosed a short, sharp laugh. "And, I say the world will wonder why your uncle did this for me when he supposedly knows nothing of me or my connection to him."

Amabella blinked as if startled. "But of course he knows of you. Wasn't it my own mother, his sister, who took you from my arms and gave you to the monks for your raising? Was it not my uncle who paid your upkeep with the brothers without my sire's knowledge? Aye, and it was my uncle who bought your place as a squire after the monks claimed you too violent to remain in their custody."

"Nay, Reiner did that." So ingrained was Adelm's habit of telling himself this that the words were out before he thought. Until the day he achieved his spurs Adelm had wondered who his anonymous patron was. On that day Reiner had appeared, greeting him as a long-lost son.

How else could his father have found him, save that he had been that patron?

The surprise on Amabella's face flattened into scorn. "Reiner lies if he says he spent so much as a single pence on you. That pig can barely feed his household through the winter."

Her words rang like the truth they were, a truth Adelm had long ago suspected but couldn't bear to acknowledge, for in acknowledging it he accepted that he'd made himself his father's tool. Reiner hadn't wanted a son but a biddable, eager thief, one capable of murdering innocent lasses.

Nor was his mother any better. Adelm looked at Amabella and saw his father's greed in her expression. He was nothing to her but a means to an end, the tool of her vengeance, such as it was. Of all his blood kin only Elianne was pure of motive, but there weren't many folk upon this earth as good and loving as his sweet half sister.

"Send my letters to your uncle," he coldly commanded his dam.

"Only yours?" There was venom enough in Amabella's voice to suggest it had always been her plan to cheat her former lover.

Adelm smiled at that. Aye, Reiner deserved this betrayal. "Aye, send them all. But how will you open that chest when you need Reiner's key along with mine to do it?"

Amabella sneered. "Your sire's arrogance is only surpassed by his blind certainty that all women are stupid. Your locks were picked the day after you installed them."

His heart cold, Adelm considered her. "Then, perhaps I shouldn't trust you."

"You have no choice," she retorted with another harsh laugh. "You never have. Your future was in my hands even before I sent Reiner to bring you to me. Now, leave me. You'll wait outside the office until the prioress returns."

Chapter 4

Keeping pace with Sir Josce, Elianne followed Lady Haydon to the broad gate leading to the nuns' garden. Beyond the portal's low arch the gentle patchwork of the vegetable plots and trees that sustained the sisters spread out before them. Long accustomed to the too-short gateway, Elianne ducked. At her side, his shoulder nearly touching hers, Sir Josce did the same. They moved at the exact instant, straightening as one on the gate's opposite side.

This synchrony of movement felt so odd that a small laugh welled up in Elianne. She clapped her hand over her mouth too late to stop the sound. Praying he hadn't heard her, she shot a look at the knight. If ever there was an event that didn't warrant laughter, this was it.

He *had* heard. Sir Josce, still matching her step

for step, eyed her, a slight frown upon his brow. Elianne's heart fell.

If he'd been like most other men, the sort like her father, who thought only of themselves, she wouldn't have cared that she'd insulted him. But even in the few moments of their acquaintance Elianne knew this man wasn't like most. He hadn't raised either hand or sword against a woman even when commanded to it by his lady. Aye, and after that he'd asked for her aid, rather than demanding it. This was a man more like Sir Adelm, a fine and loyal knight. The possibility that Sir Josce might now adjudge her disrespectful of his grief was unbearable.

"Pardon, I didn't mean to laugh," Elianne said in true regret. "It's only that you, that we, move as if we were each other's shadow." With a lift of her hand she indicated the way the very swing of their arms matched.

The frown smoothed from his brow and, despite his grief, the corners of his mouth lifted. "It is odd," he agreed. "Startling as well." Something stirred beneath the pain filling his fine blue eyes, then he turned his attention back onto his lady ahead of him on the path. "Not unappealing." This last was but a murmur.

Although the aside was surely meant only for himself Elianne caught it. He found her attractive. In that instant she was achingly aware of him, of the powerful set of his shoulders and the way he carried himself with ease despite that he wore armor weighing four stone. Exposure to the sun this day as well as all the days of summer past had given his skin a fine brown hue and streaked brighter gold into his already fair hair. Elianne's gaze marked the line of his nose, then dropped to the gentle curve of his lips.

A sigh escaped her. Lord, but he was a fine-looking man, the sort who could have any woman he wanted, yet he found her attractive when no other man ever had. Something subtle stirred deep in her, the sensation one she didn't recognize. It was a pleasant sort of urgency, not unlike the excitement she felt when she thought about the upcoming celebration planned for Knabwell's saint day.

In its wake came long-repressed resentment. Even her sisters had husbands, albeit peasants. Not she. Never she. She'd be her father's servant until he died. The reward for her service was to be left with only the prayer that there might be a place for her with these women in their constrained and walled world.

Unable to bear thinking on what she couldn't have and what faced her, Elianne forced her attention off the knight and onto the garden around her. Broad hats on their heads and hoes in hand, the sister-farmers and the menservants who aided them in working new richness into their garden paused to gawk. And, rightly so. This was a strange, silent parade: a mad noblewoman, the sheriff's worthless daughter, a handsome knight, trailed by a flock of panting nuns. Until a distant lark released its glorious song, the only sound was the rush of so many skirts through the drying grasses.

Into the leafy shade of the priory's orderly forest they went. It wasn't just apples that filled this area, a full eighth of the city's expanse, but also pears, tangled rows of blackberries and roses, bushes of sloes, even crab apples. All too quickly Lady Haydon led them to their awful destination. To Elianne the icehouse had always looked like a giant badger's den, a great, grassy hump of earth with stone steps leading down into its sunken chamber, where much of the convent's foodstuffs were preserved. Or dead bodies, although the sisters weren't often called upon to use this chamber as a morgue.

Lady Haydon stopped on the icehouse's top step, her halt so abrupt that her skirts swung around her legs. As the trailing nuns gathered into a ragged half circle a bare few yards from them, Elianne came to a standstill a foot or so behind the noblewoman. Rather than step forward to join his lady, Sir Josce, his armor jangling quietly, halted at Elianne's side.

Startled, she looked up into his face, intending no more than a glance. Instead, her gaze caught and held. His eyes were closed, his head bowed. Grief radiated from him.

Pity tangled with approval in Elianne. That he so deeply mourned his master was further proof of his good and caring nature. Sir Josce's eyes opened. Elianne started and snatched her gaze from him to his lady, hoping he hadn't noticed that she'd stared.

Lady Haydon yet hesitated at the top of the ice-house stairs, her clasped hands shaking. Her face grayed as she eyed the oaken door separating her from her kin. No longer did Elianne resent her father's call. He was right, she was needed here today, but not by him. It was Sir Josce and his lady she could serve this day. Elianne stepped forward to join the noble widow on the step.

The lady turned her head to consider her new companion. "Coward me, I cannot go another step," she said, her voice harsh and soft in the same instant. "I've come all this distance only to fail my sweet loves."

Elianne slipped her hand into the bend of the lady's arm. "If you will, we'll descend together," she offered in a quiet voice.

Lady Haydon sighed her agreement and, stair by stair, they made their way down to the ice-house door. Sir Josce followed, or so said the gentle rattle of mail and scrape of a leather boot sole from behind them. The great iron ring that served as a handle turned with a groan.

Frigid, musty air gusted past them as the door opened, then the day shot in over their shoulders to flood the chamber with warm light. Where bags and barrels didn't conceal them, earthen walls radiated a rich brown color. Packed with straw, what remained of the great ice blocks hewn from the river in winter past gleamed a translucent white. Gossamer spider silk covered the ceiling. Three cots stood at the back wall, the forms upon them already shrouded in white linen for burial.

With a sharp breath, Lady Haydon released Elianne's arm and stepped delicately toward the nearest cot, dropping to her knees. "Adelaide," she cried, her breath clouding before her in the chill air. "Oh, my sweet, sweet child. How can you bear it here when the cold always makes you cough?"

Elianne's heart broke with the noblewoman's words. If Lady Haydon was mad, it was grief that had driven her to it. As the bereft mother's shoulders began to shake, Elianne took a backward step, wanting to grant her some privacy. She collided with Sir Josce, her foot treading atop his.

Startled, she lurched to the side and whirled into a staggering step. He caught her by the arms, his hands cupping her elbows. In instinctive reaction she leaned forward, resting her hands upon his chest as she steadied herself against him.

They were nearly eye to eye, close enough that she could see the gleam of sprouting hair upon his lean cheeks. The pulse in his neck throbbed, the heat of his body reaching out to envelop her. A fire flared to life in her somewhere beneath her gullet. Her pulse lifted until her heart fair pounded. That strange urgency returned, now writhing in the depths of her belly. Mary save her, but how could his mere nearness to her make her feel so alive? Confused and not a little unnerved, she pushed back from him.

He let her go without resistance, his gaze focused not on her but on the corner of the icehouse. "Why is his armor here?" he asked, his voice harsh and barely louder than a whisper. The pained lines that bracketed his mouth deepened with his words. As he spoke he shifted backward, step by step, until he stood in the doorway.

Elianne turned to see what he meant. A narrow beam of sunlight probed past the farthest cot, on which lay Lord Haydon's still form. Half in light and half in shadow, a knight's shield stood against the wall alongside a sheathed sword. A silvery gleam escaped the careful stack next to the sword's tip.

Chain mail? In the seven years the bandit troop had plagued this shire her father had steadfastly refused to discuss their activities with her. Degraded men, her sire had claimed, were too gruesome a topic for a woman. Now curiosity demanded satisfaction. What sort of thieves left behind armor worth nearly its weight in gold?

Lady Beatrice loosed a low moan from her prayful pose beside her daughter's still form. Elianne's heart wrenched anew. It was all too much to bear—a knight who could set fire to her insides, a lord killed by thieves but still in possession of his riches, two murdered children and their grief-crazed mother. She turned to leave, only to pause in wary caution. Sir Josce blocked the chamber's doorway, his head once again bowed, his eyes closed and his mouth tight. Unlike his lady, who gave way to tears, he battled his grief with all his might, or so said his fists.

As little as Elianne wanted to disturb him, she needed to escape this place. Almost tiptoeing, she made her way as close to him as she dared. Here she paused, wondering how to slip past him without disturbing him. Sir Josce's eyes opened. Stark loneliness filled his gaze, as if he thought himself the last man upon this earth and utterly without hope of again knowing human companionship.

It was nothing more than a reflection of what tormented Elianne each and every day. The sense of kinship was unbearable. She reached out without thought, needing to comfort herself as much as him. Her hand closed over one of his fists.

He sighed. Some of the loneliness ebbed from his blue eyes, and his expression relaxed. His hand opened and turned, his fingers sliding between hers.

His palm was hard and callused. Ah, but the sensation of his skin against hers was impossibly welcome. That strange urgency returned, bringing with it the unnerving sense of being afire.

Only then did Elianne realize how wrong she'd been to touch him. This wasn't her father or even Adelm, who accepted the occasional press of her fingers with the respect a brother might give a favored sister. This man was no kin of hers and was, by that definition, dangerous.

The litany Elianne's father had drilled into her head over her lifetime played anew. Men, Reiner ever lectured, were fickle creatures. While to a one they claimed to respect virtuous women, in truth all men wanted nothing more than to relieve all women of said virtue. In this battle betwixt what a man said and what he did a woman's single touch, even one offered in all innocence, might lead him to think she no longer wanted her precious maidenhead. Aye, and if a woman were fool enough to give said man her most precious possession her lover would shortly betray her, rightly abandoning her to face alone the consequences of her actions.

She shifted back from him, her hand opening as she tried to draw her fingers from his. Sir Josce frowned. It wasn't irritation she saw upon his face but disappointment. His hand tightened on hers as if he meant to pull her close to him again.

A touch of panic lifted in Elianne. Was it too late? Did he already think her a loose woman?

"Nay, you must let me go," she told him in a frantic whisper. "It's not right that I'm here alone with you and your lady."

The loneliness returned to haunt his gaze. "Stay," he asked, his voice hoarse. "I—she—may yet need you."

His words reverberated in her. He needed her.

Within Elianne, a terrible image rose, that of this powerful, handsome man as the husband she would never have, the father of the children her virgin womb would never produce. Her loneliness grew until it tore her heart to shreds.

"I can't," she cried, tearing her hand from his grasp.

Shoving past him, she flew up the stairs to halt on the top step. There she stopped, undone. True, she was overly free with her movements, but then she needn't worry about impressing any man with her behavior. Movements aside, she'd never in all her years broken with propriety the way she had this day. She resisted the urge to look down the stairs at the knight who found her attractive. She knew how it had happened. Except for Adelm, she'd never before felt as easy with a man as she did with Sir Josce.

"Mistress du Hommet!" Prioress Gertha shot out of the now much expanded crowd of workmen and sisters gathered here. Bright red circles marked the churchwoman's fine cheeks, while enough torn grass clung to her hems to suggest that she might actually have lifted her heels a little between her office and here. "Lady Haydon is below?" At Elianne's nod, Gertha leapt around her to race down the stairs.

"Stand aside, damn you. Make way for me," Reiner du Hommet demanded, his deep bass voice loud enough to rattle the treetops.

Irritation hissed from Elianne. Wasn't it just

like her sire to bull his way through a crowd of women? Her father shoved through the last line of folk separating him from his daughter, his new scarlet gown a beacon among so many dressed in somber hues. He came to a halt before his daughter, the nervousness that had plagued him these last weeks yet dancing in his hazel eyes. What upset him he wouldn't say, but his mood had changed when he'd learned of Lord Haydon's death. After years of plaguing only merchants, the ruffians had finally killed someone of consequence.

"What is the lady doing here? Why didn't she come to the office first as she should have?" Reiner demanded of his youngest daughter. "And where were you? You were to be at the priory before the lady's arrival."

Elianne shot him a narrow look. "And so I was, standing at the gate to greet Haydon's noble widow when she arrived. If you want me to be any swifter you'll have to buy me a horse to use. Where were you? You can't blame me if you were waiting in the wrong place."

So it was between them. Her father might own her, body and soul, but that didn't keep Elianne from offering sly and surly jibes about her status along the way. His irritation was the price he paid for her servitude. An acceptable trade, as far as she was concerned.

"Now what are you doing here?" Elianne went on. "Sister Mathilde should have told you to remain in the office. The lady's escort asked that only women be present at this meeting."

A touch of outrage came to life in her father's face. "No one orders a sheriff away from what is his rightful business."

Elianne loosed an irritable breath. It had been a waste of breath to send that message with Mathilde. Her father always did just as he pleased no matter who wanted what, like purchasing a gown for his trip to court when there was barely enough in her beleaguered household purse to see them through the winter.

"Nay! Help me!" the prioress screamed, her distraught voice echoing up from the subterranean chamber.

So frantic was the churchwoman's call that Elianne leapt down the steps, leaving her father behind her. Clucking in agitation, a good part of the crowd surged after her, the press driving Elianne into the dark chamber before them. With but a few wary beams squeezing past the occasional shoulder, there was just light enough to show Elianne that Lady Haydon had left off her vigil at her daughter's side. Now, shoulders heaving, the noblewoman stood at the icehouse's center. Gone was her hat. One plait lay open, the stream of her hair down her back colorless in the dimness.

Clinging to one of the lady's arms as if to restrain her, Gertha spied Elianne. "Help me stop her," she demanded of the sheriff's daughter.

Elianne did as she was bid, taking Lady Beatrice's other arm, but her gaze was on Sir Josce, who now stood between his lady and her daughter. His expression was harsh. "Nay, my lady. Your vow won't hold me here. You won't unwind them."

Only then did Elianne see the linen puddled on the floor beneath the nearest cot. Horror woke. As Lady Beatrice once more surged toward the cot, Elianne held her back with all her might. The lady couldn't do this. Icehouse or not, these corpses were long past their time for burial.

"Nay, they must be exposed!" Lady Haydon shouted at her new captor, her tone fraught with hysteria. "I want the sheriff to look upon them and see what his laziness has cost me."

Instant silence claimed the chill chamber, the quiet so deep Elianne could hear her own breath echo in her ears. Of a sudden she understood her father's panic, and it became her own. Right or wrong, her sire would be blamed for Lord Haydon's death. Come Michaelmas court at September's end, Lady Haydon would make her complaint against him. If the king dismissed him it would mean ruin for her as well as her father. John would demand repayment of all his sheriff owed, a crushing amount that included the cost of twice purchasing the sheriff's position.

"You shouldn't blame him. He's done the best he can," Elianne said, needing to save herself as best she could.

Lady Haydon jerked as if struck. She wrenched around to glare at Elianne. "Who would you have me blame, then? Myself?" she screamed, then gagged. A moment passed and then another, her mouth opening and closing, but no breath passed into her lungs.

"Holy Mother help us, she expires!" Gertha screamed, releasing her hold on Lady Beatrice in frantic reaction to the lady's distress.

Elianne caught the noblewoman against her. "Help her!" she cried to the lady's knight.

Chapter 5

Even before Elianne called to him, Josce moved. Jesus God, he'd never forgive himself if Beatrice died and made orphans of her two surviving daughters. He tore his father's widow out of Elianne's grasp and gave her a great shake.

"Breathe, breathe!" he bellowed. His shout exploded in the unnatural quiet that held this place in thrall. To his utter astonishment Beatrice did as he commanded, drawing air into her lungs with a hungry gulp. Her head dropped forward onto his shoulder as she hung in his arms like one stunned.

"Make way," Josce snapped at those who blocked his path. "Let me bear her from this foul chamber."

With a great rustling the stunned onlookers retreated silently up the stairs. Cradling his stepmother in his arms, Josce followed them, Elianne and the tiny prioress at his heels. Once out in the world a few steps took him into the shade of an old apple tree. He lay his stepmother upon the thick grass beneath it.

Lady Beatrice's face was flaccid in unconsciousness. Each breath strained from her lungs. She looked even grayer now, sicker, the marks of her grief all the darker. The prioress crouched at his stepmother's head but aimed her gaze at the loose and respectful circle that formed about the fallen woman.

"Sister Ada? Sister Cecilia? Are either of you here?"

The convent folk shuffled around them. A single young nun stepped from their ranks. "I am, Mother," she said, her accented French suggesting a common birth. She knelt near her prioress at Lady Haydon's side.

Josce watched the way the youthful sister pressed her hands to his stepmother. It told of a close acquaintance with illness and its cures. Elianne came to kneel at his side.

"You did it. Your lady breathes again," she whispered to him.

Between the hint of pride in her tone and what had passed between them in the icehouse, the urge to take Elianne in his arms woke in Josce. Rather than look at her, he studied her hand on the grass next to his own. It was a capable hand, her nails neatly pared. Her skin wore a brown stain, no doubt from apples. The smell of the fruit had wafted from her when they'd collided in the icehouse.

Something stirred in him—not desire but another emotion, one he couldn't identify. From the time he'd come into the awareness of his manhood to this day, he'd made use of courtesans and chambermaids, peasant lasses and whores. Yet if he lived into his dotage he knew he'd never forget the feel of this woman's hand on his. Her simple, honest touch had offered him more care, comfort and connection than he'd had from any lover's caress.

"Well, there's no fever," said the healer-sister, looking up from Lady Beatrice. A touch of a frown married the young nun's smooth brow as she glanced between Josce and Prioress Gertha. "And her heart beats, steady and strong. As near as I can tell she's but fainted. Of course, I'm not as skilled in such things as is Sister Ada," she added in humble caveat.

"Thank you, Sister Cecilia," the prioress said, nodding as she eased back on her heels to look at Josce. "Sir knight, you've done your noble mistress a great service this day. Now, do her one more. Take her in your arms and bear her to our infirmary, where you may leave her, confident that we can heal her."

It was a sensible request. The shame was that he couldn't give her a sensible response. "I can do so only on one condition," Josce said. "Before we arrived Lady Haydon took from me my solemn vow not to leave her side. Where she goes I must stay."

The prioress's mouth pursed. "How ridiculous," she scolded. "You know perfectly well there's no accommodation for you in our walls. Leave her to us and retreat to the guest house to wait as all male visitors must."

There was no sense arguing, so Josce said nothing.

Mother Gertha's eyes narrowed at his silence. "Surely, you cannot be so honor-bound that you'd so strictly interpret such an oath," she chided.

When had it become wrong to be an honor-bound man who kept his word? Haydon's men had witnessed his oath. To be forsworn was to ruin himself. More to the point, to break his word now was to risk his involvement in his father's final rest. Done with this conversation, Josce lifted his stepmother into his arms and came to his feet.

Soft cries and anxious murmurings broke from the mostly female folk surrounding him. The prioress and Sister Cecilia came swiftly up after him, as did Elianne. He took a backward step.

"What are you doing?" the prioress demanded sharply. Behind the tiny woman, Elianne's brow creased in concern. She shook her head at him, the movement suggesting he should do as the prioress said.

"What else, save keeping his oath and taking his lady away from here," said a man from behind Josce, his deep voice a rough and too-loud rumble in this quiet group of churchfolk.

Startled, Josce pivoted toward the speaker. Jesu, but how could he have not seen the scarlet-clad, heavyset man? Scarlet was an expensive color, as was the fabric onto which the dye had been laid. An inkling of who this was shot through Josce. "Who are you?" he demanded.

"Reiner du Hommet, lord sheriff of this shire." The man at fault for Lord Baldwin's death gave a slight bow of his head as he introduced himself. "I have a solution for your problem," he then offered, grinning widely, as if pleased with himself.

Between the man's name and his flippant attitude, icy rage burst to life in Josce, slaughtering all else. "You dare to speak so to me? Incompetent! Idiot! You allowed murderous thieves to run rampant on lands you're sworn to protect. My lord father's death sits upon your soul."

"Father?" Du Hommet's broad face came alive with surprise.

"Father?" Elianne echoed as she moved around Josce to stand beside the sheriff.

Josce glanced between the two. There could be no mistaking who had sired Elianne; Elianne was no middling merchant's daughter, but the sheriff's child. The pieces had all been there for Josce to see—her French the same as his, her bearing that of England's upper class. Josce damned himself for thinking grateful and even lustful thoughts about the daughter of the man who had caused his father's death.

"You're right." Du Hommet's head bowed as if in shame. "Lord Haydon's death rests upon my shoulders. Mea culpa, my fault for not finding these accursed thieves."

"Here is what I think of your apology." Josce turned his head and spat, then threw his challenge. "Incompetent you are, and so says all the world. There's not a man at court who doesn't laugh behind his hand over your complaints of wily thieves eluding you. They say you're too lazy to rise from your fat arse and round up the ruffians. Well, you'll bestir yourself now, and swiftly so.

"A fortnight." Josce's need to swing his sword and purge his grief made him draft an impossibly short time period for his threat. "That's how long you have to find those thieves and bring them to me so I might dispense the justice they deserve."

Between taunt and threat, du Hommet's face reddened. The veins stood out on his neck, but it was panic that filled his gaze. "If I cannot produce them?" he asked, although his expression said he knew well enough what came next.

"You'll die in their stead," Josce snarled, offering the man the threat he expected.

Du Hommet's gaze shuttered. He bent his neck and hung his head like some palsied friar. "Then, I will not fail you," he replied. "Let me prove my sincerity by offering you what you so need at this moment. If you won't be separated from Lady Haydon, bring her to my manor, Coneytrop. Call it a sop if you want," the sheriff hurried on as if to convince, "but think on how well it serves you. My home lies but a half mile from Knabwell's walls, close enough that the nuns can send their healer to tend Lady Haydon. Close enough that you need never leave her side to make your lord father's burial arrangements."

Outrage burned in Josce's heart. "I'll not sleep within the same walls as the man responsible for my sire's death."

"Then I'll remove myself," du Hommet said, his tone strained. "To take up residence in the king's castle when there's so much to be done before court at month's end suits me well enough."

Alarm bells clamored in Josce. Why would any man invite his newly avowed enemy into his home? He glanced at Elianne, hoping for some clue from the daughter. She stared at her sire as if the sheriff stood upon his head.

"But Father, it's harvest time and I cannot leave—" she began in protest. A curt wave of her father's hand silenced her.

Those alarm bells rose in volume. Why was du Hommet so determined to bring him and Lady Haydon into his home? The puzzle demanded a cooler head than Josce presently owned. As he fought to calm himself, the sheriff shot a guarded glance at Elianne.

"My daughter is right to suggest that she cannot leave while our home is in the midst of putting away its harvest," Sir Reiner added, shooting a sly glance toward his child. "Let her stay to see to your meals and your comfort whilst you dwell in our hall."

"Papa!" Elianne cried, both shocked and stunned in the same instant.

Her reaction only confirmed to Josce how far out of character the sheriff had slipped to make this offer. That it had to do with Lord Haydon's death there was no doubting. Why else would the sheriff want Haydon's son and his wife where he could monitor their every movement?

Josce looked to Elianne. She yet stared at her father, wringing her hands. Worry darkened her expression. Worry over what? Did she know that her sire hid something, something that she didn't want Lord Baldwin's son to find?

Had her compassion for his grief been naught but mummery? Had her sire asked her to watch him, and for that reason Elianne had come with him to the icehouse instead of going to the prioress as Josce asked?

New anger surged through him. Whatever their plan, they would fail. He would go to their home, hold Elianne as his hostage, and dig until he found whatever it was du Hommet strove to conceal. It was but a single harsh nod he offered to signal his agreement.

Sir Reiner's smile sat crookedly on his mouth. Subtle triumph glowed in his gaze. "Take your ease in my home as you take my vow. I won't fail you. You'll have your thieves, my lord."

The sheriff's promise to deliver the thieves rang hollowly, the honorific by which he addressed Josce stinging like salt in a wound. "I am Sir Josce FitzBaldwin, Lord Haydon's natural son," he snapped. "That I have so much of a title is solely at my sire's forbearance and affection. Thus is his loss all the more painful for me."

The sheriff's expression stiffened, as if he now regretted his offer. Too late, the die was cast.

"Lead the way, my lord sheriff, and make haste at it. My lady stepmother needs both bed and care," Josce commanded, stepping onto the pathway that led to the gate.

The prioress and the young healer blocked his way. "Sir Josce," the prioress said, "you will not take your lady stepmother from our walls, not when doing so threatens her life."

"Stand aside," Reiner du Hommet demanded, waving at the prioress as if she were a troublesome gnat, not a woman of consequence. "The decision is made."

"Is Lady Haydon truly too ill for travel?" Josce demanded of the young healer.

Framed by her white wimple, the nun's broad English face creased. She wrung her hands and glanced between her prioress and him. That she fretted over her answer clearly said Lady Beatrice wasn't at death's door, which was just as well. Josce wasn't certain even Beatrice's imminent demise could stop him from traveling to du Hommet's home to discover what it was the sheriff hid.

"We go," Josce told the prioress. "If you care for my lady stepmother at all, perhaps you'll send your nun, here, with us to see to her well-being."

Chapter 6

Elianne and the prioress stood just inside the convent's gate, while beyond the guest house nuns and Haydon's men prepared Lady Haydon for departure from the priory. Both Sister Ada and Sister Cecilia were arranging this last and unexpected leg of Lady Haydon's journey; they would travel with the lady to Coneytrop. Never comfortable in the powerful churchwoman's presence, Elianne dared a swift and curious glance at Mother Gertha. The prioress stood with an unnatural stillness, her head bowed over her clasped fingers. Elianne knew her own reasons for refusing to aid in the lady's leave-taking, but why did Mother Gertha linger?

At just that moment Sir Adelm strode around the house's corner. Against the day's somber events Adelm had eschewed his usual military trappings for a muted brown gown that made his hair seem more silver than grayed. The thick fabric lent softness to a face that was naught but harsh crags and forceful angles. Behind him came Reiner.

Elianne's stomach soured against the satisfaction on her father's face. Betrayer! Liar! After so many years of warning her against strange men, her sire had abandoned her to one without so much as a fare-thee-well.

As if she heard the men approaching, the prioress's head lifted. Elianne caught a startled breath. Cold rage filled Mother Gertha's face.

As he saw the churchwoman's face, Adelm's brows quirked upward, just a little. It was more display of worry than Elianne had ever before seen upon his face. There was no reaction from Reiner as he stopped before the women.

The prioress's breath hissed from her. "May God forgive me for it, but I pray the devil takes your soul, Reiner du Hommet," she snarled. "How dare you undermine my authority by offering your home after I commanded Haydon's bastard to leave his lady at the priory."

Reiner's eyes widened in surprise at her attack, then, as always happened when he confronted something he didn't wish to face, he found refuge behind outrage's shield. He thrust out his chest and threw back his head. "What is this?" he demanded. "You snap now when the time for disagreeing with my suggestion was at the icehouse?"

"Oh, but you would have relished that," Gertha shot back. "Me, bickering with you where my own folk might witness. Nay, I'll give you no further opportunity to publicly subvert my authority, or anything else. I won't have you or any of yours in my domain. From this day on, our doors are closed to you and your kin."

"You wouldn't dare!" Reiner bellowed, sounding frantic at her threat. "I am the king's agent."

"And my complaint against you will be at court before you," the prioress retorted, pivoting toward the gate.

Elianne's hope of future sanctuary here shattered with Mother Gertha's words. She whirled on her sire, fear for herself and her future destroying all caution. "You've killed me!" she cried, her voice shrill. "Without refuge here, I'll have to whore to feed myself after your passing."

"How dare you speak so to me," her father snapped, then gave her a goodly shove toward the guest house's corner, propelling her a few feet from him. "Still your tongue and get around yon corner to join Haydon's troop for the journey home."

Instead, Elianne wheeled on him, closing the distance between them with a single long step. "I won't! I won't go home, not when both Lady Haydon and her stepson have pronounced themselves your enemies."

Standing behind her sire, Adelm's features

twisted into an expression that urged caution. Elianne ignored him.

"Please, please don't send me with them," she pleaded. Elianne had only intended to soften her voice into female tones of distress, but instead her words came out fraught with fear. Rightly so. If she wasn't afraid of Lady Haydon, in less time than an eye's blink Sir Josce had gone from a handsome knight who needed her to a powerful and hostile man who craved her sire's blood. Worse, he was a man she'd touched when she shouldn't have, a man whose touch had set fire to her in the most unnerving way.

"That bastard offers you no threat. What you heard from him was naught but grief's ravings. Think no more on it." As he spoke, Reiner looked away from his daughter as if to prevent her from reading something in his gaze.

It didn't work, for what he tried to hide filled his voice. Reiner didn't believe a word he'd just spewed. Nor did he care that Sir Josce might be a threat to his daughter. He wanted her to stay at Coneytrop with Lord Haydon's dangerous son.

Outrage tore through Elianne. Her father had some ulterior motive, which could only mean Reiner had once more cooked up a moneymaking scheme. "God take you, but you've at last found a way to use me, just as you did my sisters, my mother and that poor wee lass who was my stepmother," she cried.

In scheme after harebrained scheme, Reiner

had striven to generate income, but none had been as horrid as his second marriage to a lass younger than Elianne. Reiner had used Isabelle's dowry as collateral for another loan, only to have both wife and son die in childbed, which meant Isabelle's dowry went back to her family, leaving Reiner owing even more.

Reiner's hand flew. The crack of flesh against flesh exploded in Elianne's ears, pain bursting along her jaw. She reeled, staggering sideways, her hand cupped to her burning cheek. She collided with the guest house's wall.

Her father wrenched her around to face him. "Drop to your knees and beg my forgiveness, else I'll cut out your tongue to end your insolence." That he held his voice low testified to the depths of his rage. But then, rage was all he had to shield himself from the wreck he'd made of his life.

Elianne raised her head in defiance. He'd have her apology when she had his. Her father's eyes narrowed to slits.

"Hear me now, vixen. Haydon's bastard comes to my home at my invitation. There he'll stay, with you tending to him and his lady as you would any visitor, else I'll have your hide for it."

"Take my skin," Elianne shot back. "What care I for my hide when you've left me without a future?"

Again, her sire's hand lifted. Before the blow could fall, Adelm lay a forestalling hand upon his master's shoulder. "My lord sheriff," he said, his voice smooth and cool, "this is neither the time nor the place for such a correction."

Reiner whirled on his captain, no less stunned by Adelm's intervention than Elianne. It was a man's prerogative to discipline his womenfolk as he saw fit, and Adelm's interference would not prevent the beating. Once Reiner decided on a beating he might postpone it, but he never relented.

"Injure Mistress du Hommet and she can hardly tend to Lady Haydon or your house." The flow of Adelm's words was soothing and oddly insistent.

A new and far more painful betrayal scoured Elianne, eating up her anger as it grew. Adelm knew! He knew how her father planned to use her and was jogging his distracted master back onto that preassigned path.

"You're right," Reiner agreed, his gaze shifting back to his daughter. He yanked at the body of his gown, then smoothed his fingers over the bulge of his belly as if to soothe the insult he'd just done to his gown's costly fabric.

"Listen closely, vixen. You'll tend to Lady Haydon as if she were your own accursed dam. If I hear you ignored her or in any way slighted Haydon's bastard I'll disown you. After that, you can beg for your daily bread before these walls, or any walls you choose, and whore with my blessing."

His threat delivered, he pivoted on his heel. "I'm for my office," he called over his shoulder to

Adelm as he started toward the guest house's corner.

"I'll be by to speak with you, my lord sheriff, once I return from Coneytrop," Adelm called after him.

Elianne stared at her friend. For the first time in all the years she'd known him, Adelm was addressing her sire as master to servant, not the reverse.

Reiner whirled, the surprise on his face giving way to something akin to worry. "I won't have time until late this evening. I've better things to do than waste my time in idle chatter with you." Then, as if he realized his snub lacked teeth, he rudely turned his back on Adelm and strode around the guest house's corner without waiting for a reply.

"You know what he intends," Elianne said, her voice trembling with the force of Adelm's betrayal. "You're helping him when I thought there was some affection between us, you and I."

Adelm watched her, his gaze guarded, his features expressionless. He said nothing.

"Since you know all," she continued, "I pray you spill his purpose to me. How can a man use his daughter, fully intending to toss her aside when he's done like some bone gnawed clean?"

Adelm shook his head. "If you mean his purpose in inviting Haydon's widow and bastard to reside with you, then I tell you true, I don't know his plan. Would that I did." His exasperation was so honest and unexpected that it gave credence to his claim of ignorance.

Shame rose in Elianne. How could she have doubted Adelm? She should have known he had no other reason for intervening save his care for her.

"What I do know," Adelm continued, all emotion banished from his expression, "as you do even better than I, is that once your sire sets himself on a path he never leaves it. Your attempt to change him will only result in pain for you."

"True enough," Elianne said with a soggy huff. At times her sire was no better than a blundering, blinded bear in his determination to do what anyone else could see wouldn't serve him. Only this time his blindness guaranteed her future anguish and debasement.

Adelm touched his hand to his own jaw at the approximate spot that her father's blow had bruised her own. "How badly did he hurt you?"

She moved her jaw, then grimaced. The promise of blackened skin was the least of her worries. "Not as badly as staying at Coneytrop with a knight and noblewoman who both thirst for du Hommet blood."

Her friend only shook his head. "You make a mountain out of a molehill, little sister," he said, using the endearment he employed only when she was at her most distraught. "Your father is right to suggest that the knight's threats are but grief's ravings."

"How can you know that?" Elianne demanded, wanting desperately to be convinced. "You weren't there when he spewed them."

A quiet, amused gleam took fire in Adelm's eyes, then died. "I wasn't," he agreed, "but I know the sort of man who hurt others, and you know me well enough to trust my judgement on this."

That Elianne did; indeed, she was the only one who did. Adelm claimed he'd shared no part of his past with anyone other than her. She knew that in his twelfth year he had left a monastery to become the squire of a middling knight, a filthy brute of a man who craved the coins generated by training Adelm while despising Adelm as the illegitimate son of some unnamed knight.

"I think," Adelm went on, "that the noble bastard is undone by his loss." As he spoke, pain darkened his gaze. He swallowed and looked away from her.

Once again, Elianne cursed those murdering thieves. "I think you grieve for the ladies as deeply as their family does," she told him, laying a brief touch upon his arm. Adelm had known and admired the noble lasses, having made their acquaintance through Sister Amabella, from whom the young gentlewomen took most of their lessons.

Adelm bowed his head, a shielding hand keeping his face from her view. "They trusted me, and I—" His voice broke. "How did I serve them?" This last was an aching, whispered comment.

"Nay," Elianne protested quietly, "you cannot blame yourself for their deaths, not when you rode rings through the shire in pursuit of those outlaws."

In response Adelm only shook his head. When he raised it a moment later, his grief was once again well hidden beneath his usual shuttered expression. There'd be no more discussion on that matter. "Enough of me," he murmured. "Be content with my assurances. Haydon's folk won't harm you."

Elianne tried to smile, wanting to repay his confidence in her with hers in him. "What will you forfeit if you're wrong?"

Adelm smiled. Rather, his lips thinned and stretched, never quite lifting. "Here's one wager I cannot lose. Should either Haydon's bastard or lady attack you, you'll fend them off with the side of your tongue you showed your sire. Trust me, they'll retreat. What better revenge can they have on Reiner du Hommet than to leave him trapped in a house with a harridan?"

Despite her worries, Elianne laughed. "Your compliments make my head spin, sir knight," she replied, then sighed. "Well then, let's be off. The sooner they arrive, the sooner the lady will recover from whatever ails her and the sooner they'll leave me in peace."

"I am at your command, mistress," Adelm said with a bend of his head.

Chapter 7

Even with a donkey-drawn cart to slow their pace, it took but a quarter hour to lead Haydon's men to Coneytrop once they exited Knabwell's city gates. Coneytrop. Josce rolled the word over his tongue. Rabbit's village, that's what it meant. The corner of his mouth curled. An apt name for the coward sheriff's home.

The folk du Hommet ruled weren't rabbits, but they were near enough. There were less than a dozen cottages, more hovels than homes, in the tiny hamlet clinging to this overgrown track. As Josce and his men rode past, filthy children, dressed in clothing that had the shape of rags more than tunics, appeared out of the surrounding landscape or dashed from dwellings to watch.

The fields that supported them and their parents spread out over the rolling hills on either side of the pathway. On one side, goodwives and geese gleaned wheat from those plots that had already felt the scythe. From the other came the songs of their husbands and fathers as the menfolk harvested. That no mill or oven stood within view said that those two essentials lay within the sheriff's walls and that the hamlet dwellers paid him for their use.

As Josce's party rounded the thrust of a hill a bare stone wall rose up, nodes of flint gleaming black in its otherwise yellowish surface. The boundary marker of the sheriff's property, for that could be its only purpose. It was no defense, being too short for that, and it had neither hoarding, so soldiers might stand atop it, nor towers. Again, Josce's lip curled. This wasn't a manor house but a glorified farmstead.

He glanced to Elianne, who rode pillion on the back of Sir Adelm's horse alongside him. After her bold racing through town an hour ago there was something laughable about her present prim posture. As if she sensed him watching her, she looked up from the study of her clasped hands. Their gazes collided, hers darting instantly to the side.

Was it a flash of guilt he saw in her eyes? Perhaps it was the mystery of his father's death, how a ragged band of thieves could decimate a battle-trained nobleman and six war-hardened soldiers, but suspicion consumed him. In that instant her touches and her compassion became nothing more than a way to seduce him into trusting her. For what reason? To protect her sire, or herself?

Josce eyed the new darkness that marred Elianne's jaw. The bruise hadn't been there in the icehouse. That Elianne had come by her injury through her sire was a given; no other man had the right to abuse her. Despite the fact that Josce sought to ignore it, a reasoned inner voice suggested that if her sire had had to beat her to win her compliance, then Elianne was no willing player in this game.

Again, Elianne glanced at him. This time, their gazes caught and held. She bit at her lower lip, her brow creased.

In that private meeting with her sire had du Hommet told his daughter why he so badly wanted Haydon's kin at his home? If he had, then Josce would never discover what was said, at least not from Elianne. Nay, if he wanted to know what she knew, he'd have to do the seducing, not her. No easy feat that, not after the threats he'd offered her sire at the icehouse.

The thought of seduction revived the memory of the strange intimacy he'd found in moving alongside Elianne. It was a siren's song, a promise that with this woman he could create those luscious sensations men and women made between them. Josce slaughtered his reaction. Harboring desire for du Hommet's daughter didn't honor his father's memory or serve vengeance's needs.

He let his gaze shift to Sir Adelm. Du Hommet hadn't bothered to introduce them, but according to Sister Cecilia the man was a captain in the sheriff's forces. Whatever else Sir Adelm was, he was an ugly man, made so not by his features, which were harsh for certain, but by his lifeless expression; beneath the fall of his gray hair the man's brown eyes were without spark.

Aye, but at least Sir Adelm was comfortable. In order to ride, the knight had stripped off the ankle-length formal tunic he'd worn at the convent to make this short journey in only his long shirt and chausses. Sweat trickled down Josce's back. As little as he liked coming to the sheriff's house, he couldn't wait for the chance to disarm. Between his mail and the woolen garments he wore to protect his skin from his metal armor, he fair roasted.

Ahead of him Sir Adelm pulled his horse to a halt before Coneytrop's narrow gate. As was the custom for places like this only one side of the gate's double doors stood wide, so the hamlet dwellers could come and go as they needed. Elianne slipped down from her perch on the captain's horse, then hurried to the closed gate. With a push she sent it swinging inward, iron tenons groaning as it moved, so the cart might pass into her home.

The instant the door reached its inner stop she lifted her skirts and dashed out of sight. It was no more than Josce expected and as much as he dreaded. Patience and time were what he needed to win her confidence, but he hadn't much of either.

Rather than follow his master's daughter into the gateway Sir Adelm turned his horse, walking the beast back to the cart. He stopped when his mount stood nose-to-tail alongside Josce's horse. For a moment the captain eyed his fellow knight, rudely studying him, then he gave a brief nod.

"I'll leave you to Coneytrop now, sir." His voice was as emotionless as his expression. Good to his word, the sheriff's captain put his heels to his horse and cantered off without a backward glance.

Having had enough of all things du Hommet for one day, Josce only looked at the cart's driver, one of the convent's menservants. "Ply your prod, good man," he commanded. "My lady stepmother needs a more comfortable resting place than a cart."

The servant did as he was bid, the snap of a lash above the donkey's ears startling it back into motion. Behind the wee beastie the cart jerked, jostling its occupant. There was no response from his stepmother. Instead, Beatrice lay as one dead atop the cushion of thick blankets borrowed from the priory's guest house. Her loosened plait, hair the same coppery color that she'd passed on to all her daughters, streamed across her shoulder and onto the bedclothes beneath her. In that moment his father's widow looked no older than Emma and more vulnerable than her youngest daughter, the baby, Alice.

"How does she fare?" he asked of Sister Cecilia, who perched on one long edge of the cart.

"She yet sleeps," the young nun responded, her French proficient despite her English roots. As she spoke, her gaze glanced across his face to the side, so it seemed she addressed the air beside him.

"Aye, and about time, too, from the look of her," Sister Ada added from her seat on the cart's opposite side. "Tell me, sir knight, when did she last eat or sleep?" This was a chide, as if the nun thought Beatrice's stepson might have withheld food and bedding.

Startled by her question, Josce frowned in thought. "I cannot speak for her sleeping habits, for she was given her privacy whilst we journeyed. As for meals, there was food at every stop." His words died off into silence.

Aye, there had been meals, both before Lady Beatrice left Haydon and while on the road, only now Josce couldn't recall one where she'd done more than pick at her meat. In confusion he eyed the nuns. "Are you saying Lady Haydon is only starved and exhausted?"

Sister Cecilia cocked her head at him. "Of that we cannot yet be certain, sir. However, even if that's all that plagues her it's hardly petty, especially when she grieves so deeply. Until her heart mends we must guard her health carefully, indeed."

Considering this, Josce turned his attention to the courtyard before them. As farms were wont to be, Coneytrop's buildings clutched together, crowding each other. There were two barns, their roofs made of thatch, sheds and lean-tos cluttering their sides. A cock crowed the alarm, then the geese took up the warning, alerting all within the yard that there were strangers at hand.

Just as Josce expected, the mill and oven stood within these walls. At the mill a grunting and sweating ox walked a never-ending circle, turning the stone that ground grain into flour. Not far from him the final outcome of the beast's labor baked; hot air steamed from the great mound of an oven's chimney, the yeasty aroma of baking bread wafting from it.

Purring and cooing, doves circled and swooped over a similarly shaped cote, while bees buzzed around hives of the same rounded form. The stable was small, no more than four stalls, but behind it there was a wide and grassy paddock, cut through by a substantial stream. It was space enough to serve the needs of Haydon's horses for the short time they might linger at this place.

Three lads, all of them dressed in brightly colored castoffs too large for them, appeared in the stable door. At the sight of strangers in their courtyard, the tallest of them raced across the yard. "Mama!" he shouted as he went.

Mama stepped out of the kitchen, a square

shed with a tiny sheltered vent set atop its roof, the opening meant to allow the fire's smoke to escape while preventing rain from dousing the precious flames beneath it. A dark-haired woman of substance, Mama wore a gown the same cut and color as Elianne's, save that an apron topped it. Gathered around her were two pretty, well-endowed lasses with thick, dark hair, also wearing blue, and a scrawny child whose sodden and colorless attire suggested the scullery. Mama's eyes narrowed as she watched so many soldiers and an armed knight riding into her world. Snatching the girls to her, she lay protective arms about them.

"Go fetch your father from the house," she told her lad in their native English.

That Josce understood her words with an ease many of his French-speaking peers didn't own lay at the feet of his nurse, the woman who'd served as Josce's mother after his own dam's death in his first year. She'd been of the mind that a bastard, even one with noble blood, needed to master more skills than most if he was to thrive in this world.

The boy dashed for the house. Josce's lip curled. Du Hommet's home might have been a peasant's abode, save that it stood on a tall stone foundation. Not tall enough. The door wasn't even lifted the full storey above the courtyard necessary for proper defense. The roof was thatch, the walls, plastered wood. All it had to recommend itself was the ell, which suggested private chambers.

"Papa, Papa! There are soldiers and nuns in our yard!" the lad shouted as he streaked up the steps to the house's raised doorway.

The cart creaked and rumbled to a stop near the steps. Josce dismounted, Haydon's men doing the same. Sister Cecilia leapt down from the cart's edge with ease, while Sister Ada groaned and leaned heavily on the cart driver's arms to dismount.

Nick came forward to stand beside his lord's son, leading his mount behind him. "Not much this place, not after what we've known, eh, sir?" asked Haydon's master-at-arms. Short and solid, black of hair, with bright blue eyes, the master soldier studied the compound, shaking his head. "Exposed and vulnerable. Too much sky, not enough stone. I expected better of a sheriff."

His words stirred Josce to once again glancing about the place. Not all sheriffs were rich men, but the position was too expensive for a man completely without resources. Nick was right. A sheriff ought to have better. Du Hommet must have better. That garment had been far too expensive for one who dwelt in such a place. "Perhaps this isn't du Hommet's only property," Josce said, his gaze shifting across the yard until he looked in the direction that Elianne had run.

Questions piled up in Josce's brain. Would that he'd known Elianne's relationship to du Hommet before he'd spewed his threats. Now, instead of plying her for the answers he needed, he had warned her against him.

Nick turned toward the stable. "Hey you, lads," he shouted in English command, in case those here didn't speak the tongue of their betters. "Come and take my master's horse."

Rather than leap into the task, the lads both ducked back into their stable to hide. Haydon's master-at-arms made a disgusted sound. "What sort of man keeps only children as servants?" he said, once more speaking in the Norman French of his betters. "Never mind them, Sir Josce. I'll have one of our own see to your mount while you see to our lady. When you're ready I'll aid you in disarming."

"Who are you and why are you in our yard?" The man's challenge rang out over the yard, his English accent so heavy that his French was almost unintelligible.

Both Nick and Josce looked to the porch at the top of the house's stairs. Papa was hardly what Josce expected. The man was an oldster, at least twice his wife's years. Moreover, he was better dressed than Elianne, in a green tunic and costly red chausses on his bandy legs.

"Richard, it's me, Cecilia," called the younger sister in English. "Our lord sheriff offered the use of his home to this lady, who is both newly widowed and ill."

Surprise started across the old man's face. "He

did what? Why would Sir Reiner send folk here? Where is Mistress Elianne? She went to meet her sire at Knabwell. Why doesn't she return with you now?"

"Your mistress ran off, she not being overly happy with her sire's invitation to these nobles," Sister Ada called, also speaking the commoner's tongue despite her Norman blood, as she gathered her bundles.

"Nobles! These are nobles?!" Richard's eyes widened until he looked about to swoon.

"Steady yourself, Richard," Cecilia warned. "The lady is in need of bed and care. Come you, or you, Aggie," she said looking toward Mama, who yet stood in the kitchen's doorway, "and help me carry her into the hall."

"I'll bear my lady stepmother within doors," Josce replied in their tongue, startling those in the yard who hadn't expected him to know it.

Reaching into the cart, Josce once more lifted Beatrice into his arms. Her eyelids didn't even flicker as he settled her against his chest. Josce offered a quick prayer that the nuns were right, and there was nothing amiss with her that time wouldn't heal.

"Where do I take her?" he asked of Coneytrop's Richard as he climbed the stairs to the door.

Hesitation marked the old man's face, then he shrugged. "I suppose if she's exalted you'd better put her in the master's bed."

With the nuns at his back Josce followed Richard through the house's main doorway. A few feet beyond the door rose a screen, a long wooden panel, which meant the hall had a central hearthstone. Because a fire needed air to breathe and the hall's inhabitants needed a draught to carry smoke out through a ceiling vent, not unlike the one piercing the kitchen's roof, the hall's external door had to remain ajar no matter the season. The screen prevented winter from howling into the chamber, even as it kept summer breezes from offering relief to a stuffy and overheated room.

Sweat broke out on Josce's brow as he crossed the hall. It was warmer in here than outside. Who built a hall without so much as an arrow slit? Windowless room and thatch roof aside, du Hommet still owned his pretensions. A massive chair sat at the head of the hall, a master's seat, raised above all those who served him no matter how few or low they were.

At least Coneytrop had a careful housekeeper. The rushes covering the floor were fairly fresh, no cobwebs clung to the walls, while the room's few shelves were without dust. Not a fleck of ash stained the empty hearthstone. Nothing save repainting would cover the smoke stains on the exposed rafters overhead, but, given the fact that the fire almost always burned, that would be a useless waste of paint and time.

Richard led him to the hall's corner, then

opened the door that stood there, moving aside so his visitors could enter ahead of him. It was as Josce suspected. The ell was du Hommet's private bedchamber. He stepped into the doorway only to stop in abject surprise.

The bed at the center of the room was a treasure beyond the apparent means of plebeian Coneytrop. Carved ivy and trailing wooden flowers decorated each of its four posts. Precious green brocade curtained it. The fabric was shot with so many golden threads that even with the shutters closed on the room's wide window it glowed in the room's low light. The sheriff had untapped resources, indeed, to afford such a piece.

"Pretty, no?" Richard said, reverting to his own tongue now that he knew Josce spoke it. He squeezed around the knight to cross to the bed, where he lay a proud and proprietary hand against one of its posts. "Four years ago, Sir Reiner's second cousin, nay, third cousin I think it was, died and left this to his kinsman. Here," the man invited, pulling down thick coverlets to expose bedclothes that seemed fresh enough, their whiteness a testimony to the power of this summer's sun. "Lay your lady upon its mattress. She'll find naught but comfort in its embrace, sir."

Josce did as suggested. There was still no response from Beatrice, not even when strands of her hair caught in his mail. Cecilia, a heavy bag in her arms, came to stop beside him as he disentangled those strands from the metal rings that were the fabric of his hauberk. Ada, yet huffing after climbing the stairs, joined her fellow. Once Josce smoothed Beatrice's hair back into place, Ada looked up at him.

"You may leave her to us now, sir, content that we'll care for her." Having dismissed Josce, her gaze moved on to Richard. "Since Mistress Elianne is not about," she said, this time speaking to the man in the language of her betters, "tell Aggie that we'll need her or one of your daughters to aid us."

"Aye, sisters," Richard replied, already turning and starting for the door.

Josce followed him. When they were out of the bedchamber he lengthened his stride and caught the man by the sleeve to stop him. "I am Sir Josce of Haydon, stepson to Lady Haydon, who is widow to the murdered Lord Baldwin," he offered, including this information in his formal introduction to see what reaction it might tease from du Hommet's servant.

Nothing but compassion darkened the old man's eyes. "Ach, a horrible thing, that," he said to Josce. "My condolences to you and your lady on your terrible loss."

Josce's teeth gritted against his desire to throw the man's sympathy back into his face. It wouldn't serve Beatrice or his men if he alienated du Hommet's servants. Against that Josce needed to keep his tone cordial and be careful as he pried.

"My thanks," he said, then shook his head. "No offense against your master, but I'm beyond understanding how thieves can run unchecked in this shire for so long." Again, he watched for a reaction.

Richard's mouth twisted as furrows formed on his already creased brow. "Your frustration is ours, sir," he replied. "You cannot know how my master has worked to find them, but they're a wily bunch for certain, canny beyond even his ken." Honesty glowed from the man's face. Whatever secrets Elianne's sire owned, his servant wasn't privy to them.

Josce shook off his disappointment. Only a fool could believe he'd simply ride into du Hommet's home and discover all without effort. Nay, whatever the sheriff concealed would be well hidden and certainly not within reach of his invited and dangerous guest, a guest abandoned by his hostess. That reminded Josce that he'd have to tend to his troop's comfort.

"The men in your yard serve Lady Haydon," Josce told the servant. "They need something decent to fill their bellies and at least barley water to drink. Ale would be better, if what you have is fresh. So, too, will our horses need water and fodder."

"I'll see to it, sir," Richard replied with a nod. He would have turned, but Josce still held him by the sleeve.

"Have you accommodations for bathing?"

Josce asked, only to swiftly amend his question. "A tub and somewhere private in which to bathe?" A place as rude as this one wasn't likely to have a bathhouse.

God grant the tub big enough that water would do more than puddle around his ankles if he had to stand. It wasn't just to scrape off sweat and filth that Josce craved a soak, although he did long to be clean. From the moment Josce had reached Haydon to hear his stepmother confirm that his sire was truly dead, his entire being had centered on confronting the sheriff. Now that this aim was accomplished, he felt oddly drained and at a loss for what next to do. He needed time and quiet in which to absorb all that had happened this day.

"A tub?" Richard made the noun sound foreign, as if he'd never before heard it spoken. "Nay, we've got no bathing tubs here. What need have we of that when we have the pool? It'll suit you well enough, sir. It lays over to the north a ways, where there's a fold in the hills." The wave of his hand indicated a direction behind the house. "I'll see you get soap and such. My lad, Will"—he pointed to the boy who peered around the screen's edge at Coneytrop's newcomer—"can lead you to the place."

Will gave an *eep* at this and ducked back behind the screen. His sire paid him no heed. "Once you're there you can stay as long as it pleases you. You'll need no guide to find your way back from the place, not once you've walked it. I'll see no one disturbs you."

With this day so hot nothing could have sounded better to Josce than a swim. He'd stretch his muscles and rid himself of filth. Aye, and when he was clean, he'd ponder out his next step.

Chapter 8

Anger clung to Adelm like Coneytrop's dust to his chausses as he climbed the stairs that led into Knabwell Castle's hall. He'd stopped in the barracks only long enough to shed his better gown and don the short tunic that was part of his yearly pay. Not next year. Next year his pay would be different, because, if he wasn't dead, he'd be deputy here even if his mother's plan to buy him an estate didn't work.

A tense smile claimed Adelm's lips. Because of Lady Haydon's decision to go to the icehouse, it was now time to turn the tables on his father. Giving a nod to the porter at the hall's door, he stepped into the room.

So crowded was this long, narrow chamber that the noise was fair deafening. A few of these folk were servants, townsmen hired to see the king's soldiers fed and to keep the vermin that infested the castle to a minimum. Everyone else was a petitioner seeking either to settle his account with the king's sheriff or have Reiner bear his business to court for him. Among their ranks Adelm spied one of Reiner's sons-in-law, who was in a boundary dispute with a neighbor.

It was a harsh reminder of all Adelm had learned this day. No matter that Reiner had arranged his daughters' degraded marriages, he now considered them beneath his notice. Elianne wasn't allowed to visit them, or they her. Reiner had no less of a fate planned for the son he refused to acknowledge.

That his sire might attempt to use and discard him didn't surprise Adelm. Such was life. Only the strong survived, doing so by whatever means necessary and taking what was needed when it was needed. Thus, if he wanted to survive, it was up to him to prove himself his father's superior.

Adelm passed the dais at the hall's head. That the chair used by the sheriff and traveling justiciars for court sessions was missing meant Reiner was in his office. Entrance to that private chamber was through a door in the wooden wall behind the dais. Pushing his way through the folk crowded before the sheriff's office, Adelm stepped past the single soldier to open the door. Those behind him surged forward, trying to follow. The soldier threw his fists. A few well-placed thrusts of Adelm's elbow drove back the most persistent.

Shutting the door on the hall, Adelm turned to face his sire's office. A narrow window slit pierced the far stone wall, taming the intensity of this afternoon's sun to a single beam. Parchments were strewn across the table Reiner used as a work space. Although the clerk was absent, his gray quill yet balanced on its rest, ink oozing from its tip. Someone's unwary hand had toppled the sand pot. The spilled grains flashed like tiny jewels upon the table's dark wood surface.

Caught in the sunbeam, his father's scarlet gown glowed as red as blood. Standing beside Reiner was one of his deputies. Adelm sneered inwardly at the lad, the fuzz-faced scion of a local knight. Despite their supposedly refined blood, young Gilbert's family wasn't much better off than Reiner; a wealthier relative had provided what the youth had needed to purchase his position. That charity hadn't extended to the purchase of chain mail for the young knight, something Adelm's uncle had anonymously purchased for him. All Sir Gilbert could afford was a boiled leather vest sewn with metal rings.

Both men watched the sheriff's captain in surprise, then young Gilbert sniffed and turned his attention back to the tally stick in his hand. "As I was saying, my lord, Gledstyn's payment is short its required amount by—"

Ordinarily, being dismissed by a shit-assed babe would have amused Adelm, a man who could remove Gilbert's head with one blow. Not today. Heady with the certainty that he owned Reiner, a lifetime's worth of snubs and rejections by Gilbert and his ilk made Adelm careless.

"Gilbert," he said interrupting the youngster, "you and our lord sheriff are finished for the moment. Leave."

The youth whirled to stare at one he judged worth barely more than the manure that befouled his boots. The deputy's hand fell to his sword's hilt. "I'll have your tongue for disrespect, bastard. You'll use my title when you address me."

The challenge was suicide. Having bested Lord Haydon, a man Adelm felt he could rightly claim in every way his own better, only fed Adelm's confidence. He bowed. "I am at your convenience."

The young knight hesitated, new concern in his gaze. Never before had Adelm reacted to one of his slurs.

Reiner made an impatient sound. "Enough, both of you. There will be no dueling at Knabwell save the sort done in our customary practice bouts. Sir Adelm, we agreed to speak this evening. Retreat and seek me out then."

"It won't wait," Adelm replied, his tone demanding his father's compliance.

Reiner's brow darkened. The panic returned to his gaze. Adelm knew the moment his father decided he couldn't afford *not* to know what his son had to say. Reiner snatched the tally stick from Sir Gilbert's hand and tossed it into the basket behind his desk. "We're done for the now. Go," the sheriff said to his deputy.

Sir Gilbert swiveled on his sheriff, his other hand opening to display the three tally sticks he yet held. "But, my lord sheriff, we have hamlets left to review."

"Then you'll have to wait outside the door until I'm finished with Sir Adelm, won't you?" Reiner snapped. "I'll call to you when I'm ready."

Still agog over this untoward chain of events, the glowering youngster stormed across the room, circling around Adelm as if he feared bastardy might rub off if he came too close. As Gilbert pulled the door wide, those outside again surged forward, crowding the opening and jabbering, each calling for the lord high sheriff to please hear him. "Get back," Gilbert shouted at them, his tone vicious as he bulled his way into their midst.

The door slammed behind him, the noise level descending once again to a muted rumbling. On the other side of the table Reiner crossed his arms, one hip leaned against the table's edge. It was a casual pose, but there was nothing calm about the sheriff's expression. Years of acquaintance told Adelm that even as Reiner panicked he was calculating how he might use this conversation to twist his son back into blind compliance.

"What's so urgent?" Reiner demanded, his brusqueness camouflaging his worry.

Adelm warned himself to set his trap with care.

"Why in God's name did you send Haydon's bastard to Coneytrop? The man's out for your blood, my lord." He gave a sarcastic edge to his father's purchased and temporary honorific. "Do you think he'll sit on his thumbs and do nothing? Nay, he's bound to poke and pry."

"Which is why he has to be at Coneytrop, where Elianne can watch his every move," Reiner retorted.

The reminder of how his sire misused his sister woke a different sort of anger in Adelm. "And what if the knight chooses to avenge himself on you by using her? Too long have you let my sister run wild. She's long since forgotten a woman's natural caution. She won't think to secrete herself where he cannot reach her."

Reiner only smiled at the suggestion of his daughter's potential debasement, the movement of his mouth lacking any amusement. "May God prevent her from remembering how a woman should behave. Why do you think I insisted she stay at Coneytrop with him? You didn't see how he looked at her at the icehouse." Reiner sneered as he spoke, as if he thought it impossible a man might find his too-tall daughter attractive. "If the bastard seduces her, good enough. A man reveals things to his paramour he wouldn't share elsewhere, and she'll share it with us."

"Elianne won't give way to seduction," Adelm protested, pitying his sister. Her kindness and caring deserved better than having Reiner as her sire.

"Then pray that he rapes her," Reiner shot back. "So great will Elianne's hatred of him be that she'll likely slaughter him. Once again, our dilemma's resolved. Now, don't waste my time or your breath worrying over Elianne." Reiner's jaw hardened. "Worry instead for us. If the noble bastard turns out to be an honorable man, Elianne won't be able to sniff out what he plots, and we'll be done for."

A harsh breath of amusement left Adelm. "How easily you sacrifice your children, Reiner. Now that you've found a use for Elianne, that leaves only me as a potential tool. So, when and how was I to be slaughtered to serve your needs?"

"Are you mad?" his father snapped, straightening, his arms opening. "I dare do nothing against you. We're bound forever by the acts we've committed, you and I."

"Are we?" Adelm cocked a scornful brow. "You've been very careful, Reiner. I thought you wise when you insisted we take no profit from the robberies until long after we ceased to commit them. All these years, you steadfastly kept our blood relationship secret. I'm the one who paid the men who serve me in our plot. Amabella has sent goods to her family and received credit in return. Who would believe me now when I say you conspired with me, or that we are kin?"

Here, Adelm paused before continuing. "I hear Haydon's bastard demands you produce the murdering thieves or pay with your own life. To save yourself will you conveniently discover that your captain has been committing these robberies and expose me?"

Enough guilt flashed across Reiner's face to suggest he'd considered doing just this. "You make me sound more clever than I am," he protested, trying for innocent outrage and failing.

Adelm loosed another harsh breath. "In that you may well be right. I was the fool who came to you fair begging for you to use me. I even convinced myself you were the one who paid for my upbringing, when I could see with my own eyes that you hadn't the means to be my benefactor."

Reiner sneered. "So your mother finally told you all, did she? Don't blame me because you assumed what hadn't happened. If you'd asked I'd have told you that Amabella's family paid your way in life." He shrugged.

The belittling movement of Reiner's shoulders cooled Adelm's rage into burning ice. "Tell me this, then. If you paid nothing to raise me, what was your purpose in fetching me to Knabwell and keeping me at your side? It wasn't to advance my career or acknowledge me, for that you refuse to do." Adelm's voice softened into the tones of a threat. "That leaves but one thing. You needed a thief."

And a man who'd not balk at murdering innocent children. Once again, the little ladies' blood burned on Adelm's fingers, just as their foreshortened lives burned in his heart. He once more rubbed his hands on his tunic, trying to escape the sensation.

"So, what of it if I did?" Reiner demanded, outrage filling his face. "You could have said me nay when I lay the plot out before you, but you didn't. Nor did I tempt you from saintliness into sin. Your foster father was quick to point out that you'd more than once lurked in shadowy places to rob those unfortunate enough to cross your path."

There it was, sitting in the open air where day's light might show its every ugly facet. What little bond had ever existed between Adelm and his sire died.

"Bah!" Reiner cried, bracing his hands upon the table's surface as he leaned toward his eldest child. "Don't you blame me now because years ago you were as eager as I to make yourself a rich man."

"Aye, and what have you managed to do," Adelm chided, "but see to it that neither of us will have anything to show for all my years of effort? You had to goad Prioress Gertha one last time, and our wealth is now out of our reach." It was hard to pretend distress over this when the prioress's command worked so well in his favor. Behind those locked gates his dam had the time and privacy she needed to strip Reiner of his portion of their ill-gotten gains and give it to her son—if she truly meant to do as she promised and not betray Adelm as she meant to betray Reiner.

Across the room the sheriff snatched his cap from his head and dragged a hand through his hair. "What was I to do, leave Haydon's bastard unwatched, when he intends to destroy me? That stupid, pompous, religious bitch. Until Gertha relents we're right back where we were before the first robbery. Only now that Lord Haydon is dead there can be no more attacks by our 'thieves.' "

"You may be where you were," Adelm replied. "I, on the other hand, will be given the position of deputy, replacing Sir Gilbert." His mouth twisted in sour amusement. Aye, Gilbert deserved to lose his place, if for no other reason than his rudeness toward those he believed beneath him.

"A wise move on your part, Reiner," Adelm went on as if his father had agreed, when Reiner stood across the table from him with eyes wide and mouth agape. "I'll serve you far better than that babe-in-arms ever could. Promote me, Father," he finished, calling his sire by that title for the first time in all the years they'd known each other.

"Are you mad?" his sire cried, the shake of his head nigh on frantic. "I can't dismiss Sir Gilbert in your favor. There'd be an outcry across the shire."

Adelm shrugged. "As you will. But know your refusal leaves me no choice but to go to Sir Josce and tell him what we've done."

Reiner loosed a loud bark at the threat. "Do it. You just said there's nothing to connect us."

Crossing his arms, Adelm eyed his sire in disbelief. Reiner still didn't realize what he'd done. "Nay, I said only that you were careful to distance yourself, at least until you panicked. Where are the spice merchant's goods?" It was a gentle question.

Amabella had refused to have anything to do with the loot from the final robbery after she'd learned of Lord Haydon's death. Adelm had suggested destroying the stolen wares, fearing the connection as much as his mother. Reiner wouldn't hear of it. The spices were incredibly precious, the peppercorns alone worth a pence a corn. Moreover, all they'd taken wouldn't have filled even the bed of the priory's donkey cart, which, Reiner had insisted, made the stolen goods that much easier to conceal.

Terror now sapped the color from the sheriff's face. Wicked amusement tugged at Adelm's lips. In the end, despite all Reiner's complex twists and turns, greed had betrayed him. Lost in his frantic need to control Haydon's bastard, Reiner had actually forgotten where the goods were hidden.

"You must retrieve them," the father cried to his child, his panic at a new and higher pitch. "God help me, but I cannot do it."

"Now Father, that wouldn't be very clever of me, would it," Adelm said with a shake of his head, "not when their location ties the nobleman's death to you. Nay, they'll stay right where they are, for as long as they remain in that spot I own your loyalty and will be your deputy come the end of Michaelmas court."

As the trap snapped shut around Reiner, hot color blossomed on the sheriff's cheeks, the red as bright as his gown. "I'll see you dead for this, you son of a bitch," he roared.

The insult made Adelm smile. "Tut, what a thing to call my dam when she only partially deserves it. Better that you said I was the son of a son of a bitch. As for my death, I am at your convenience, Reiner, but beware my will and what is writ within it." An empty threat, but his sire didn't know that the document didn't exist.

Reiner's fists slammed against the surface of his table. The quill fell from its rest. Spilled sand bounced upon the wooden planks. Caged as he was, it was all the reaction the sheriff dared. With triumph as his companion, Adelm turned on his heel and left his sire's office.

Chapter 9

"Not that way. Can't ye hear the tumbling water? Come around the trees as I do, else ye'll soak those fine boots of your'n."

Only a voice as high and piping as Will's could have pierced the steady bass thrum of water as it cascaded down the hill's side. Standing up to her waist, wet hair streaming down her back, Elianne pivoted in the pool to look behind her. Some thirty feet from her, greenery thrashed. Branches on the overgrown willows and alders shifted, the height and violence of their movement suggesting Will led someone far larger than himself.

This was what came of running to the pool without warning Aggie where she intended to hide. All Elianne wore was her chemise. The sodden undergown clung to her like her own skin.

Her gaze leapt to the alder at the pond's edge.

There, in the same fork she'd used from the day of her first, toddling journey to this place, her clothing waited. Although they weren't that far from her, she'd never reach them and dress before Will and whomever he led were upon her.

There was but one option. Elianne dove, the cool water closing over her head. Eyes closed, three powerful strokes and years of acquaintance took her behind the sheeting falls. Here, time and cascading water had carved a hollow from the hill's side, leaving a submerged shelf. When she put her knees upon that rocky ledge, her head rose from the pool's surface only as far as her lower lip.

The water made a lacy curtain in front of her, distorting everything she saw through it. What it did for her, it did for those looking in this direction. As long as she knelt here and was careful with her movements, no one would be the wiser to her presence.

On the bank two figures stepped out of the greenery. One was small and dark, the other tall with a gleam of gold where his head should be. Dismay ate Elianne alive. It couldn't be him, not when Will was speaking English. Nay, she wouldn't allow it to be him.

"See? Isn't this wondrous?" Will said, his awed tone demanding agreement. "It's better than any tub ye might use, this I vow, Sir Josce."

It was. Elianne closed her eyes in hopelessness. God save her, but the man she most fervently hoped to avoid meant to bathe here whilst she was trapped behind the falls.

"Have a care, though," Will was saying to her father's enemy. "If ye've a mind to dive, ye cannot do it from that side."

Elianne frowned at Aggie's son. What sort of loyalty was this? He chatted with the strange knight as if they were the dearest of friends.

"And why's that?" A touch of laughter resonated in Sir Josce's voice. His English was without accent, as if he'd spoken the tongue all his life, just as she had.

"The pool's not deep enough to that side, but 'tis on the other. Of course, to dive from there ye must scale the wall to the top, there, and it's a goodly drop from there. Enough to make a man's bones turn to water," the tone of Will's voice suggested that he'd perhaps experienced just such a fear against all his mother's warnings against diving. "Our mistress has done it, but not many can swim or climb as well as she." There was pride in his voice now, despite the fact that it was untoward for him to find virtue in her unfeminine abilities.

"Now, have a care here as well, for there's a great frog that lives amongst these rushes. Me brothers and me keep him as our'n. We'd thankee kindly for leaving him be."

Bittersweet memories stirred in Elianne. Once, not so very long ago, all the frogs here had belonged to her and her sisters. So, too, had the slender grass snakes, the water bugs and the newts. This place and its magic had been their refuge and their playground.

This time, Sir Josce did laugh, the sound a warm rumble of amusement. "My thanks for the warning. I'll have a care not to disturb him."

"Yer a good knight and true, sir," Will replied, his tone content, as if he'd assessed Coneytrop's guest and was well pleased by what he saw. "Well then, here's yer towel and the soap pot. Ye can use it all if ye wish. Mama knows how to make more. Papa says ye may take yer time as it pleases ye. We'll be having us a bit of a sup come sundown, but there's naught for your sort to do until then." With a cheery fare-thee-well, Will crashed back into the greenery and departed.

Elianne bubbled her groan out into the chill water. What if the knight took Will at his word and spent hours here? She'd either freeze or drown waiting for him to leave, that's what.

The water tumbled. In the distance, a kingfisher called. Nothing else disturbed the silence. Easing back on the shelf, she rested her head upon the base of the narrow, vertical fissure that cracked open the hill's face. The crack was as tall as she and just wide enough for a thin person to enter. The opening led into a cave, the forechamber of which she and her sisters had years ago turned into their own castle, making chairs of rocks and tables of sticks with rushes upon the floor.

On more than one afternoon they'd woven poppets from reeds, dressing them in flowers and giving them milkweed fluff for hair. Aye, and in the pageants they'd staged for their playthings those poppets had lived far different lives than the ones that had befallen their creators.

Moments passed and still there was no splash to mark Sir Josce's entry into the pond. What was taking him so long? Elianne shifted on the shelf to peek around the edge of her liquid curtain.

The knight had one foot raised upon the log that served those who used this pool as a seat. He was removing his chausses, a garment that all men wore despite their station. The long stockings covered him from his toes to past his hips, a string holding it up at his waist. Just now, Sir Josce was unwinding one of his garters, the strips of cloth that fitted his stocking's legs to his calves.

His back was toward her, and his shirt was off, not for the first time over this past summer if the sun-darkened color of his skin told the tale. There was something about the span of his shoulders and the gleam of his bare brown back that made Elianne's breath catch. As had happened at the icehouse, that strange urgency stirred in her, this time with enough strength to make gentle wings take flight in her stomach. She ducked back behind the water and pressed a hand to her belly. Much to her relief the quivering stopped.

It seemed that forever passed and still he didn't enter the water. When she could bear it no longer, Elianne again peered around the fall at him. He faced her now, not a stitch on him. Sunlight glowed against the hard planes of his chest and the strong curves of his upper arms. His belly was flat, his hips narrow, the muscles of his thighs powerful. Her gaze caught on his manhood.

That urgency grew stronger still, while the wings within her stomach became a fair-sized flock. Once again she jerked back behind the concealing fall of water. What was wrong with her? She'd seen more than one unclothed man before this day, whether it be her sire, or Richard, or men from Coneytrop's hamlet as they swam or bathed. Never once had the sight of any of them caused such a reaction in her.

At long last Sir Josce splashed into the pool. Blinking away the fall's distortion, Elianne watched his head rise above the surface only a few feet from her on the other side of the cascade. He blew and huffed against the water's coldness, the toss of his head shifting wet hair out of his face. For a goodly while he alternated between diving and floating upon his back on the water's surface. Despite that she now shivered, his ability to swim won Elianne's grudging admiration. There weren't many as comfortable as she in the water, not even her sisters, who'd spent as much time here as she had.

Time crawled. She gave herself up to freezing solid, when he finally sloshed from the pond. Thank heavens. Her fingers were so cold that she could barely feel them. She marked off what she thought was long enough for him to dress and leave, but no branch cracked, no greenery crunched.

Impatience and discomfort forced Elianne to once more duck low into the water and lean out from behind the water's concealment. Disappointment only worsened her shivering. He wasn't leaving. Unlike everyone else, who washed while in the water, he stood upon the bank with his back to her as he applied his soap.

Frowning, she watched him stroke the thick stuff down the length of his arm. In that instant she again felt how his fingers had threaded through hers in the icehouse. As if he yet touched her she felt the strength of his palm and the warmth of his skin against hers.

She swallowed, those wings again taking flight. Then, reality and imagination tangled. As if it were her and not himself Sir Josce touched, Elianne swore she felt the stroke of his hand up her arm.

Heat exploded in her. From deep within her, a throbbing began. Elianne jerked back into hiding, shifting uncomfortably on her rocky perch. Oh, this was absolutely impossible. He had to leave. Nay, she had to leave, but how, when he blocked her path?

She glanced above her. Right here, over her head, was escape and concealment. Aye, at hand but beyond reach. She'd have to climb the wall to enter the cave, and that would expose her to Sir Josce.

Water splashed again as he reentered the pond. Perched stiff and still, Elianne waited, counting every breath as her desperation worsened. He'd soaped, now he was rinsing. He had to leave once he was done.

Once again, he swam until he was just beyond the water's curtain. The angle of his head made it seem as if he looked right at her. Elianne caught her breath and sank a little deeper into the water.

His head disappeared beneath the pond's surface. A moment passed, then another, and still he didn't rise. Good. If he drowned, she could leave.

Water bubbled beside her. Sir Josce's head broke the surface. His knee hit hers on the shelf as he came to rest on it beside her. His skin was warm against her own chilled leg. Shocked, Elianne stared at him.

He smiled. "So, were you planning to stay in hiding until you wrinkled like an old woman? Lord, but it's cold back here. Come back out where it's warmer and the sun shines."

With a shriek, Elianne dove through the fall. Kicking with all her might, she drove herself toward the bank and escape. She was halfway there when his arms closed around her, pulling her back. Thrashing against his hold, she screamed underwater. He dragged her to the surface.

She came to her feet, once more standing in water to her waist. Sputtering, she dug her toes into the mud beneath her feet and thrust away from him, reaching for anything, even a willow's trailing branch, that might aid her escape. He grabbed her wrists and pulled her back against him, wrapping his arms around her. With her hands caught in his, her arms were trapped alongside his as he held her.

Elianne strained. It was hopeless. He wasn't just taller than she, but far stronger.

A shiver shot through her, this one having nothing to do with the cold. They were indecently close, her back to his front, her breasts resting on his forearms. Wet linen was no barrier to sensation. His chest was warm and solid, his thighs like stone behind her own. She arched her back to keep her hips from touching his. Oh Mary, but what if he meant to wreak vengeance on her sire by misusing her?

"Let me go," she demanded, coughing out what she'd swallowed in her panic.

"How can I when I know you'll only run from me?" he said, his mouth so near her ear that she felt his breath against it.

"I run for good reason," she threw over her shoulder. "You want to kill me and my father."

"Not you," he said, his arms tightening around her. "It was never you I meant to threaten."

"I don't believe you," she shouted, her raised voice hiding both her fear and her own disconcerting reaction to their nearness. "Now, let me go!"

Her demand rang in the trees that surrounded

the pond, startling the birds into silence. Beyond that, no one else heard. Nor would anyone. The fold of the hills around this place kept it private and quiet.

"After what you heard me say to your sire I cannot fault you for your fear, but give me a moment to explain and apologize," he offered, his tone quiet, even placating.

As if she had any choice in the matter. Until he chose to release her he owned her. "A moment, but no more," she told him, her voice harsh.

"Forgive me," he said. They stood so close that she felt the words rumble in his chest as he spoke them. "I was overwrought at the icehouse. My lord father was dear to me, and seeing him bound for burial was—" His voice trailed off into a pained silence.

The memory of the grief radiating from him at the icehouse assaulted Elianne's fear. He'd loved his sire, even though the only life Lord Haydon could give his bastard was a tainted one. Hadn't she been beyond bereft when her own mother died? Aye, and in her grief she'd behaved just as Sir Josce, accusing her father of murder, saying his debts and all his schemes to win coins had caused her dam's passing. That Reiner hadn't struck his daughter for her insults stood as proof that he knew he'd wronged his wife.

Twisting a little in his hold, Elianne looked over her shoulder at him. The water had darkened his golden hair to a warm brown. Sunlight sparked against the droplets clinging to his skin. Honest grief glowed in his clear blue eyes. Beneath the pain lurked the loneliness that had drawn her to him at the icehouse.

"He was the last of my close kin," Sir Josce whispered, as if to explain what Elianne saw in his gaze.

All her fear ebbed with his words. What took its place was that subtle sense of connection she'd known. She relaxed in his hold. As she did, something sparked beneath the pain and loneliness in his gaze.

"Can you forgive me?" he begged softly of her. "I'd not have you despise or fear me, Elianne du Hommet."

It was the way his deep voice curled around her name that did it. Her heart skipped a beat, her pulse lifting until it sang. "All I can forgive is your vehemence, and you must be content with that," she warned, yet looking over her shoulder at him as she waited for him to release her.

He nodded in agreement, but his arms around her didn't loosen a whit. A shiver shot up Elianne's spine. "I have given you what you want. Now, you must free me." Her voice was no louder than a whisper.

Tantalizing heat sparked deep in his gaze. "Must I?" he breathed in return. As he spoke he pulled her closer still, his arms no longer imprisoning her.

Elianne should have shoved away from him.

Instead, she stood still against him. His mouth lowered until his lips rested against the spot just below her ear. She gasped.

His kiss was warm, his beard soft. He smelled of Aggie's soap. Her knees weakened as the heat of his body flowed into her, until he once more set her afire. The sensation grew, pulsing, as heady as if she'd drunk too much hard cider.

Only then did Elianne identify what that urgency within her was, and she was stunned that she hadn't recognized it before this moment. The good Lord knew she'd certainly heard enough warnings and lectures on this subject. Holy Mother save her, but it was lust for him that worked on her senses.

Oh, but that made him far more dangerous to her now than when she'd thought he meant to harm her. If she was to remain a virtuous woman she needed to end the contact between them, and right quickly, too. Even as she opened her mouth to command him to cease, envy stirred.

Was this pleasure what other women—women who'd been fortunate enough to have sires who'd found them husbands—knew? If so, then she'd been doubly cheated in her life. The need for a taste of what she'd been denied spiraled even as her father's threat of abandonment echoed in her. If she gave way to this man she'd be begging for her bread. Or, whoring.

Anger lifted its vengeful head. For years she'd held tight to virtue to honor her sire, and what had it bought her but the opportunity to become his pawn as he destroyed her future? No matter how she lived her life, from this moment forward she'd end it disgraced or abandoned, come that fate this week or years hence. Against that her sire no longer deserved her honor or her loyalty.

The need to repay his betrayal with a betrayal of her own grew. Her eyes narrowed. Aye, from this day on she'd do as she pleased and what pleased her right now was to know more of this.

Josce savored the cool freshness of Elianne's skin as he traced his lips along the line of her jaw. He'd been angry when he'd found her clothing in yon tree. It seemed too fortuitous, Richard sending him to the pond to meet his master's daughter, who waited in hiding there for him. He'd stretched out his bathing against the certainty of her seduction attempt, giving her the opportunity to reveal herself.

But she hadn't come forth. Instead, she'd remained behind the falls until he'd truly feared for her. Then, when he did "find" her, she'd tried to run. Was she truly innocent of any involvement in whatever her father plotted? Or was she more clever than Josce expected and meant to let him seduce her?

Either way, the seduction was going well, indeed. He touched his mouth to the spot beneath her ear. She loosed a breath, the sound fraught with pleasure. All remaining resistance drained from her.

As she relaxed against him, their bodies melded as if made one for the other. Startling hunger roared to life in Josce, consuming him in its fiery embrace. God help him, but he needed Elianne to touch him, and he to touch her, as much as he needed breath in his lungs. In passion's cleansing heat could he forget all, at least for this moment.

He moved his mouth to the curve of her neck. She tilted her head to the side, inviting him to do more of this. His pulse lifted. Releasing one of her wrists, he cupped her breast in his hand. Heat, glorious heat, washed over him as he closed his fingers over the hard bud of her nipple.

She gasped and thrust away from him. Every fiber in his being shouting in complaint, Josce reached to grab her back. He couldn't let her go, not when all that mattered just now was joining with her.

Rather than run she turned to face him. He swallowed as he looked upon her. By God, but he'd been wrong to think she wasn't beautiful, for he'd never seen a woman more lovely. Wet hair streamed in rich strands over her shoulders. Thin fabric clung to her, revealing and concealing her in one glorious instant. Her nipples were dark circles beneath transparent linen.

Need ate up all sense and purpose. Reaching

out, he pushed a strand of her hair back behind her ear, then traced his fingertips along the curve of her breast. She shivered and caught her breath in surprise. Up his hand went, following the line of her neck to her cheek. Her skin was smooth and cool to his touch.

Sighing, she lay her cheek into his palm. For reasons Josce couldn't name, that she did so made his heart twist in the strangest of ways. He threaded his fingers into her wet hair, the pressure of his hand urging her closer. She did as he bid, then took another step. Nipping at her lower lip, she hesitantly lay her hands upon his chest.

Josce caught his breath. Passion's needs flowed from where her fingers touched him, seeping into every corner of his being. Aye, more of this, that's what he craved.

Leaning forward, he touched his mouth to hers in a tiny kiss, a bare brush of his lips across hers. It was enough to set lightning to dancing in his heart. She trembled against his caress and eased another step closer to him. Her hands slipped up until she clasped her fingers at his nape. Her breasts came to rest against his chest. With nothing between them save her chemise he could feel every inch of her against him. His ready shaft lay against her belly, the sensation close to heaven.

Josce shook. At this moment he wanted her more than he'd ever desired any other woman. It took all his will not to grab her to him and take what he so needed. He cupped her face in his hands. A desire to match his own burned in her green eyes. When he stroked his thumbs over the jut of her cheekbones, her expression softened, desire's promise filling her face.

"Tell me to stop. Cry that I must cease," he whispered, trying to save himself from becoming her tool. He followed this with another brush of his lips across hers in an effort to convince her to give herself to him.

She looked at him, a tiny crease marring her smooth brow. Fear—nay, concern—lurked beneath the heat in her gaze. "And if I do not stop you?" she asked, her voice so low that he barely heard her over the tumble of water down the hillside.

"Then I will kiss you again," he breathed, his body afire with the very idea of what would follow. "After I've kissed you, I'll take you. If that isn't your intent, then say me nay now and leave. Stay, and I'll not warrant that I can stop myself, even if you later beg me to cease."

She considered his warning for a moment, then loosed a shallow sigh. With that breath her breasts shifted against his chest, sending the most wondrous sensation spinning through him. She lifted her lips to his.

"Kiss me again," she breathed against his mouth.

Josce groaned. It didn't matter why they did this, only that they did. He caught her lips with his, his mouth slashing across hers.

* * *

Elianne gasped beneath his onslaught, all the while praying that he never ceased what he did. Her heart raced, her skin burned. Everywhere they touched, heat grew. The feel of his shaft trapped between them fed the demanding throb that now lived in her womb.

He released her face. Wrapping one arm around her, his other hand went to once more cup her breast. The stroke of his thumb across its peak set her to quaking. She panted. In all her life she'd never felt so alive.

Just when she thought she couldn't tolerate his caress another moment he ceased his torment and slid his hand down her belly. His fingers halted against her nether lips. Before she knew what she meant to do Elianne shifted, her legs opening as her body invited him to touch her most private part. And when he did, even with the fabric of her chemise between her and his fingers, she melted.

Something about his caress demanded movement from her. She reacted to her body's bidding without thought, shifting against him. He groaned, then grabbed at her chemise, wrenching it up from between them until its hem floated in the water around her waist.

Her mouth yet clinging to his, Elianne gasped when his hands came to rest against the bare skin of her hips. He lifted her a little, far enough that her feet left the pond's floor. His shaft slid between her legs.

Startled, Elianne fell against him. Without the muck to anchor her toes, her legs floated. Needing more security than this, she wound her calves around his thighs.

He stiffened. His fingers tightened on her hips as if he meant to hold her just where she was. He tore his mouth from hers to gasp. Beneath the heat that filled his eyes, awe blossomed in his gaze.

"Oh my God," he breathed, "I've never—this is—" he gasped. Raw need for her blazed in his eyes. "Touch me," he begged. "Want me."

She did as he commanded, stroking a hand down his nape, only to shiver at the feel of his skin against her hand. With her lips she traced the line of his neck as he'd done to her. The taste of him was intoxicating. Even with her chemise between her breasts and his chest she could feel the springy hair that grew from his skin. When she shifted against him she learned that the brush of those hairs against her breasts made her tingle all the way to her toes. He groaned, the very sound feeding her roaring need for more of this. She touched kisses to his neck, his ear, then caught his mouth with hers.

"Jesu," he breathed against her mouth. "Love me," he begged, his voice gruff and quiet, then claimed her mouth as his own.

Against the heat of his kiss that throbbing within her became an insistent pulse. His shaft moved between her legs, finding its way between her thighs to the entrance to her womb. Josce freed her mouth. His breathing rough, he pressed a kiss to her cheek, the tip of her nose, then caught the lobe of her ear in his mouth. Elianne melted, pure and simple.

He shifted, his shaft pressing into her, only to have her maidenhead bar his path. Not until that instant did the enormity of what she intended hit Elianne. How could she have forgotten the terrible rending that both the nuns and her father assured was the price of losing her virginity?

As if startled, Josce released his hold on her hips. In instinctive reaction Elianne tightened her legs and arms around him, even though there was no chance she might fall when the water buoyed her so. It was enough to move his shaft farther into her. There was but a tiny pinch, then she held him within her, the fullness both foreign and welcome in one astonishing instant. Beneath the strangeness a new warmth woke, whispering that there was yet more pleasure to be discovered in this lust of hers.

Josce groaned. He kissed her ear as he held her against him. At his caress that throbbing within Elianne demanded she be closer still.

She shifted. Her legs tightened around him. He growled. The sound rumbled deep in his chest, then he moved within her.

A wave of delight crashed over Elianne. Again and again he moved, creating still more of what pleased her. His breathing grew ragged and hoarse. His body tensed. His heart pounded against her own.

Then, with a harsh cry, Josce clutched her against him and thrust a final time. A moment later, he relaxed. Gasping, he once more lay his mouth on her, but the passion she now craved with all her heart was gone from his kiss. From her womb came a demanding pressure, the sensation clamoring for something else, something that Elianne couldn't begin to name.

It was this nagging unfulfillment that brought home the idiocy of what she'd just done. Giving her father's enemy her maidenhead hadn't repaid her sire's betrayal. All she'd achieved was to completely ruin herself.

Elianne lowered her legs, releasing Josce from within her as she once more rested her feet upon the pond's mucky floor. Struggling against shame, she let her arms fall to her sides. Josce straightened. Concern darkened his blue eyes. So, too, did the knowledge of what she'd given him fill his gaze.

He raised a hand to trace his thumb across the fullness of her lower lip. Rather than comfort her, this gentle caress woke mortification. God help her, but what could he think of her now save that she was a whore? She whirled and splashed for the shore as swiftly as the water would allow her to move.

"Elianne," Josce called after her.

Ah, but this time he made no attempt to stop

her. Why should he? She'd already given him the only thing of value she'd ever owned.

The thought that he might come to loathe her because of her flawed character and morals made tears sting at Elianne's eyes. She clambered out of the pond, then leapt to the tree that held her clothing. His garments lay atop hers, the nearness of their belongings like a chide, a reminder of what had just occurred between them.

Behind her water splashed, marking his progress toward her. "Wait," he called to her.

Needing to escape him and everything wrong she'd done here, Elianne snatched her clothing, leaving his attire tangled as she went. With her gowns clutched close to her chest, she raced along the pathway that led away from the pool.

Before Josce could reach the bank Elianne had disappeared into the greenery. Even though he knew it was futile to follow her, he snatched for his clothing. His shirt snagged on a twig. Cursing, he yanked.

The sound of rending fabric was loud in the silence around him. He stared at the torn shirt in his fist. Ruined, just like he'd ruined Elianne.

Josce dropped to sit upon the log at the pool's bank, his shirt crumpled in his fists. When she'd agreed to lovemaking, he'd assumed that she did so for her or her father's purposes and that experience served as her guide. Instead, she'd been virgin.

That du Hommet might have commanded his untouched daughter to give herself to his enemy was beyond impossible. Then why had she agreed, spending her maidenhead on him? The better question was why he hadn't stopped himself when he realized that she was untouched.

Here, at last, was a question to which he knew the answer. With his thinking already fogged by desire, by the time he'd understood the meaning of the barrier that stood between him and his entry into her she was past saving. But, God help him, between her wrapping her legs around him and the novelty of making love in the water, he'd been out of his mind with need for her.

"Damn, damn, damn," he muttered, burying his head into his shirt.

This hadn't worked out at all as he'd intended. Not only had he destroyed any chance that she might serve him instead of her father, in his passion for her he'd forgotten all his father taught him of caution and sowed his seed with abandon. Jesu, but what if he'd planted his bastard in her?

Chapter 10

Under massing clouds and with a cool breeze at his back, Josce rode toward Coneytrop from Knabwell. After confronting his sire's body in the icehouse yesterday he hadn't believed his spirits could sink any lower. He'd been wrong. Today, he'd arranged his father's and sisters' burials.

The sister who served the convent's dead had been matter-of-fact when she'd suggested Josce return only the seats of his kin's souls to Haydon for burial. Of course she was right. Distance and the time since their deaths really left no other choice. Thus, most of his father's and sisters' remains would find their eternal rest in the priory's cemetery, while their hearts, packed in plain clayware with salt for preservation's sake, would return to Haydon for interment in the family chapel.

Never had Josce considered himself squeamish; it wasn't a characteristic a knight could afford. But when Josce plied his sword it was with the heat of combat upon him. Such a state left room for no other emotions. To coldly cut open a body felt so disrespectful that he'd insisted on overseeing the deeds. His stomach lurched, even though it was well into the afternoon and he'd eaten nothing but a bit of bread and cheese this morn. God help him, but he prayed there was no slaughtering going on at Coneytrop this day.

"Sir Josce, the gate?" called Nick from behind him.

Pulling himself out of his stewing thoughts, Josce found he'd ridden past the entrance to the sheriff's home. He turned his mount to face Nick and the three soldiers who'd accompanied him for today's grisly duty. Like him, Haydon's men had forgone yesterday's armor, their helmets and hauberks replaced by more comfortable attire. Their short tunics were of Haydon's green, a hue the color of spring grass, worn atop yellow chausses.

Josce's clothing was the color of the forest, hunting attire. It was all he had with him. When the news of his father's demise had reached Josce at Rafe Godsol's manor, Josce had rolled his armor into his pack to ride hell-bent for Haydon, leaving everything else behind him, including his servant. Rafe and Josce's other friends had all assured him that they'd see that his servant, Perrin, had the coin and supplies he needed to follow after his master.

"Pardon, Nick, I was paying no heed," Josce said, although there was no reason to offer an excuse.

Josce had known Nick for all the years of his life, so long had the man been Haydon's master-at-arms. In all that time Josce had never once seen the soldier's expression as sad as it was at this moment. Today's chore sat no less heavily on Nick than it did on his lord's son.

"No need to beg pardon, lad," the master soldier said quietly, and, not for the first time this day, he blinked away his pain.

Harboring his own ache, Josce turned his mount and rode into the yard. So many horses staying at Coneytrop gave Will and his brothers plenty to occupy their time. They were hard at their currying at the yard's center. No doubt that frog of theirs was grateful for the respite.

Will grinned when he saw them come. "Yer back at last, sir," he called out in greeting. "We've all been awaiting you."

"Aye, now we can eat," cried Rob, the middle lad.

"Dinner," squeaked Dickon, the youngest. He dropped his brush and dashed forward to catch Josce's reins.

Josce swung down from his saddle and started toward the house. As he passed the kitchen, Aggie's girls appeared in the doorway. It yet astonished him that any place could exist with but ten servants to its name, six of those being only children. The only two not related to Richard and Aggie were the pigherd, a hermit of a man who preferred his charges over humans, and the shepherd, a lad from the hamlet outside Coneytrop's walls. The scullery lad was the son of Aggie's deceased sister.

Aggie's daughters were called Mabil and Pippa. Of them, Mabil was a truly winsome lass. She also had her eye on the best-looking of Nick's younger soldiers. For that reason had Josce taken the lad with him into Knabwell this morn. A flirtation between Haydon's soldier and Coneytrop's maid would only worsen an already hopelessly complicated situation.

Standing in the kitchen's doorway, Mabil giggled, then leaned against the jamb. There was nothing subtle about the promise in her posture. Aggie appeared behind her, a frown on her face.

"You'll come in here right this moment, missy," she scolded, grabbing her daughter by the back of the gown and dragging Mabil into the concealment of the kitchen. Mama was no less intent than Josce on keeping Harry and Mabil apart. Aggie took a stance in the doorway, arms crossed, feet planted, her posture daring Harry to get past her to her daughter.

As Josce crossed Aggie's path he peered

around her into the darkness of the kitchen, only to realize that he sought Elianne. He straightened with a disgusted start. He wouldn't look for her.

He hadn't seen Elianne since she'd left him at the pool, not at the communal dinner last even, or when the household had broken its fast this morn. He tried to tell himself that this was a good thing. After all, it suggested he'd been wrong to suspect her. If she truly was the innocent she seemed, then vengeance's dictates demanded he keep his distance. It didn't honor his father's memory to lust after the sheriff's daughter.

That didn't stop subtle anger from stirring in him. She was avoiding him, as if she blamed him for what had happened between them.

What right did she have to blame him? He'd given her the right to choose, and she'd made her own decision. Anger grew at a slow seethe. Josce embraced his outrage, letting it cleanse him of pain.

Looking neither right nor left, he climbed the stairs, entering the hall's doorway just as something struck the screen's inner face. The distinctive clatter of dice across a wooden floor followed. One man groaned, while a goodly number more hooted in triumph.

Josce stepped around the screen. It wasn't just Haydon's men squatting about that panel. Aggie's Richard looked cozy indeed with the forces belonging to his master's enemy.

All of them scrabbled to their feet as they saw who came. Richard grinned at his guest. "God be praised that you're back. Your lady stepmother has awakened several times and called for you. Best go to her at once."

Right this moment? Josce eyed the waiting tables and their benches at the hall's center, longing for time and peace in which to settle his thoughts. What if Beatrice yet clung to madness? His head throbbing, Josce strode across the hall for the ell and bedchamber. At the door, he stopped, his hand raised to knock.

"Out! Out!" Although Lady Beatrice's raised voice was barely more than a hoarse croak, there was no mistaking her hysteria.

Against it, Josce reached for his sword. Before he could yank it from its sheath, the door shrieked open. Elianne, fabric clutched in her arms and her gaze aimed behind her at the bedchamber, stepped into his arms.

Instinctively, Josce grabbed her to him, dragging her back against him to protect her from whatever threat had Beatrice screaming. Elianne cried out and struggled against his hold. Josce tightened his arm around her as he scanned the bedchamber. All he could see were Sister Cecilia and Sister Ada staring back at him, their faces alive in surprise.

With the realization that there was no danger, Josce's awareness shifted to the woman in his arms. Elianne yet strained against his hold. He could feel her breasts against his arm. As tall as she was, her hips pressed against him. He shuddered.

God help him, but she felt as wondrous in his arms fully clothed as she had at the pool. Every nuance of the sensations they'd made between them washed over him. It wasn't wine he needed to cleanse him but Elianne's hands once more stroking his skin. Lost in that thought, his arm around her loosened.

Elianne exploded from his embrace and whirled. Panting, she clutched her hands to her heart, a half-formed garment crushed against her chest. Sunlight streamed out of the bedchamber's open door behind her to find bright blond in her honeyed hair. Shadows marked the pretty lift of her cheekbones and the fine line of her nose.

Color, hot and red, burst to life on her cheeks. "What do you think you're doing?" she cried out, her complaint a hoarse croak.

Josce frowned at her. She acted as if he'd tried to rape her, not protect her from harm. "I heard Lady Haydon shout."

That color deepened. "Aye, she shouted, at me," she said shortly. "Now, let me pass."

Her tense tone only provoked Josce's anger. "Is this how you speak to all your sire's guests?"

Distress dashed through her green gaze. "Everyone watches. Just let me pass," she cried in a low voice. As she spoke, she turned her body to the side so she might slip past him without touching him.

There was no mistaking her message. Not only did she blame him for what had happened but she'd give him no chance to explain. Her rejection cut through Josce's chest to his heart just as the nun's knife had done to his kin.

Anger rose to a full boil. He turned on his heel and stepped into the bedchamber. What she wanted he'd give her. After all, she was nothing to him but the useless spawn of the incompetent Reiner du Hommet.

Chapter 11

As Josce strode into the room he was startled anew by the bed. With the room's shutters thrown wide, the sun streaked through the window to spark in the golden threads of its closed curtains. So detailed were the carvings on the bedpost capitals that the wooden roses entwining them seemed to grow before his eyes.

Sister Cecilia and Sister Ada stood at the bed's foot. Not far from them stood three stools, placed beneath the window, where they could use the light. A basket of handwork stood beside the stools.

The bed's curtains were pulled wide. Lady Beatrice lay close to the edge. At some time between yesterday afternoon and now they'd stripped her of her traveling attire. Sunlight glowed on the pale curve of her bare shoulders where her streaming hair didn't cover them. Her face was still a sickly white, the rings beneath her eyes just as black as they'd been yesterday.

Her expression was hard as she eyed her stepson. For the first time, no doubt because Josce now accepted the fact that his sire truly was gone, he regretted not having done more to win her affection. Where her emotions went, so went his connection to his remaining half sisters, his only surviving kin.

"Come close," Beatrice called to him, her voice rasping, as if it cost her to speak.

"I'll bring you a stool, sir," Sister Cecilia said, rushing to do as she offered.

Two steps took Josce to the bed's side. Cecilia put her stool in place and he settled upon it. Beatrice sent her caretaker a commanding, sidelong look.

"Perhaps we'll wait outside?" Cecilia said, the matting crunching beneath her shoes as she backed away from the bed. "Come, Sister."

Beatrice waited until the nuns closed the chamber door, then rolled farther onto her side to face him. "Why are we here?" she demanded, the animosity she ever bore him filling her quiet words. "Why do I lay in the foul sheriff's bed? Why must I endure the presence of that wretched man's wretched daughter?"

"Because the prioress wouldn't allow me to stay at your side and the vow you wrenched from me wouldn't allow me to release you to them," he replied flatly.

Beatrice's brow creased as if she didn't remember the events of yesterday, then a touch of sheepishness took light in her eyes. "That was wrong of me," she murmured. It was a quiet admission.

Then, as if she'd surprised herself, her gaze once more hardened. "No matter why we're here, I won't stay another moment. Damn them, but those two sisters wouldn't remove me from this place without consulting you first. At least they heeded me when I bid them change the linens. Now you go out there and tell them that we return to Knabwell and the priory this very afternoon. I'll not tolerate another moment in that man's bed, or his home."

"On the contrary, my lady, you'll stay just where you are," Josce replied, too angry to tolerate her high-handedness just now.

Her eyes widened. "Upstart! Do you dare refuse me?"

"I do, and when I've told you why, you'll agree." Giving her no chance to protest further, he launched into his explanation.

"It wasn't until after you lost your senses that the sheriff came to the icehouse as you suggested he would. When I met him I offered the man the threat we intended, giving him a fortnight to produce the murdering thieves. Despite my harshness toward him he insisted I bring you to stay in his home, even excusing himself from staying with us. Now, madam, ask yourself why the sheriff would invite a hostile force to live in his house."

Beatrice blinked and frowned. Irritation and dislike dissolved. When it was gone, there was nothing to disguise her native intelligence.

"Ah, so our sheriff has some hidden purpose," she replied, "and thus must we remain lodged here despite our feelings for him. So, what have you learned of his secret intent thus far?" she asked of him, a new sharpness in her gaze.

Josce gave a shake of his head. "Nothing, but then it's been only one day. However, I do know much more about the thieves who did this deed."

Aye, he now knew that the bandits had coldly murdered his sisters. The means of their deaths had been his to see when the bindings were removed for the extraction of their hearts. His sweet sisters' throats had been slashed. Rage simmered over the depth of the horrible insult done to them. Against their innocence and youth, his own oath to collect payment for their lives at the expense of his own seemed like a holy vow.

"Tell me." The eagerness to deal out her own revenge lent new color to Beatrice's pale cheeks. "If you think to spare me by holding back a word, think again. I'll not have you coddling me."

"As you will. These thieves attack but once a year. Until this last attack their victims have always and only been merchants traveling alone, men who've been separated from the usual pack trains that traverse the shire." It was the members of the town council who'd confirmed what the sheriff had told Josce. "In this last attack a spice merchant was the chosen victim, a man who rode with five armed guards and three journeymen. Knowing that your lord husband traveled with six of his own soldiers and discounting the journeymen as more merchant than warrior, that means the thieves must have been at least twenty in number. Any less and they couldn't have bested the combined strength of Haydon and merchant.

"Aye, and if I'm right in this guessing," Josce went on, "then the bandits lost half their own. I spoke to Knabwell's coroner, who is no lover of his lord sheriff, by the by." Like the other royal servants Josce knew, the shire's coroner also scorned his sheriff as inept and boorish. "A bonfire was set at the battle scene. Along with the burned bodies of the spice merchant and his men were the skulls of twelve more."

"But six of those were our men, no?" Lady Beatrice interrupted.

"Nay, none were our men." Josce hesitated, for this is where the tale turned peculiar. "All of our men's bodies and their belongings were left untouched, from their weapons to their purses to their horses. Nor was your lord treated any differently. His armor was complete, not even his signet missing. Haydon's own now rest in St. Stephen's churchyard, one of Knabwell's parishes.

The town council saw to their burial, absorbing the cost, no doubt hoping to escape Haydon's anger over the murder of our lord and ladies. They also stored our soldiers' possessions until all could be returned to us."

Digging into the purse that hung from his belt, Josce pulled out his sire's heavy silver ring. Two small rubies were inlaid at either side of its carved face. He held it out, offering it to Lady Beatrice.

She reached for it, but before her fingers curled around it she snatched back her hand. "You keep it. Whoever next holds Haydon's title will have their own ring made."

When her words were out, Beatrice's breath caught. Tears glistened in her eyes for the first time since Josce had joined her at Haydon. Her face softened in grief. "He was a good man, your sire," she said quietly. "Shame on me for the cold wife I made him."

His throat tight, Josce's hand closed about the ring. "Madam, I will wear this proudly all the days of my life, grateful for the man who made me and the fine and loyal woman who was his mate."

Beatrice blinked the pain from her gaze, then loosed a breath of harsh amusement. "Don't think one act of kindness indicates that I've softened toward you. You remain the bane of my existence. Why couldn't you have been like other bastards, grasping and demanding? If you had, then your lord sire would long ago have set you out into the world to make your own fortune. Instead, you adored him, while he doted on you, treating you as if you were his heir." Much to Josce's surprise, there was little of her usual bitterness in this speech.

"Enough maudlin sentiments," she said, waving away her words and softness as if they were nothing. "Instead, tell me what sort of thieves leave such valuables behind them."

Josce leaned back on the stool a little as he spoke. "Would that I knew. All I can conjure is that the bodies and wealth of our dead were left untouched as an apology, or a message."

Beatrice looked askance at him. "That's mad. What sort of message would murderers and thieves want to leave?"

All Josce could do was spill his own confused thoughts on the matter. "Each time I consider it I see someone trying to convey that they didn't choose to attack our kin and wouldn't have drawn swords against your lord husband if he hadn't forced the confrontation."

As he heard the words exit his mouth Josce had to agree with his stepmother. It was mad to think there was any sort of method to this. If the thieves hadn't wanted to slaughter a nobleman they could have retreated when the baron joined forces with the beleaguered spice merchant. After all, if the twelve dead attackers were any indication, the two forces had been well matched.

Against that any sensible commander should have withdrawn. Seven years of careful robberies committed without detection said that the commander of these bandits was both sensible and cautious. So, why had he and his men fought on?

Lady Beatrice shuddered. "Why would anyone burn their own dead? It isn't human to leave them naught but cinders, with no countenance for God to look upon come Judgment Day."

Josce grunted as her comment stirred him from the pondering of his conundrum. "The coroner says that over the past seven years there have twice been bonfires out of which have come more skulls than members of merchant parties. Against that I can only surmise that they burn their dead so that none may see their faces."

It was as if lightning struck. Josce caught his breath, then leaned forward, grabbing the edge of the bed against the force of his comprehension. "Papa recognized them." His words were a raging breath.

"What? How do you know that?" Beatrice demanded in confusion.

Josce looked at her, his head spinning against his new understanding. "My father knew his attackers. That's why they couldn't retreat. Once he'd seen them they had no choice but to fight on to protect their identities. In doing so, they sacrificed many of their own."

Excitement took fire in Beatrice's gaze. "Aye, it makes sense," she cried. "Against what you assume of their troop's size, we must believe this the best armed and trained band of thieves in all England. That takes resources beyond the reach of cast-off soldiers or the gaggle of rogue bachelor knights who ofttimes plague travelers and merchants. And, with that thought in mind, we also know where we must look to find these 'thieves.' "

Her smile was grim. "Right here in this shire, among those of Baldwin's own class. Baldwin was acquainted with most of the knights and all his peers in this shire. As he should be, since my dowry lands lie here," she said, telling Josce something he already knew well enough.

"Who?" she demanded, hatred's heat firing in her eyes. "I want to know who among the shire's well-to-do can afford to maintain such a troop. Who among my neighbors took my babies' lives simply because they traveled with their sire and could bear witness to who did what?"

Josce shook his head. "Nay, it's not who can maintain such a troop, but who until a few weeks ago had more men than they needed but are now missing half of those they should have."

"Aye," Beatrice said, sounding pleased indeed at what they'd uncovered. "It's absent men we seek."

That his sire might have been betrayed by one of his own class stirred Josce's need for vengeance to a new heat. "Then upon the morrow my purpose will be to discover who's unexpectedly gone missing in this shire. By tomorrow's sunset, my lady," he promised, "we'll be far closer to those who committed this outrage."

"Why wait so long as a day?" Beatrice sniffed. "Ask the sisters right now." She waved away her own suggestion. "Nay, Sister Cecilia's common born and has lived all her life within Knabwell's walls. And, although Ada's father was a knight, after all her years at the convent she's not likely to know how many men someone at the shire's far edge might keep. It's the sheriff we need to ask."

Josce laughed at that. "Is that why we're here? Does the sheriff suspect, or even know, which of his betters commits these acts? It could be he allowed the robberies to continue in order to protect his own position."

It made sense and explained much. Caught between the powerful man he dared not betray and the kin of the powerful man who'd been slaughtered, du Hommet would do what he could to soothe both sides, all the while hoping he survived his predicament.

"I'll place our questions before the sheriff upon the morrow's morn, my lady." Feeling their interview at an end, Josce started to rise.

"Not good enough," Beatrice said, laying her hand over his on the bed's edge as if to hold him in place. Josce stared at her fingers as they rested across the back of his hand. In all the years he'd known her she'd never once touched him.

"If you're right and the sheriff knows," Beatrice was saying, her eyes narrowed and her mouth a thin line, "do you think he'll simply admit to what he's done? Nay, he'll shift and sidle, trying all the while to throw you off the scent. That tall lass, she's his daughter. It might surprise you to learn that women know far more about their menfolk than you men suspect. Ask her about her father and her shire."

Not at all liking the direction this conversation was taking, Josce gave a shake of his head. "My lady, she's none too happy at having us in her home. She won't tolerate being in the same room with me. I doubt she'd answer any questions I put to her. Nay, if anyone is to approach her it must be you."

Outrage filled Beatrice's gaze. "You want me to approach her when her father is involved in the deaths of my babies?" Her anger died into a quiet moan. Tears welled in her eyes. "How can you even ask that of me?"

Josce sighed. She was right. He couldn't ask it of her, even if it meant they lost whatever information Elianne held within her.

Beatrice scrubbed a hand over her face to wipe away her pain, then caught a ragged breath. "You must do what I cannot. You're a handsome man. Surely, you've more than once chased reluctant maids and brought them swooning to your feet. Pursue her. Charm her. Bed her, if that's what it takes to win her confidence, then use her to pry open the lock on her sire's secret."

Josce's eyes narrowed as resentment again stirred. Bedding Elianne—if lovemaking afoot, as they'd done at the pool, could be called bedding—he'd already done. What had it won him except more distance between him and the sheriff's daughter, destroying any chance of using her against her father? That didn't mean he needed to confess to his stepmother what he'd done.

"Madam, I can but try, but don't invest too much hope in my success. It's best that I plan to confront the sheriff on the morrow," he told her, dodging her suggestion.

"Fair enough," Beatrice said, the corners of her mouth almost lifting as she removed her hand from his. "You've done well to know so much in only one day's time. Glad I am that I chose you to accompany me here instead of Martin." Martin of Peterborough was Haydon's steward. "Not only do you understand what I need, you have the cunning and strength to win it for me."

When she smiled this time the curve of her lips was almost natural. Another first, Beatrice smiling at him.

"You cannot know how Martin protested," she told him, her tone fair conversational. "He wanted you at court, saying that your connections to the toadies who make their living from our king would better serve the settling of your sire's will than even the heaviest of purses I could give him to spend."

Josce frowned at her. "Martin's already in London to present my lord sire's will?" If he'd noticed that his father's steward hadn't been at Haydon before he and Lady Beatrice had left for Knabwell, he didn't remember it. "What sort of hurry can there be in the matter?" he asked his stepmother.

In all truth, any haste was useless. No matter what his father had written in his will—and Josce had no idea what that might be, having never wanted to know—both his stepmother and unmarried sister would find themselves wards to King John.

England's king knew well the value of a coin, especially when the same pence now bought less than it had ten years ago. Against that, John never lost an opportunity to take one, even if that meant snatching it from someone else's cold, dead fingers. Until little Alice was ripe for marriage in another eight or ten years, John would control her half of Haydon's income, less what he spent for the child's upkeep. In fact, Alice might find herself a nun without a convent, her entire lifetime spent as an unmarried maid in the king's court. She wouldn't be the first of John's royal wards to linger in fruitless celibacy; the longer the king kept his heiress-wards unwed, the longer he controlled their dowries. And when he wasn't milking their wealth, he was making them gifts to those foreign mercenaries he favored over his own English peers.

Nor would Lady Beatrice's fate be much different. She, too, might languish in the royal court never to remarry. Once again, it was to John's profit. As long as Beatrice remained an unwed widow, the king could make use of the income from her dower, the portion of Haydon's lands she kept to support her for her life's time.

"Oh, there's more than enough reason for haste," Beatrice said. "With Michaelmas Court nearly upon us a good number of England's barons find their way to Westminster. Martin will carry the news of your sire's death to all those peers who were Baldwin's friends. With my purse and their loyalty to support him, Martin will then demand our John honor the warden my lord chose for us."

Here, his stepmother paused, her lips taking an ironic twist. "You."

"*What?*" Josce stared at her in astonishment.

"Aye," she said, the twist of Beatrice's mouth tightening until she looked as if she'd swallowed something sour. "Baldwin didn't want the king bankrupting his estate, so he committed us into the care of the one man he trusted above all others. And, however much it pains me to say it, I agree with my lord husband's choice. You are the only man I'd trust with my daughter's fortune." Her last words were nothing but a gentle sigh.

Overwhelmed, Josce shook his head. What she and his sire wanted was impossible. "The king will never accept me as your warden. Not only am I landless but at only seven and twenty, he'll name me too callow to do a proper job as administrator." Never mind that there were younger men managing the properties of the king's wards; it was the fact that Josce might be more loyal to his family than he was to his king that would deter John.

"You're no longer landless." Beatrice's voice was quiet now and not in the least harsh. "With your sire's death, you gained control of Blauwstyn for your life's time."

Josce swallowed. Blauwstyn was a prosperous farmstead, not unlike Coneytrop, with two mills and a great flock of sheep. True, he'd only ever be the property's manager, incapable of passing the lands on to his heirs, but ownership of his sire's property was beyond any bastard's reach. Once Josce died, the land would revert to Haydon's legitimate line.

Aye, but he only had this property because his father was dead. The image of his sire's torn and broken body rose in his mind's eye. Once again, Josce watched the nun add insult to injury and remove the heart that had cherished him. Grief welled, trying to consume him.

Shooting to his feet, Josce turned his back on his stepmother. Blindly, he made his way to the door. Once outside the chamber, he walked, not caring where he went.

Chapter 12

A big basket hung from each of Elianne's arms, jostling and joggling with her every step. In one lay days' worth of sewing, the chore she'd chosen to do whilst she hid from Sir Josce. Nay, that wasn't fair. It wasn't the knight she sought to hide from but herself.

All it had taken to set her body into a new lustful flight had been the feel of Sir Josce's arm around her. Every one of the wonderful sensations he'd made in her had returned. No wonder nuns had holy vows to bind them into celibacy. Although Elianne had only just made lust's acquaintance it already owned her body and, most likely, her soul as well. That was dangerous, indeed.

In her other basket were onions for braiding, the preparation of these fragrant roots for winter storage one of her most portable food-related chores. It was also something she could do after it grew too dark to sew. Tucked in with the vegetables was a loaf of bread, a pot of cheese, and fruit, a poor replacement for the formal meal Elianne would forsake to hide from Sir Josce.

Bundled before her was a blanket and the pallet she'd used last night in the kitchen after having been displaced from her usual sleeping arrangements because of Haydon's visit. The scent of straw escaped the pallet's casing, stirred to it by the way she'd bent the mattress, the smell strong enough to tickle her nose.

There'd be no tossing and turning in the kitchen for her tonight. Nay, she meant to sleep in her garden. To sleep under the stars was no burden, not for her. As long as it didn't rain.

Elianne cast a calculating eye heavenward. It was cooler today than yesterday and clouds filled the sky, but they weren't the sort that promised moisture. Now, the morrow might be a different tale, but she'd deal with that when the time came. At this point in her life the morrow seemed years away, especially when she yet had hours left before this day's sun set.

Chuffing against her awkward burdens, Elianne made her way around Coneytrop's kitchen garden, the great expanse of soil behind paddock and barns that kept vegetables on her table. As she went she eyed the newly emptied rows, evidence of what had been harvested this day. Another chore weighed in on her overburdened and hopelessly disrupted schedule. It wouldn't be long before the garden was empty. When that happened, the soil would need turning, the remains of this year's bounty worked into the dirt to feed the earth. Aye, and the doing of this was one chore that wouldn't wait. The soil needed to sleep a little before Saint Martin's Day and the planting of next year's garlic.

Reaching the back of Coneytrop's garden, Elianne passed through the sheepfold to the farthest corner of her home. Here, a wall shorter than that enclosing Coneytrop extended out about twenty feet to claim a bit of ground that had no other use save that of pleasure. What had once been her mother's private space now belonged, every bush and bloom, to Elianne. Unlike the pool, which everyone in the household used, no one, not even her sire, entered Elianne's garden without her permission. Here, in the arms of the beauty she'd created, would she be safe from Sir Josce for as long as he remained at Coneytrop.

As Elianne made her way down her garden's wall toward its gate, she smiled. Her lungs filled with the melded scents of lilies, stock and marigold. But mostly there were roses. At her bidding did the twining, tangling bushes now tumble over the garden's enclosing wall in showy display.

She stopped before the gate and frowned. The door stood ajar, when Elianne was almost positive she'd closed it after hiding in here all of yesterevening before finally finding her rest in the kitchen. She shrugged away her carelessness, turned her back to the doorway and started into the garden, pulling what she carried as far forward as possible.

It wasn't the gateway that caused this maneuver but her precious arbor, which lay just inside her garden's gate. She'd woven willow branches into a supporting skeleton on which she'd trained her rose canes, turning a simple doorway into a four-foot-long tunnel of fragrance, a tunnel that was just a little narrower than the doorway.

As she backed into the arbor, Elianne eyed its crest. The canes that lay across its roof were in desperate need of pruning, their weight enough to bend the fragile framework. Aye, but they yet flowered, and she didn't have the heart to remove them. A few more weeks, she promised herself, and it would be time for their autumn pruning.

Juggling and shifting her burdens, Elianne was almost clear of the arbor when her onion basket caught. Stopping, she gave the basket a careful tug. The whole framework wobbled.

She studied the basket. It was a wayward cane, having slipped beneath the onion's basket handle, that trapped her. If she wanted to free herself she'd have to walk back toward the gate a little. Elianne took a forward step, only to have the basket on her opposite arm catch. She twisted, trying to see what held her this time, but all that met her gaze was roses.

This is what came of trying to do too much at

once. With a breath of frustration, she once again juggled what she held. Pallet straw crunched. The arbor jiggled. The sewing basket stayed fixed outside the willow work.

"Mary save me," she cried in rising irritation.

"Go away," Sir Josce growled from the garden behind her.

Gasping, Elianne started, her arms opening. Her pallet fell. Her onion basket tipped, spilling the precious vegetables onto the path. Willow supports snapped. Elianne leapt back as, with a creak, the overladen roof of her bower crashed down at her feet. It lay before her, a tangled mass of broken, thorny roses and shattered willow.

"Nay," she cried in heartbreak, then whirled. There, on her very own mother's bench, a rustic construction of piled stones with wooden planks for a seat, sat Sir Josce. He wasn't even looking at her. Instead, his head was bowed, his elbows braced upon his spread knees.

"This is my garden, mine alone," Elianne scolded, striding to stand before him, her hands on her hips. "You've no right to command me gone from what belongs to me. Nor do you have my permission to be here. Be gone with you."

He looked up at her, an anger to match her own filling his gaze. "I don't need your permission to be anywhere within this house when I already have your sire's. He gave me the use of his home and this is the space I choose to use. You leave."

"Would that I could," she snapped back. "If you haven't noticed, the gate is now blocked. Because of you, my arbor is now ruined." Her voice broke a little against the destruction of something so cherished.

With a seething breath Haydon's son came to his feet. Elianne took an instinctive and protective backward step. Oh Lord, but he was bigger and stronger than her sire. Any blow he landed was likely to do more than sting.

Rather than attack her, Sir Josce stepped past her as if he meant to depart. Startled that he might do as she bid, Elianne turned to watch. He stopped at what remained of her bower, grabbed a piece of the broken framework, and yanked. Torn leaflets flew. Fragrant petals fell like rain as he dragged the canes through the framework, stripping the branches of what grew on them.

Elianne's heart jerked. "Stop," she cried, rushing to his side. "You're killing what I worked so hard to grow!"

"Stop?" he snarled, turning on her. His blue eyes were fair afire with what raged in him. "Make up your mind. You want one of us to leave this place because you cannot tolerate my presence. In that case, I need to carve a path through this mess."

Eyes narrowed and jaw tight, he took up another piece of the broken skeleton and pulled. Elianne yelped as canes cracked. She grabbed at his hands to save her precious plants.

"Stop," she cried more gently, her fingers closing over his as she met his gaze.

Beneath her hands, his fingers tightened into fists. His strength flowed into her. If he chose to ignore her there'd be nothing she could do about it. Against that, she added a quiet "Please?"

He sucked in a surprised breath. Dropping what he held, he tore his hands from hers and grabbed her by the upper arms. "What were you thinking yesterday?" he nigh on shouted at her. "Why did you let me do that to you? You were maiden still."

His questions startled Elianne even as shame burnt like hell's fire in her heart. The urge to once more run from him, not to escape him but to hide from what she'd done, returned. A useless effort. It was too late for hiding her sin, at least from him. She forced herself to look up into his face.

Anger yet touched the lift of his cheekbones, but what filled his eyes was a goodly dose of guilt. That surprised her. He shouldn't feel guilty, not when he'd only taken what she'd offered him.

"Why?" he begged of her more gently this time.

She drew a shaken breath. Without anger to shield her from it, his nearness reawakened that warm throbbing she'd known at the pool. "Because you made me feel—" Her whisper died off into silence. She had no words to describe how he had made her feel—only that it was just the same as he made her feel right now. She offered a helpless shrug.

His face softened. His grip on her arms loosened. A breath of laugh left him.

"Aye, that's how you made me feel, as well," he said, his voice low. A touch of hurt returned to his gaze. "If you don't blame me, then why do you run from me?"

"Blame you?" she cried. Before she knew what she intended, she lifted her hands to rest them upon his chest. Beneath her palms she felt his heartbeat, steady and strong. "I can't blame you, not when you made what we did between us my choice."

With her words, shame once more rose to heat her face. "And that is my reason for running. How you must despise me. Not that I don't deserve it," she sternly reminded herself. "It must seem to you that I carelessly gave to a complete stranger what I should have cherished."

He shook his head. "Nay, I won't condemn you. I shouldn't have lingered at the pool once I knew you were there."

"You saw me hiding?" she asked, a little piqued that she'd nearly frozen solid when he'd known all the while just where she'd been. But of course he'd known. He'd laid his clothing on top of hers.

Amusement lightened his eyes a little. "Not at first. It took me a while to discern just where you hid." He smiled, but it sat askew on his lips. "There are reasons why fathers keep their daughters fully clothed and well guarded in the presence of other men. The passion that overwhelmed us yesterday is one of them. It's I who am at fault for this. You bid me release you, and I refused."

Elianne blinked, wholly stunned. Her father was wrong. Not all men loathed and shunned the women they deflowered. Here was Sir Josce apologizing, even taking blame, where he owned no fault at all.

That only set her own guilt to writhing. Shame on her for using such a good man in a childish and futile attempt to strike back at her sire. Not that she wanted to admit to Sir Josce what she'd done, any more than she'd tell him how she yet longed for more of his kisses and touches.

Her shame burned a little brighter at that thought. Perhaps she wouldn't starve to death in the future. It seemed she was a whore by nature.

"You are too kind," she murmured. "No matter what you say, the fault and the sin must remain mine."

Releasing his hold on her arms, he lifted a hand as if he meant to stroke her cheek. Before he touched her, his hand fell back to his side as if he thought the better of a caress. He was right to do so. Elianne let her hands fall from his chest, then folded her fingers before her as if in prayer. A sham. All she prayed for was a chance to once more be held by him.

"Nay, we'll both have to share the wrongdoing," he said, taking a step back from her, "each doing our own penance once we've confessed to it. God grant that penance is all we have to do." Concern darkened his gaze. "So great was the pleasure you made in me that I forgot myself. I can only hope I didn't plant my seed in you yesterday."

Elianne's knees weakened. The thought that she might already harbor his babe filled her. It wouldn't be long before she knew. Her hand dropped to her abdomen as she reminded herself that her courses were due to start in the next few days.

At her movement, he whirled, his shoulders tensed. "Damn, damn, damn," he muttered, then strode away from her.

Elianne watched as he made his way to the garden's far end, which wasn't far, considering how small her little piece of the world was. He stopped at the perimeter, his back to her, his feet crushing sweet violets. With his arms braced against the wall he leaned toward the cold yellowish stones. Grief radiated from him.

Knowing that she couldn't control her lust for him, Elianne should have let him be. Good manners demanded that for privacy's sake she leave him to his own emotions. She couldn't. As had happened in the icehouse, the need to soothe him grew until she couldn't stop herself.

She followed him, coming to halt right behind him. At the priory she'd caught back her touch. There was no longer any point to that sort of caution, not after what had happened between them at the pool.

Daring much, she put her arms about his waist. With her front to his back, she rested her cheek upon his shoulder. "Tell me," she whispered. "Tell me all of what makes you ache so. In the spilling of your tale I pray you find a little peace."

Chapter 13

Josce drew a sharp breath as Elianne embraced him, only to relax in the next instant. There was naught of desire in her touch. Neither did her arms about him suggest that cloying sort of ownership some women adopted after they'd given themselves to a man. All she offered was comfort, and this he accepted with a gratitude beyond words.

"You cannot imagine my day," he murmured. "I commanded that those I love be further mutilated. Their hearts were removed for later interment at their home."

"Ah," she replied, the sound owning no judgement in its syllable. Somehow, the fact that she didn't condemn what he'd done went far to ease what ached in Josce.

She stirred against him. "Their home, not yours?" It was a gentle question.

"Not mine. Never mine," he retorted softly. "Bastards don't have homes, not unless they buy one for themselves." The corner of Josce's mouth tightened against what his sire had given him. "Or, by some miracle, inherit one," he muttered.

"Your sire forgot you in his will?" she asked.

"On the contrary." It was guilt's harshness he heard in his own voice. "My lady stepmother has just informed me that I now own one of my sire's finer hamlets, a place not unlike this one, which I'll hold for my life's time."

"You didn't expect this."

She made the comment a flat statement, as if she believed he'd never owned a whit of ambition in all his life. What else should she think? Only a fool would pine after an inheritance when his birth denied him hope of one. Josce supposed that made him a fool, then.

"Nay, I expected it, even longed for it when I had no right. My sire incurred great expense in my upbringing, sending me to court and King John as if I were his legitimate heir. He even purchased my horse and armor when I came of age. And still I betrayed his affections to long for what couldn't be mine."

He drew a ragged breath. "In the most secret part of my heart I coveted Haydon's title. I wanted to be my father's heir. I wanted men to thrust their daughters at me for my consideration rather than stand between their lasses and Haydon's far less desirable bastard."

Elianne's head lifted from his shoulder. Josce breathed out against the absence, wanting her cheek's pressure once more against his back.

"You wanted no more than what other men desire," she said. "How can harboring such thoughts be a betrayal of your sire? Did you demand that he make you his heir?"

"Nay, of course not," he retorted in impatience. "It would be pointless, when bastards cannot inherit the way other men can." He shouldn't have to tell her this.

"Then, you demanded that he provide this piece of property to support you throughout your life." It was another flat statement.

Josce stiffened in outrage. "I did not."

"Just as I thought," she replied, a touch of amusement in her voice. "Well then, it seems to me you've done no more than to wish for what wasn't. There's no sin in that. Lord knows, if there were I'd have been damned to hell long ago." The amusement in her tone was now flavored with a little bitterness.

Once more leaning toward him, she this time set her chin upon his shoulder. In doing so, her plait curled forward, its bulk coming to rest against his neck. The warm smoothness of her braided hair against his skin sent a shudder through Josce and left him aching to comb his fingers through her tresses the way a lover did.

"Don't you think," she went on, "that the reason your sire remembered you in his will is because you satisfied all his earthly expectations? If you'd behaved badly toward him or disappointed him or betrayed him in some other way, surely he'd have excluded you."

She made it sound so simple when it was anything but that. "Do you think I told him what I expected and longed for?" Josce demanded. "Nay. Bad enough that I owned such illicit longings. I wasn't about to repay his affection by confessing such a thing to him."

Her laugh was deep and rich. A slight turn of Josce's head was all it took to let him look into her face. As had happened yesterday, he found that her unusual height and bold mannerisms filled him with subtle pleasure. Here, something within him seemed to say, was a woman who could be his equal, his partner, in all things.

She watched him, her green eyes alight, her smile wide enough to display the pretty line of her teeth. "Here you are, telling me you kept your longings to yourself while accepting the life your father gave you with grace and ever reflecting gratitude for the gifts he settled on you. I think me that's all the more reason for him to reward you."

The rightness of what she said washed over him. His father had never promised an inheritance, but then again neither had Lord Baldwin suggested there'd be nothing for his only son in his will. In all truth they'd never discussed it. Now Josce wondered if his own unease over the subject had caused his father to avoid any mention of his final arrangements.

With that in mind Josce revisited the details his stepmother had provided of what was now his. Gratitude stirred beneath the pain of his sire's loss. Not only had Baldwin of Haydon revealed how much he'd trusted his son by placing his legitimate heirs into Josce's hands but his father had also bestowed upon his beloved bastard the seed from which Josce's own fortune might sprout.

Elianne was right. What his father had given him was nothing more than a reflection of a sire's pride in the son he'd raised and loved. As Josce accepted this, he felt closer to peace than he had since learning of his father's death.

Josce once again eyed his reluctant hostess. "How came you to be so wise that you can decipher the message one man sends another in his will?"

It was a quick laugh that escaped her even as the amusement swiftly dimmed from her face. Her arms around him started to open. Josce caught her hands to hold her against him. She couldn't leave him yet. Her touch was more welcome and necessary than any woman's caress he'd ever known.

"Stay," he commanded her.

At his bidding she again leaned against him, but there was a new tautness to her body that suggested she was no longer comfortable. "I suppose it's because I know what it is to long for an inheritance without hope of ever having one."

Josce sighed for her. "Then you're a younger daughter with a brother who takes all."

"Nay," she said with a tiny shake of her head, "I'm the youngest daughter of three." When the words were out she turned her head upon his shoulder, hiding her face from him.

"If that's so, then you and your sisters divide Coneytrop and the lord sheriff's other properties between you when he's gone," he said. This was commonly done when there were only daughters to inherit, indeed common enough that he shouldn't have to explain it to her.

"What other properties?" Elianne retorted, her voice harsh, her head yet turned. "Coneytrop and the hamlet beyond these walls is all my sire owns."

Josce frowned. How could Coneytrop be the sheriff's only possession? Someone who had so little could never afford that bed and the fine red gown. Needing to see her face so he might read the answers in her gaze, Josce stepped from her embrace and turned.

Her head bowed, Elianne let her hands drop to her side. He crooked a finger beneath her chin to lift her face, then studied her features. Fear for her future mingled with anger and frustration in her expression. A touch of moisture made her eyes gleam.

"There's nothing for me," she told him, gently

shifting her head off his supporting finger, "nor anything more for my older sisters than what they took with them into their marriages. Indeed, they may even lose those few virgates after my sire passes. Upon his death what my father borrowed from two different kings to twice purchase his position must be repaid along with other debts."

Josce sighed again, this time in new understanding. The country's previous king, Richard, known as the Lionheart, had treated the offices of England's sheriffs as trade goods. Twice in the ten years he'd reigned had he sold them to the highest bidders, each time demanding higher fees from the buyers than was traditional, thereby cutting into the position's customary profits.

When John had followed his brother onto the throne, the last of old Henry's cantankerous brood had been even more desperate for coins. Not only had John maintained the fees his elder brother had applied but he'd also added myriad other fines until he'd stripped away a goodly portion of the profit from a position that had once been a guaranteed route to wealth. Aye, but however small, there was still profit to be had unless a man was spendthrift, which explained the bed and fine gown. Reiner spent what he earned, setting nothing aside for his daughters.

Josce's heart tugged over Elianne's predicament. Left without resources, she'd beg for her living if her married sisters didn't open their homes to her. And, if their father's death replaced expected inheritances with new debts, her sisters' husbands weren't likely to offer to feed yet another impoverished woman.

"Shame on me for burdening you with my problems when your life's by far the more difficult," he said. "There's not much hope for you, is there?"

Elianne's mouth twisted. Her cheeks took fire. She bowed her head to again consider her folded hands.

"And thus did I say you aye yesterday," she whispered. "I coveted a taste of what other women know. Fool that I am, in my longing to discover what my sire's poverty denies me I didn't consider that you might set your seed in me."

"Neither did I," Josce said with a wry laugh as the longing to once more hold Elianne against him stirred in the pit of his being. "All I could think was how wonderful you felt in my arms."

Her head lifted. The need to know she was special beyond his simple need to copulate filled her green eyes. "Did I?" she whispered.

Even thinking about the sensations she'd wakened in him was enough to send a shudder through Josce. "You have no idea," he said, his voice suddenly hoarse.

Her smile was slow. This time the fire in her cheeks held desire's hue in its color. Her mouth softened.

"How strange," she said, a new huskiness in

her voice. "Who would think that knowing you were well pleased with me might please me so deeply?"

What she said rattled Josce to his core. The promise of passion that filled her face only fed his own reaction to her. Once again he craved to lose himself in her arms, and in her body.

Lifting a hand, he cupped her cheek in his palm. Just as she'd done at the pool she leaned her face into his hand. Her skin was like silk against his. Before he could thread his fingers into her hair and draw her closer to him, she caught his hand by the wrist and pressed her lips into his palm. Her mouth against his skin fair weakened Josce's knees. Then she stepped back from him.

"No more," she said quietly. "I think me you and I are safer when there's a bit of space between us."

It wasn't a laugh as much as a mingled sound of longing and frustration that left Josce's lips. Still, she was right. Their attraction was strong indeed. Hadn't they ended up embracing despite the fact that he'd wanted to toss her over the garden wall when she'd first appeared in here?

"Pardon," he said. "I promise to keep a decent distance. Not that such a separation is what I want, mind you," he added with a smile.

She laughed, her eyes bright against his compliment. "What an accomplished swain you are," she teased.

Her words were but an echo of his stepmother's demand that he charm Elianne into their tool. The need to know more of her sire's debts followed. Such money worries went far to support his suspicion that Reiner du Hommet had done more than turn his back while one of the shire's baron's went a-robbing. He needed information, and, surely, locked within Elianne was everything he wanted to know.

"I'm no swain, not, at least, as far as you're concerned," he replied, taking care with his words. "You've been kind to me today when I thought myself without a friend. Say you'll stay with me a little longer."

"I'll stay," she replied with a nod, then started toward the bench.

Her movement wasn't fast enough to hide the pleasure that his words had awoken in her. Guilt nibbled at Josce's conscience. Her affections were already settling on him, when she could have no place in his life.

That was, if he even had a life past the fulfillment of his vengeance. Josce frowned as the reminder of his coming demise warred with the responsibilities his father's will wanted to set upon him. An instant later he shook off the thought. Just as Josce was certain he'd die for what he planned he was equally certain King John wouldn't honor the dictates of Baldwin's will, not when so much wealth was at stake.

"Come, sit with me here," Elianne called to him from the bench. "If you're on one end and I the other, we ought to be safe enough."

Set on his vengeful course, Josce didn't hesitate to join her. As he took his seat at the bench's far end, Elianne smiled at him. "Would you care for a bit of something to eat?"

His stomach growled against her offer. "Aye, indeed I would. You brought food with you?"

"I brought everything with me," she replied with a laugh, leaving the bench to stride across the body of the garden. She stopped before what remained of her arbor and lifted a pallet from the ruins. "Look upon how determined I was to keep my distance from you."

Heat stirred in the pit of Josce's being as he stared at the makeshift mattress. Oh, but he could conjure ways to use yon rustic bedding that would well please both of them. Aye, and guarantee that he got himself a child.

"You meant to stay the night in here?" he asked, trying to distract himself from his inappropriate thoughts.

She sent him a chiding look. "Not just this night, sir, but all the nights of your visit. Aye, and I came to the garden because this is the only place in all of Coneytrop that belongs solely to me. Here, I should have been safe from you, only someone forgot to tell you that you weren't allowed in without my permission," she finished with a laugh.

"You're safe with me," Josce assured her. It was a lie. For revenge's sake, he meant to use her to destroy her father, destroying her in the process.

Dropping the pallet, she grabbed up one of her baskets and returned to sit on the bench's opposite end. With a toss of her plaits, she dumped out the onions, then took out a wrapped packet along with a stoppered skin. Opening the packet, she set her bounty out on the bench between them: bread, a pot of cheese, three raw apples.

"What will you have, Sir Josce?"

"Josce," he insisted. "We know each other too well now for titles, Elianne."

Bright color once more took life in her cheeks. "Aye, Josce then," she murmured.

"I'd have a piece of that bread, then help myself to the cheese."

"As you will," she replied, breaking off a hunk of bread for him.

Pulling his eating knife from its sheathe on his belt, Josce spread some of the potted cheese onto the piece. "I'll thank you for this. I've not eaten since this morn."

"Then, eat it all if you please. I only want an apple," she replied, choosing one of the fruits.

Taking a bite, Elianne turned a little on the bench to look out over her garden. A moment passed, then another. She said nothing.

A little startled, Josce eyed her. Where was the chatter with which other women filled silences? Not that he begrudged them their tongues. Words were the only power a woman owned. Once a man showed his interest in her, the only way she could bind him to her was to talk ropes around him.

Not so Elianne. As she chewed she lifted her face toward the sun, watching the birds darting above them. It was a moment before Josce understood, and when he did, he sat where he was, flummoxed.

Here was the only woman in the world who lacked even a trace of artifice. From the back of his brain came the memory of her bold run, of the way she'd wrapped her legs around him in the pool. Now, today, she'd embraced him not for lust's sake but because he had needed comforting. With her every honest movement and touch, she told him who she was.

Against that his decision to misuse her felt all the worse, like beating a child who'd done no wrong. Trapped between the needs of vengeance and what he knew was right, he tossed his last apple core into the beds, a feast for the birds and insects, then trod polite conventions into the ground by leaping for what he needed to discover.

"Since you've already helped me once to straighten my thoughts this day, help me again if you will." The pleasure his request sparked in her gaze made Josce flinch.

"If I can," she replied with a tiny smile.

He paused to marshall his thoughts. Of one thing he was certain: what he told Elianne here would most surely reach her sire's ears. Therefore, she must carry only the messages he wanted the sheriff to hear. When he was ready, he tossed his words like a knife, his statement coming to a quivering halt between them.

"My lady stepmother believes Lord Haydon knew the thieves who attacked him."

Elianne's brows lifted in surprise over her eyes. "Why ever would she think such a thing?"

"Because the thieves didn't retreat when Haydon's party joined the set-upon spice merchant. She and I reckon the only reason for doing so could be to conceal their identities. Why else fight on, only to lose twelve of their own?"

"Twelve?" Elianne's brows remained high upon her forehead. "How do you know how many the thieves lost?"

Josce's hopes of learning anything new from her faltered. He countered her question with his own. "Has your father told you nothing about the bandits he chases?"

"Not a word," Elianne said with a shake of her head. "He says the activities of degraded men are an indecent subject for a woman. I must admit to wondering, though. I saw your sire's armor in the icehouse, left in its entirety. What sort of thieves leave behind something so valuable as that?"

"My question exactly," Josce replied, then eyed her for another quiet moment.

Innocence and ignorance glowed from her face. Aye, but if Reiner thought keeping his daughter unaware protected her, he was a fool. Nothing would shield Elianne if a connection between du Hommet and the bandits was revealed. Nay, for what remained of her days she'd be reviled as the spawn of a base and dishonorable man.

That her father might leave his daughter so completely bereft, without either coin or name to protect her, stirred a need to shield Elianne the way her sire hadn't. If Josce had no harbor to offer her, there was another one.

"Tell me, for I cannot help but wonder," he said to her. "That's a fine bed your sire owns. Since there's no acreage to give you for an inheritance, why doesn't he make that bed your inheritance? It's fine enough that the prioress might accept it as your dowry and give you a position among the nuns. Not that I think you should take your vows," he added. The idea of Elianne locked in a barren cell and beyond his touch made something within Josce twist in the strangest way. "It's only that yesterday you seemed at one with the sisters, and they were content with your presence."

What could have been a quiet cough broke from Elianne. "That assumes my father values me above a bed given to him by some distant relative whose face he cannot recall."

Josce blinked at confirmation that du Hommet had inherited the bed. If he hadn't purchased it, then where had all the profit gone?

"As for the priory," Elianne was saying, "until yesterday I was, indeed, comfortable in its embrace. A number of sisters had promised to petition Prioress Gertha to offer me a place upon my sire's death, even though I have no dowry. Yesterday, my father's invitation to you resulted in your lady stepmother leaving the priory when the prioress wanted her to stay. In doing this he alienated Mother Gertha beyond hope of any such offer."

Catching a broken breath, she stared at her fisted hands upon her knees. "He gave away my only chance for a decent future, and he won't tell me why he did it."

Josce eyed her in astonishment and triumph. That du Hommet had ruined his own daughter's future to invite his enemy to stay in his house nigh on screamed that the sheriff was connected to the thieves. Josce strained to arrange his fragmented bits of insight into a whole, only to give up in frustration. Too many pieces were yet missing.

What followed was the strangest desire to tell Elianne all he knew. Startled, Josce swallowed the urge, only to be flummoxed all over again. It wasn't just to warn Elianne against her sire that he wanted to confide in her. Nay, he longed to convince her that his own vow to kill her father was right and just, when no daughter could accept such a thing.

"Well, against that I can see why you weren't overjoyed to have Haydon avisiting in your home," he managed.

Elianne shot him a sidelong look, one corner of

her mouth lifting. "Aye, and then all went even more awry when you came to bathe at the pool."

Josce drew a quick breath as his poorly controlled desire for her once more took flight. God help him, but he wanted to hold her in his arms one more time. As if she felt what stirred in him, new heat came to life in Elianne's gaze. Her face softened. She bit at her lower lip.

"Mistress! Mistress, come you now and swiftly so!"

The shout from one of Aggie's girls jerked Josce out of lust's grip. Across the bench from him, Elianne fair sprang to her feet to face the gate. Pretty Mabil appeared in the opening, doing her best to peer past the wreckage blocking the gateway.

"Oh mistress, what happened here? Ach, look at your lovely arbor!" she cried, failing at her attempt to pick her way through the mess into the garden. "A shame, after all the work you did on it. Sir Adelm is arrived and would speak with you. He also brings with him a messenger for Sir Josce."

Only then did Mabil see Josce sitting on the bench. "Oh, but here you are, sir. We've been looking all over for you."

She smiled at him and blinked, or was it a wink? A touch of revulsion shot through Josce at this, only to be followed by another raft of surprise. Why would one woman's bold ways disgust him, while another's only left him wanting more of her?

"I think your messenger comes from companions of yours who've taken up lodging in town," Mabil called out with enough force to make her words ring against the garden walls. "I think they expect you to come to them on the morrow."

Josce's disgust gave way to dismay. In polite society a messenger delivered his news only in the presence of the one to whom his words were addressed. Apparently, every man and his brother received any and all news here at Coneytrop. Forewarned was forearmed. Unless there was no way to avoid it, he'd send no messages to Lady Beatrice should his quest for vengeance take him from these walls.

Only then did the full meaning of what Mabil had said register. His friends had left their holiday at Glevering to join him? Gratitude lifted him from the morass of emotions that owned him these days. The need to know who had come of the friends he so valued brought him to his feet.

"Well, that's the end of it, then," Elianne said, her voice low and flat as she turned to look at him.

That stopped Josce. "The end of what?"

"Your visit," she replied, regret and longing filling her pretty eyes. "Once you leave us to join your comrades, your lady stepmother will return to the priory. She wants to go, now that she's a little improved."

"Nay." The word fair leapt from Josce's mouth, startling him. He told himself it was his need for vengeance that prompted his denial. The truth was that he wasn't ready to bid Elianne farewell.

"Nay," he repeated, this time burying his passion. "My lady stepmother and I concur. We prefer to remain at Coneytrop throughout Lady Beatrice's recovery. If she returns to the priory the sisters will separate us, and neither of us wants that. I know it's a burden for you, but might we stay a little longer?"

The joy that blossomed on her face both took Josce's breath and worried him. Would that she weren't so honest. Her affection for him filled every inch of her expression.

"But, of course," she agreed.

"Mistress, what are you doing in there with Sir Josce, anyway?" Mabil called to them, her voice alive with curiosity. "I thought you went to the garden to avoid him."

Yet smiling, Elianne whirled and strode toward the gate. Josce watched her walk, once more enjoying her straightforward and capable pace even as he felt the beginnings of responsibility for her settle onto his shoulders. He had an inheritance and the promise of new wealth at his fingertips. How expensive could it be to see her pensioned to the convent should his vengeance leave her orphaned and without resources?

"So I intended," Elianne called to Aggie's daughter. "Unfortunately he was here before me.

Mabil, from your side, do what you can to untangle the roses from the wreckage and make a path. I think Sir Josce would like to hear the proper version of his message sometime before nightfall."

Chapter 14

Adelm took his ease at the hall's high table, a cup of Elianne's fine ale before him. As he waited for his half sister to join him, he watched Haydon's men game. Richard, Coneytrop's bailiff, diced along with them. If the bailiff's whoops were any indication, Richard was fully enjoying this visit by his master's enemies.

The corner of Adelm's mouth tightened. It was a good thing he'd insisted Reiner keep their illicit activities from Coneytrop's bailiff. Richard was a worse gossip than any of Knabwell's midwives. It hadn't been easy to do. Where Elianne respected a man's privacy, never asking about what she had no right to know, Richard poked and pried with niggling questions.

Behind the hall's screen the exterior door opened, then Elianne rounded the wooden panel. She smiled at him as she strode toward his table.

Adelm stared. Something was different. It wasn't her hair or her clothing, but she looked softer, more feminine, somehow.

An instant later, Sir Josce followed her around the screen's edge and into the hall. Haydon's bastard wore hunting attire this day. Oddly enough, the knight looked more powerful dressed in the rough woolen garments than he had in his mail.

As Adelm studied the tall man he gave thanks his fellow bastard hadn't traveled with Lord Haydon that day. One more sword plied with the nobleman's skill and the battle might well have gone to the "thieves'"detriment. As it was, Lord Baldwin and his men had come close to decimating his handpicked band of soldiers.

Grief stirred in the pit of Adelm's stomach. Until that day he'd lost only four men over the full seven years of thieving. To lose so many all at once cut him to the core. Those men had been his to care for, and he'd failed them just as he'd betrayed the trust those little ladies had put in him. It galled him that, were he to die now, the sum of his life would be murder, failure and betrayal.

"Sir Josce!" cried the servant called Perrin, whom Adelm had led here from Knabwell. The man rose from the crouching dicers, where he'd been welcomed as one of their own. "God be praised, we've finally caught you."

The knight stopped beside his man. "And glad I am you've come, Perrin. I'd dearly like something other than this to wear," he said, touching the breast of his rough tunic.

Another start of surprise shot through Adelm. Yesterday Haydon's bastard had worn his thirst for vengeance on his face the way some knights painted their successes on their shields, for all the world to see. This day no sign of that blood lust showed. Adelm doubted the knight had given up his dark ambition. That meant the man hid his emotions. To what purpose?

Elianne reached Adelm's table. Not a trace of yesterday's unease showed in her face. Instead, his half sister looked beautiful in a way she never before had. Her eyes fair sparkled, while there seemed to be a new lushness to the bend of her mouth.

Only then did he recognize the signs. Adelm drew a quick breath. She was virgin no longer. That bastard had had his way with Elianne!

Even as the thought formed, Adelm discarded it. That Sir Josce yet lived said he hadn't laid an inappropriate hand on Elianne. Reiner was right to think she might slaughter a man for even attempting rape. As for a seduction, although deflowering Reiner's daughter might serve Sir Josce's vengeful ambitions, a year wouldn't be long enough for a determined stranger to tease Elianne into sin.

His sister was oblivious. More than a few men had cast their nets in Elianne's direction over the past years only to gnash their teeth in frustration when she'd failed to notice their advances. Nay, Elianne couldn't be anything but the maiden she'd always been. Then what was different?

"Mabil says you wish to speak with me," Elianne said, naught but welcome for him in her voice.

"Aye, so I do, but not so much for conversation's sake, but yours," he replied, yet gnawing over her change. "Is all well? Do you yet fear Haydon's stay at Coneytrop?"

With his words Elianne shot a glance across the hall toward Sir Josce. As her gaze lit upon the knight, her face softened even further. Adelm caught another startled breath. Jesus God, it wasn't Sir Josce pursuing Elianne but she him!

Far beneath Adelm's astonishment and his own base need for self-preservation a strange mingling of gratitude and pride woke. Such was the purity of his sweet sister's heart. Elianne fixed her affections on yon knight not caring a whit for the fact that the man was bastard born.

When she returned her gaze to Adelm, her expression was a touch sheepish. She gave a tiny shrug. "Perhaps I overreacted a mite. Haydon's men are well behaved and good natured." She laughed a little. "Mayhap, a little too good natured. Our Mabil has her eye upon one of the soldiers."

Adelm's astonishment grew. By his sword but

his ofttimes dour sister was fair giddy with her newfound affections. He shot another look at Sir Josce.

The knight had retreated a bit from the dicers. With his back toward the room, he and his servant were opening a pack between them. There was no message for Adelm to read in the span of the noble bastard's broad shoulders. Then again he didn't need a message from this man to know Elianne's fate. Once the knight's business was done, Sir Josce would leave, and his sister's heart would be broken.

Adelm's jaw tensed. If there was a hell, then Reiner should rot there for how he'd used his children. Fretting for his sister, he looked back at Elianne. She might be wise enough to recognize that Sir Josce could offer her nothing; not only was the man Reiner's enemy, but in this world property married property, no matter what a man or woman's heart might desire. A bastard without inheritance would never offer for a woman with nothing to her name. Ah, but was Elianne's heart strong enough to recognize this truth?

"And, the knight?" he asked gently. "He also behaves himself toward you?" Here it was, her opportunity to confess, if there was aught to tell.

The girlish softness drained from Elianne's face to be replaced by shades of sorrow. Adelm sighed for her. Aye, his sister knew very well the pain she faced by fixing her heart upon her sire's enemy.

She shrugged a second time, as if the loss of a

lass's customary dream of home and family were nothing to her. "He's calmer today than yesterday." There was an odd flatness to her voice, then she offered a puzzled frown. "Do you know he has the strangest ideas. He believes his lord father knew someone among the thieves, if you can fathom it."

The hairs on the back of Adelm's neck stood upright. Like the crying of some awful haunt, Adelaide's sweet voice echoed out from his memory, as she'd called out his name to her sire upon the battlefield. Sir Josce was wrong. It wasn't Lord Haydon but his daughters who'd known one among the thieves.

With that thought, death came to breathe behind Adelm, hot, hungry and horrible. He, a common woman's unacknowledged bastard, had slain nobles. If he were exposed, it was drawing and quartering that would send him into eternal blackness. Adelm mentally recoiled from the prospect of such pain. Sir Josce must be kept from the truth even if that meant using his sister as a spy, as Reiner intended.

Hating himself anew, Adelm set himself to the task of winnowing information from Elianne. "Why would he think such a thing?"

His sister's brow remained creased. "Sir Josce says the thieves fought on and lost many after Haydon's troop joined the spice merchant. I didn't think bandits owned that sort of courage. Shouldn't they have run when they found themselves outmanned? Why battle on and lose so many, unless they had something to protect, such as their identities?"

"Who would a nobleman from outside this shire know among such riffraff?" Adelm countered, his fear abating a little. What Elianne related was nothing more than the conclusion any battle-trained and intelligent man might make when dissecting what little was known of that day.

"I think it more likely that Lord Haydon somehow trapped the troop, leaving them no choice but to fight their way out of his net," Adelm went on. "Don't forget that this is the first time those thieves faced a knight with well-schooled soldiers instead of a merchant's simple men. It's logical that the bandits might lose more than a few in that case."

"Aye," Elianne replied slowly, her brow smoothing, "so it is."

Then she shuddered. "Ach, those poor lasses. It chills my blood to think on what they endured before our Lord finally took custody of their souls."

Adelm flinched. If only he'd known Lord Haydon and his party had been in the vicinity when he'd attacked the spice merchant. If only the nobleman hadn't tried to rescue the beleaguered merchant. If only Haydon's womenfolk had stayed far from the battle scene.

The need to beg Elianne's forgiveness filled him. Adelm longed to tell her how he'd made the lasses' passings as swift and painless as possible. Hadn't he covered their eyes so they wouldn't see their deathblows approaching? Aye, and as their lifeblood had flowed he'd rocked each of them in his arms, trying to soothe their fears as they'd entered whatever afterlife was set aside for the innocent. He let the urge for Elianne's absolution die. How could he expect her to forgive him when he couldn't forgive himself?

"Why does Sir Josce make you his confidante after he's told the world your sire is his enemy?" he asked instead.

New color burst to life in Elianne's cheeks. She lowered her gaze to the table, using her fingernail to scrape at remains of the midday meal left on its surface.

"I doubt I'm his confidante. I think grief over his sire's death made him hungry for a sympathetic ear. As for his threats toward my father"—again she shrugged—"I wonder now if they, too, were nothing but a reflection of his grief. It seems he and his sire cared deeply for each other."

Adelm's response was a noncommittal grunt. Coward or not, Reiner wasn't one to mistake a threat. Nor had anyone misread Sir Josce's black expression yesterday each time the knight had looked upon Knabwell's sheriff as the noblewoman's cart was being prepared. Sir Josce wouldn't be at peace with his sire's death until he'd spilled blood. Elianne, on the other hand, was far too quick to forgive, and to trust.

Raising her head, his sister looked at him. "I hope I'm not out of place in suggesting this, but perhaps you should confer with Sir Josce over these thieves. If you tell him all you know it might set his mind at ease."

Adelm could have kissed her. Elianne's suggestion was just the excuse he needed to broach the subject with Sir Josce. However, it wasn't the knight's mind he wished to ease but his own. He needed to tease Sir Josce into revealing all he knew, or thought he knew.

"So it might," Adelm said to his sister, forcing his lips to lift into a smile. "Sir Josce has some novel ideas. Against that I'd do well to hear him out. Mayhap his fresh eye will find that little piece we need to finally run these villains to ground."

"Go to him now and speak with him," Elianne insisted, already stepping back from the table as if she expected him to rise immediately and do as she bid. Then her affection for him took light in her eyes to drown out her newborn feelings for Sir Josce, if only for that moment. "But before you go I'll thank you for calling on me."

"I seek only to repay your continuing care for me," he replied, his heart twisting with that aching warmth only Elianne had ever stirred in him.

His sister smiled. "Will you stay for the evening meal?"

Adelm shook his head. To remain close to Coneytrop and Elianne would surely stir Sir

Josce's interest in him, and just now his life couldn't bear the scrutiny. "Would that I could, but your sire claims to have need of me this night."

That Elianne sighed in disappointment over this only further warmed Adelm's heart. "As you will," she replied. "I'll bid you farewell then. My arbor just collapsed in the garden."

A startled bark of a laugh slipped from Adelm's lips. "No surprise that! Nay, that it lasted as long as it did is the astonishing thing."

She made a face at him. "You're supposed to commiserate over what I've lost and what that loss costs me, not laugh. Take pity! I vow I'll be pruning until the morrow."

"The morrow," Adelm said, only now deciding to pass on his father's message to his sister. "I almost forgot me. Your sire asks that you come to him on the morrow an hour before terce, bringing a clean shirt and something other than his best to wear. He'd also like linens for the king's bed."

As was Reiner's right as sheriff, he slept in Knabwell Castle's sole bedchamber, the bed being the one their king would use should he ever make a royal visit to this bucolic corner of his kingdom. However, the sheriff's right didn't extend to use of the royal linens.

Irritation blossomed on Elianne's face. She crossed her arms. "He needs *me* to bring these to him, and on the morrow? And, not just at any hour, but the one before terce? What is this? Why can't I send Richard into Knabwell with them right now?"

Knowing that Reiner wished to pick his daughter's brain over Sir Josce's activities and was choosing a quiet moment in which to do it, Adelm could offer his sister nothing more than a wry look and a shrug. "What can I say? He was specific. He wants you, not Richard, and on the morrow when he stated. He also reminds me that you shouldn't come without an escort."

"An escort?" Elianne spat the words at him as all the softness departed from her expression. "What need have I of escorts now that my sire has thrown away my future? When you return to Knabwell you may tell my sire that I'll come to him as it pleases me and no other way. If he doesn't like it he may choke on it."

With that parting jab for their father, she turned and started for the door. Adelm smiled at her back. Thus did Reiner get what he deserved from at least two of his children.

His attention shifted to Sir Josce. Haydon's bastard had shucked his hunting tunic in preparation for donning a new garment. However, Elianne's departure had caught the big man's interest. Sir Josce watched Elianne cross the hall. Adelm wasn't so far from his fellow bastard that he could mistake desire as it took light in Sir Josce's face.

Adelm's lips tightened. His hand fell to his sword's hilt. Here was one who needed a reminder to behave himself around other men's women. In the next moment, Adelm let his hand fall from his weapon's hilt. What point was there to warning Sir Josce away from Elianne when the knight was already doomed to failure? Adelm knew his sister. No matter Elianne's longing for Haydon's son, she was too sensible to give up her purity.

Amusement stirred. It really was a shame she wouldn't. It would serve Reiner rightly to become grandsire to a bastard's bastard.

Content that Elianne was and would remain safe, Adelm came to his feet and started across the hall toward Sir Josce. It was time to meet the man most likely to be his opponent if this drama of theirs played itself out to its worst outcome. As he walked, Adelm assessed his adversary. Haydon's bastard stood half a head taller than himself and had more bulk in muscle. Neither trait was an advantage unless the knight owned his sire's ability with a sword.

"Well met, Sir Josce," Adelm said as he came to a stop near the man and his servant.

As the knight presently had his head inside a fine yellow tunic trimmed with green braid, Perrin made the announcement. "It's Sir Adelm, Sir Josce. The sheriff's captain led me here from Knabwell."

Sir Josce's head appeared out of his garment. A tenseness that hadn't affected his expression when he'd looked upon Elianne now owned his face. His chin lifted in a sure sign of aggression.

Adelm almost smiled. As usual, Elianne judged wrongly. Sir Josce's need for vengeance was no less intense today than it had been yesterday, only concealed for his own reasons.

"Sir Adelm," Coneytrop's guest said, offering his titular equal a brief nod.

Adelm reciprocated the gesture. "I understand that Lady Haydon is a little improved. Do you plan to remain at Coneytrop now that your companions have arrived and she can retreat to the priory?"

"We do. My lady stepmother is fain to stay," the knight replied, his tone almost too polite, "and Mistress du Hommet has given us leave to do so. That is, if her father agrees, of course," Sir Josce finished, the confidence in his voice saying he knew full well Reiner wouldn't refuse him.

Nay, there was more than confidence in the knight's face; Sir Josce's expression said he knew he was here because Reiner hoped to control him. Against that, a reckless desire to taunt stirred in Adelm. What better way to learn a man's limits than to push him past them? Aye, and Elianne had given him just the weapon he needed to prick the man.

"Mistress du Hommet spoke with me a moment ago about your beliefs regarding the thieves. Dare I say I'm astounded to learn you think your sire recognized someone among that band of ruffians? How can that be, when there could be no one in that foul troop worth the dirt beneath your lord's shoes?"

When neither disappointment nor chagrin came to life in Sir Josce's steady gaze, the cockiness drained from Adelm. Death once more breathed upon his nape. Sir Josce didn't care that Elianne had shared this information with another man, which could only mean he'd expected her to spread it. And that meant Adelm had no idea what this man's true thoughts were. Worse than that, the knight now knew that someone other than Reiner was interested in his activities.

Lord Haydon's son gave a careless shrug. "I keep telling myself such a thing can't be possible. Still, what other reason did the thieves have to remain and fight once they were set upon by a small army? Protecting their identity seems logical to me." Sir Josce sounded every inch the reasonable but confused man.

The tall knight paused to cock his head. "Say, you may be just the man I need to ask. Are there any among this shire's gentry who kept more men than they seemed to need last week but this week lacks that surfeit?"

Relief surged through Adelm. He'd fully expected Sir Josce to ask for a headcount of Reiner's troops. For the moment the knight yet followed the wrong scent. Aye, and it was up to Adelm to see that his fellow bastard kept moving in that errant direction.

"Well now, there aren't many in these parts who can afford to keep more than they need. There's Sir Thomas le Hearne. He has five knights at the moment, but three of those are his own kin. Blood demands he feed them all even while they strip his larder bare. Beyond that no one comes to mind."

"Nay, not knights but soldiers, and it'd be more than three gone missing," Sir Josce countered. "I'm looking for a man who ran with eighteen, twenty, or even as many as two and twenty at his back. Now he'd be hard-pressed to account for ten or mayhap even as few as eight of those he once kept."

Adelm blinked, startled at how close this came to the truth. He'd started that day with two and twenty and now had but ten remaining in his troop. That no one had yet noticed their absence was solely due to the frenzy that came with preparing for Michaelmas Court. When anyone asked about the missing men, they were told the soldiers were across the shire gathering this or that bit of information.

"My apologies, sir," Adelm said with a shake of his head. "As I said, no man springs to mind. Do I take it from your questions that you'd have one of our shire's better folk acting as the bandit king?"

Sir Josce's eyes narrowed just a little. "Let me say I but toy with the idea to see where it leads me."

Adelm did his best to make the lift of his shoulders seem unconcerned. "Now, that's something I never considered. Hmm, but if some grand knight or one of our barons was responsible for these attacks I doubt he'd parade his excess men across the shire. Doing so would only call attention to himself, wouldn't it?"

Frustration flashed through his opponent's gaze, then it was gone. "I suppose. Ah well, as I said, I but toy with the thought."

Despite Sir Josce's words, there was nothing in his tone to suggest that reaching a blind corner meant defeat. Instead, the knight smiled, the curve of his lips tight. "Oh, and by the by. Bear a message to your lord sheriff for me if you would. Tell him that my threat stands. When the sun sets this evening, he'll have a fortnight less two in which to bring me my sire's murderers or pay my price."

It was in every line of the man's body. Either Reiner produced the thieves or Sir Josce extracted from the sheriff the blood he needed to sate his grief. The threat rankled, then it reminded Adelm of Sir Josce's face as he looked upon Elianne. Armed with this new weapon, Adelm dropped what he hoped would be at least a stunning blow.

"What's this?" he demanded in pretended outrage. "Would you be so swift to threaten Mistress du Hommet's sire if you knew that the sheriff's death leaves her a penniless orphan with no future save that of begging?"

The attack surprised Sir Josce, or so said his sudden flush. "The fate of du Hommet's daughter is none of my concern."

"Is that so?" Adelm persisted. "I'd have guessed you felt otherwise after the way you watched her a moment ago."

His adversary's eyes narrowed. In anger, or because he wanted to hide his expression? "So, we're past the pith and into the pit of this fruit, are we?" Sir Josce asked, his voice low. "Do I tread too near a lass you'd claim for your own? If so, be at ease. I've no ambitions in her direction."

"No ambitions?" Adelm retorted, allowing a touch of scorn to fill his voice in the hopes of unsettling his fellow bastard a little. He needed a weakness to use against the man. Nay, he needed to know what Sir Josce truly thought.

"It wasn't harmless interest I read in your face a moment ago. Were I Mistress du Hommet's guardian I'd be asking after your intentions toward her. Since you seem not to have noticed what's happening to you, I think me I'll offer this warning. Watch your heart, for it's slipping from your grasp."

The knight stiffened, his expression almost startled. Triumph shot through Adelm. At last, he'd found a chink in the man's armor. That it might be an affection for Elianne was sheer irony.

Giving his erstwhile opponent no chance to respond, Adelm offered a brief nod, then whirled and made his way from Coneytrop's hall. Success's warmth lasted only until he took his horse's reins from Will. As Adelm lifted himself into the saddle, death once more panted at his back.

And why shouldn't it? His life wasn't worth those of the two sweet lasses he'd killed. Now he was using his sister to save himself.

Everything in him rejected this. He couldn't use Elianne, not when doing so betrayed the affection and respect she'd ever shown him. In the time it took this thought to register, Adelm's future shifted. No longer was it *if* he would die for killing these nobles, but when. A surprising wave of peace followed, lapping around him like warm water.

He turned his horse as Elianne stepped out of the toolshed with what she needed for her pruning. She offered him a cheery wave. Adelm nearly sighed as he once again read the caring for him written upon her face. If only there were a way that his passing could save his sister from her future.

Chapter 15

Watch his heart? Sir Adelm's words of yesterday drove Josce across a hall yet trapped in predawn darkness. Shoes in hand, he wore naught but his thigh-length shirt. Tossed over his shoulder were the rest of his garments. Enough people had already been disturbed by his insomnia this night. Dressing could wait until he reached his destination.

At the screen Josce stepped over Richard of Coneytrop's blanketed form. He rounded the wooden panel to stop before the door, then took care lifting the bar. There was but a wee creak as the panel opened. Josce shot a glance back around the screen at what he could see of Richard. The man responsible for guarding his master's hall snorted and rolled onto his side. Such were Coneytrop's defenses.

Closing the door behind him, Josce donned his

shoes, then made his way down the stairs. Sir Adelm's statement nipped at his heels all the way. *Watch his heart?*

Exactly what had the knight meant by that? It was Elianne who was infatuated with him, not he with her. Aye, but if that were so, what Sir Adelm had said shouldn't have kept Josce from his rest this past night. It was the meaning of his sleeplessness that worried Josce.

In the courtyard he started toward Elianne's garden, that being the farthest he could go from the hall at this time of the night. Come prime, the service that marked dawn and the opening of the city gates, he'd ride to Knabwell, but right now he couldn't even saddle his horse. Will and his brothers slept in the stables, supposedly standing watch over their paddocked four-legged charges. If Josce roused them, they'd surely wake their mother. If Aggie woke, so would Elianne, and the last thing Josce wanted at this moment was to face her.

So he might tell himself, but that didn't stop his head from turning toward the kitchen, where she slept. Even after Josce had asked Beatrice to keep Elianne within the hall and under their protection, his stepmother had refused to allow her enemy's daughter into the bedchamber. That left Elianne no choice but to sleep with her female servants outside the hall, which in itself was unusual.

Customarily, the soldiers and male servants belonging to visiting guests took residence in an estate's outbuildings, leaving the hall and its barred door for the womenfolk. However, there wasn't enough room in all Coneytrop's barns and sheds for the soldiers who accompanied Haydon's noble widow. Thus had the sleeping arrangements shifted, Richard's wife and daughters retreating to the kitchen, taking Elianne along with them.

Despite night's depth the kitchen's door stood wide. That vulnerable women might leave the door open startled Josce. As he strode past he caught the glow of a banked fire through the portal. No doubt even so faint a light lent those within the kitchen's flimsy walls a bit of company and a sense of security.

Once past the kitchen Josce made his way around the estate's vegetable plot, then through the sheepfold to Elianne's garden gate. Lifting the latch, he pushed, expecting resistance, only to have the door swing wide with ease. Elianne must have returned yestereven to clear away the wreckage of her arbor. The recall of her broken roses brought with it the memory of her hands on his as she'd pleaded for her precious plants. There had been nothing subtle about the sensations that had streaked through him from her touch.

Desire stirred anew. So did the indignity of Sir Adelm's charge. *Watch his heart?*

Josce left the gate open behind him to pace across the grassy expanse to the bench. Tossing his clothing onto the seat, he dropped to sit beside them, then kicked off his shoes in preparation for dressing. Just who was Sir Adelm to make such a charge to him?

Someone who apparently knew Elianne well enough to speak of her like an uncle or a brother. Josce's eyes narrowed. It didn't matter who Sir Adelm thought he was to Elianne, the man was wrong. There was nothing at all for anyone to read upon his face. He wasn't enamored of the sheriff's daughter. Or at least he hadn't been until that cursed knight set his ridiculous seed into Josce's brain.

Driven to it by Sir Adelm's charge, all the night long Josce had relived his every encounter with Elianne. Again and again, he took that walk with her across the priory's yard, enjoying the odd intimacy of their matched pace. This was inevitably followed by the image of Elianne standing before the wreckage of her arbor, holding aloft that pallet of hers.

Josce's eyes closed. He breathed out against the promise of pleasure. Oh, but the things they could do, that he would love to do with her, upon that mattress.

Which, as had happened more times than he could count this night, led him back to the pool. Right on cue remembered sensations stirred, then grew until every inch of him craved her. God help him, but he longed to be in the water with her again. This time, he wanted her legs higher, fastened about his hips, not his thighs, as they made love.

So great was this desire that his shaft stirred. Growling in frustration, Josce stared down at his feet as he dug his bare toes into the moist sod. Wasn't his physical reaction proof that all he harbored for Elianne was carnal need? It had to be lust. Elianne was his enemy's daughter. To hold even a shred of affection for her betrayed his vow of vengeance.

"What are you doing out here at this hour?"

Josce's head snapped up at Elianne's soft call. Framed in the night the form in the gateway was humpbacked and misshapen. Even though Josce knew very well who stood there, he found himself foolishly hoping this was some ogre pretending to be Elianne. Far better he battled a mystical creature than meet the woman herself.

"I saw you walk past the kitchen only because it was too hot in there to close the door and Aggie won't douse the fire," Elianne continued around a yawn as she crossed the garden's expanse to join him. "Is something amiss? Does your lady stepmother worsen?"

Half considering running, Josce came to his feet as she appeared next to him out of the darkness. The night turned her loosened hair into black threads around the white circle of her face. Her humpback was a blanket bunched up around her shoulders. Held closed by only her fist, the woolen sheet cloaked her to her knees. Her feet were bare.

Josce looked at her naked toes and swallowed as his lust stirred, this time with uncomfortable strength. Elianne would sleep unclad; why would she do differently than anyone else in the world? Did the swathing blanket mean she hadn't paused to dress before following him here? He shook against his need to peel back the covering and see for himself.

God save him, but he was drowning in want of her. Lust. That's all it was.

"Lord, but the kitchen floor's harder than anything I've ever before slept upon," she went on, her voice a little tighter now. "That's why I noticed you. I was once again rearranging my pallet hoping for a softer spot."

Her voice died off into silence, then she gave a nervous little laugh and took a backward step. "I'm intruding. My pardon. I'll leave you to your thoughts."

She couldn't leave him! Reaching out, Josce caught her by the arms. Even as he told himself he shouldn't, he drew her closer, wrapping an arm around her back. She sighed as she came to rest against him, her hands braced on his chest.

Josce's longing for her grew until it was beyond need. Right now. He'd take Elianne upon the dewy grass. Aye, and when he finished his lust would be sated and he would be free of the spell she'd woven over him.

The heat of her body pulsed from her to envelop him in her warmth. Her hair tumbled over his arm, thick and cool where it touched his skin. His fingers curled into the fabric of her blanket. Lord, but she was wondrous tall. He barely had to bend his head to touch his lips to hers.

Their mouths met. Her lips softened beneath his, then she shivered against his kiss. Josce's eyes closed as her tremor sent sensation streaking through him.

Wanting so much more he lifted his other hand to her nape. With his fingers threaded into her hair he cupped her head in his palm to trap her mouth against his, then let his kiss deepen. What need had he of words when the very pressure of his lips on hers urged her to give herself to him?

Just as he prayed she might, Elianne relaxed against him in feminine surrender. Need became throbbing heat. He swore that even through the fabric of his shirt and the bulk of her blanket he felt the mound of her womanhood resting against his shaft.

His mouth slashed atop hers, demanding that she cede to him what he now needed more than breath itself. Her hand caught in his shirt as she pushed herself back from him, just a little. Her lips left his.

"Josce," she breathed, her voice shaken as she turned his name into a plea.

Frustration and need howled in him, trying to drown out her voice. It didn't matter what she said. He knew she desired him as badly as he wanted her, else she'd have truly pushed him or fought free of his embrace. Another kiss and she'd let him do as pleased him, as pleased them both. Such was the thinking of a man who but lusted after a woman.

Pulling her close again, Josce lowered his head to give her that kiss. Once more, she melted into his embrace, ready to yield all to him as she'd already done. His lips stopped but a breath from hers.

Images of yesterday filled him, of Elianne seated on the garden bench as they ate. In his mind's eye he again saw how her honesty of character glowed from her like some saint's halo. Josce's eyes closed in defeat. Misusing Elianne would be akin to defiling a church. God help him, it wasn't lust he owned for her, but the beginnings of something far more dangerous.

Pinned next to him, Josce's mouth so near to her own that she felt his breath against her skin, Elianne waited for him to release her. He would, of that she was certain. Josce was too good a man to press himself on her, especially when he knew how wrong it was for them to sin again.

She could make it easier for him if she took a step back from him. It was the right thing to do, the sensible thing to do. After all, he wasn't hers to keep.

Pain stabbed through Elianne as she again confronted a truth she'd visited often this night. Not even if Josce loved her with all his heart could he ever claim her as his own. To wed a worthless woman betrayed his father's gift to him. Nay, Josce's wife would be well endowed with either property or wealth.

Elianne marked time's passage by the thud of her heart's beat. Still, Josce held her. It was a seductive swirl of joy that filled her at this. He wanted to let her go no more than she wanted him to release her.

It didn't matter. She had to move. To repeat their sin was to double her chances of bearing his child.

Bearing Josce's bastard meant a lifetime of shame for her and his child, even if he did as his sire had done and claimed her babe as his. Wasn't the torment Adelm endured proof of that? Her father would be shed of her. Knabwell's folk would call her whore. The very thought of standing before Mother Gertha in Church court and admitting to fornication terrified Elianne.

Still, not so much as her fingertip shifted. How could she reject Josce when doing so meant she'd never again know the wondrous pleasure of his caresses? It didn't matter that what she wanted was wrong, or even sin. She craved another taste of what the world forbade her.

In the end it was she who moved. She leaned forward to touch her mouth to his. Josce tensed, his lips almost hard atop hers, then, almost as quickly, he sighed and relaxed.

As his arms around her tightened, pulling her against him, her kiss became his. There was such urgency in the caress that Elianne wanted to laugh and cry all at once. He needed her. Like her, he needed the pleasure they could make between them.

A moment later, his mouth left hers to trace a blazing line of kisses down her neck. His hand descended from her head into her blanket's opening. His fingers were warm against the bareness she hid beneath that woolen sheet. When he curled his hand around the fullness of her breast, Elianne gasped, quaking. That throbbing returned to her womb, stunning in its intensity.

Knowing this must be their final tryst made Elianne bold. If this was to be the last, then she'd spend it learning all she could of him and the joy he made in her. Releasing her grip on her blanket, she let it drop onto the grass at her heels, baring her unclad form to the stars.

Josce sucked in a startled breath, then leaned back from her as if he meant to study her. Just as well that he moved. Now that she was bare, she wished to feel his skin against her own.

She caught the hem of his shirt, tugging at the loose-fitting garment. When Josce realized what she wanted, he snatched it off of him. The shirt was all he wore. Elianne sighed in appreciation.

Lord help her, but she liked the way he looked, especially right this moment with his form framed against the jeweled velvet of the night sky. There was something about the powerful bulge of his shoulders and the strong curve of his arms that fed what pulsed in her.

He reached out as if to once more take her into his arms. She held up her hands to stop him. "Nay," she murmured, "let me know you first."

"Know me?" he replied, his voice as low as hers.

That they should whisper when they were so far from the house that no one could ever hear them even if they screamed almost made Elianne smile, then it made her sad. Such was her fate. What she and Josce shared must always remain secret.

"I know we haven't long before we must part, you and I," she said, her voice still low.

His sigh acknowledged the truth of her statement. The sound cut into her heart. She reached out to lay her fingers upon his shoulders.

"If this is all I'm to have of joy in my life I would memorize all of you, so I might keep the recall as my own once you're gone." As she spoke, she traced her hands downward, exploring the muscular landscape of his arms.

He shivered at her caress. When she reached his hands he caught them in his own. Lifting her trapped hands to his lips, he pressed kisses to each finger, then placed her palms against his chest, inviting her to touch him as she would.

It was enough to set Elianne to trembling. That heat at her woman's core redoubled. She drew her hands down the contours of his chest, smoothing the hair that covered his skin. When her fingers reached his waist she slid her fingers to the sides of his torso, then stroked a pathway down either side of him to his hips.

He caught a shaken breath. Not even the night was dark enough to hide the way his shaft reacted to how she touched his body. Elianne watched in fascination as it jerked and lifted, rising as if it had a life of its own.

This wasn't the first time she'd seen a shaft at salute. By necessity Aggie's boys had often gone without breeches or breechcloths once they began to toddle and before they were trained to use the latrine. At times their wee members had looked like arrows in search of a bow. Aye, but this was the first time she'd seen a man's shaft rise for want of her.

She touched the tip of her finger to that part of Josce most male, then stroked its length. To her surprise, his skin there felt silken soft. Now curious indeed, she closed her whole hand around his shaft and stroked.

Breath huffed from Josce. A tremor shot through him. Elianne smiled. There was no mistaking his pleasure. Against all logic the knowledge that she pleased him fed her own enjoyment until her womb fair melted.

Oh, but she was liking this well indeed. Again, she stroked his shaft. He panted, then reached out to cup her breasts. In a caress as bold as hers his thumbs shifted across her nipples. It was her turn to pant. She released his shaft to shake her hair back over her shoulders so it might not impede him, should he want to do more of this.

A quiet laugh rumbled from Josce. "Lord, but everything you do astounds me," he whispered. As he spoke, he used his fingertips to outline the fullness of her breasts.

Even as his caress sent waves of feeling washing over Elianne, she eyed him in surprise. Her, surprise him? How, when she was a woman whose life was nothing but crushing daily routine?

"There is nothing unusual about me," she breathed.

"You're wrong in that, Lianne," he returned, then leaned forward to rest his forehead against hers. "Touch me again," he commanded at a whisper.

Elianne happily complied, once more curling her hand about his shaft. As she slid her fingers down its length, he moved his hands upon her breasts to rub his palms against their crests. The thrill that shot through Elianne was so great that her body arched, her hips thrusting toward his. Startled, she released his shaft and fell against him. From deep within her came a primal knowing that it was this sort of sensation she wanted from Josce.

With a quiet growl, he wrapped his arms around her and pulled her hard against him. Every inch of them touched. Her thighs met his, her hips rested against his. Elianne's breasts throbbed as they flattened against his chest.

Trapped between them, his heated shaft sought to move against her belly. To her astonishment this sent another wave of that strange thrill washing over her. Aye, more of this!

Without thought, she lifted her mouth to his. He accepted her invitation, his lips once more slashing across hers. Her skin took fire. Clasping her hands behind his neck, she shifted against him and knew another thrust of joy.

His hand slid between them, his fingers slipping between her thighs. Elianne's whole body shook at this caress. Lost in what he did to her, she didn't notice they were no longer afoot until she felt the damp coolness of the grass against her back. His fingers yet sending waves of joy careening over her, Josce lay half atop her. Not that she cared where they rested. Nay, as long as he never ceased what he did, Elianne could have made gravel her bed.

His mouth lowered to claim the peak of her breast. She cried out and shivered, beyond all thought. Freeing a quiet groan, he shifted to lie atop her. His shaft slipped between her already open thighs as he once more lay his mouth atop hers.

With his kiss he begged her to accept him within her. Of their own accord, Elianne's legs spread to give him what he craved. There was but a memory of yesterday's pinch as he entered her. Instead, she shook against the wondrous fullness that came from taking him within her.

Using his mouth to taunt and tease her, he shifted atop her, thrusting a little deeper within her. So great was the sensation that flowed through her from his movement that Elianne cried out against his mouth and caught her arms around him. "Again," she begged. "Move within me again."

A breath of a laugh left him. He touched his lips to her ear, sending shivers dancing down her spine. "With the greatest of pleasure," he whispered, then did her bidding.

And pleasure it was. Heat spread all the way to her toes. A new urgency took hold of her. At her body's command, her hips lifted to meet his next thrust. She gasped as her joy expanded yet again.

Atop her, Josce groaned. There was nothing playful about his kiss when his mouth claimed hers this time. Again, he thrust into her. Greedy for more of what his movement made in her, Elianne once more lifted her hips to meet him.

Josce gasped. Bracing his forearms against the ground, he raised himself above her just a little.

Elianne cried out. She needed the wondrous weight of his body atop hers.

"Don't leave me," she begged, reaching up to pull him back down atop her.

He laughed. Catching her face in his hands, he pressed a kiss to her lips. This was sweet, when more heat was what she craved of him.

"How can I leave you when you're driving me gloriously mad with what you do?" he murmured against her mouth.

That he might be enjoying this as much as she startled Elianne, then it filled her with new power. To think that she, a mere woman, had the ability to drive so powerful a man mad with pleasure. Thus it was that when he again moved within her she once more rose up to meet his thrust with one of her own.

A low moan left him. He dropped atop her, then began to move in earnest. Joy tumbled atop joy in Elianne with his movement, yet still her body screamed for more. At its urging, her arms around him tightened.

It wasn't enough; she needed to be closer still. Lifting her legs, she clasped them about his hips and pulled herself hard against him. Josce cried out, the sound loud enough to echo against the garden walls. His breathing harsh and ragged, he drove into her again and again.

Of a sudden, and even with her eyes closed, Elianne felt the night sky explode above her. And still, he moved. She clung to him, letting his every thrust carry her into a glorious place she never dreamed existed.

With a final cry he rolled over, pulling her with him, until she lay atop him. Panting, he caught her face in his hands, kissing her cheek, her brow, her eyelid, the tip of her nose. Between the joy he made in her and the joy in his kisses Elianne laughed.

"Lianne," he breathed against her mouth. "My astonishing, wondrous Lianne."

That sobered her. Easing back in his embrace, she shifted until she could lay her head into the hollow of his shoulder. His heartbeat thudded into her ear.

"Would that I were yours," she whispered.

Holding her close to him, he once more shifted, this time rolling onto his side so they faced each other. Elianne pillowed her head on his arm to look up into his face. Behind him the eastern sky lightened in false dawn. It was illumination enough to see that his expression was tight. Did she see sadness or longing in his gaze?

He lifted his free hand to comb his fingers through her hair, brushing strands back behind her ear. "Will you put your arms about me?" he asked quietly. "For the now I need to feel your heart next to mine."

A part of her shattered with his words, leaving behind an ache that was a terrible mix of bitter and sweet. She should leave him. From this moment on, every touch and kiss they shared would make their eventual parting all the more painful. Instead, she put her arms around him. Just as he asked, she held him close to her heart until she slept.

Chapter 16

Dawn's pinks and golds exploded along the horizon behind Josce and Perrin as they rode up to Knabwell's walls. As early as the hour was, they weren't the first to reach the town's eastern gate this morn. A handful of peasants dressed in brightly colored homespun waited before the city's massive doorway. A bent old woman carried a great bundle of faggots on her back. One man's sack held strong cheeses, judging by the pungent stink wafting around him. Another drove an oxcart filled with wheat.

Halting his horse behind them, Josce glanced at his servant only to find Perrin watching him in return. Confusion painted his servant's face. The instant their gazes met Perrin looked down at his horse's mane, staring at that stiff hair as if it were the most fascinating thing he'd ever seen.

Worry, chagrin and a touch of very untoward

amusement all tumbled in Josce. Such was the price he paid for trying to negate the truth of Sir Adelm's words.

Josce had been vehement yestereven in describing the sheriff's incompetent, and most likely dastardly, actions to Perrin. At the same time he'd reaffirmed his intent to end du Hommet's life. Aye, and when Perrin had awakened this morn and sought out his missing master, where had he found Haydon's son? Naked in the arms of du Hommet's daughter at the center of the sheriff's garden. The only positive thing about all this was that Elianne had slept through the discovery.

Covering her with her blanket, Josce had left her where she'd lain. God be praised that none of the rest of the household had been up and about at that hour. She didn't deserve the shame the world would surely lade upon her were their relationship revealed.

Surprise blinked through Josce. Relationship? In the next instant, he sighed in acceptance.

What they'd done between them at the pool had been but an encounter, happenstance and nothing more. Last night they had done something far more significant. Rather than expunge Lianne from his thoughts, the experience had left Josce only wanting more of her.

That he might yet long for Elianne astounded and dismayed Josce. This is what came from losing himself to passion. That his heart might now fixate on his enemy's honest daughter was beyond irony.

God knew he'd played the game of slap and tickle often enough. There had been chambermaids, rich widows and other men's wives, but whether or not he'd succeeded in his seduction he'd never once given any of those women so much as a sliver of himself. That included his seed.

Out of the depths of Josce's memory came the echo of his father's voice, warning his son not to do as he'd done. Baldwin of Haydon lectured that while a man of principle always lived up to his responsibilities, a wise man never put his seed where it didn't belong.

And what had happened to the caution his father had taught him? For the second time Josce had let the sensations Elianne made in him wash away all thought until he once again had sowed seeds where they had no place being. What if one of them took root in Elianne's womb?

Lost in the complexity of what he'd done to himself, Josce stared at the city's yellowish stone walls. Wood and coal smoke, the result of so many kitchen fires burning all at once, snaked and curled above the city's skyline into an ever thickening brown cloud. Clinging to that acrid smell were hints of hundreds of breakfasts all being cooked at once. Cocks crowed from within the walls, greeting the sun with the same arrogance they displayed everywhere else in this world. Not far from the apron of dirt fronting this gate, the river that served as both Knabwell's water source and sewer chuckled as it spilled through the town's water gate, glinting and sparking in day's newborn light.

A single treble peal broke the morning's peace. A deep bass boom followed, then bell after bell rang until all five of Knabwell's churches were reminding the city's faithful that prime service was at hand. With each bell's note at war with all the others, the invitation became more clatter than carillon.

The gatekeepers didn't hesitate. With a rhythmic song to mark their pace they put their hands to their ropes and lifted the massive bar that closed the gate. When it was out of its braces the gate moved, bellowing out a groan with its inward swing.

Before the door came to a rest against the gatehouse wall the waiting peasants surged into the opening. Well-known to those who guarded this portal, the commoners were within the city walls almost before Josce and Perrin had time to urge their horses into movement. Reaching the porter, Josce reined in his mount, expecting to be called to a halt and asked his business. Instead, the man waved him on with a "Good morrow, sir."

Startled that he might be known after only a few days' time, Josce did as the man suggested and rode into the city. The street he traveled ended in a fork only a dozen yards ahead of him.

Where was he going? In his exhaustion he'd forgotten where Perrin had said his comrades resided.

Perrin urged his palfrey ahead of his master. "It's the home of Alfred the Goldsmith we want. This way, sir."

Josce gratefully put control of his life into someone else's trusted hands. He needed time to gather his energy. It wasn't just his friends he met this morning; he wanted to confront du Hommet again and reissue his threat. This he did to convince himself that despite his growing fondness for Elianne he hadn't forgotten he meant to avenge his father. Besides, the more he threatened the sheriff, the more unsettled du Hommet was likely to be. That increased the chance that he might err and betray himself.

The house before which Perrin halted was as narrow as its neighbors, but it towered over the rest, rising three storeys in height. Even that hadn't been enough space for the wealthy goldsmith. Beneath a cap of expensive slate the house's upper storeys hung out far enough into the lane that tall men would have to step to the street's opposite side to pass.

Warned to expect Josce's arrival this morn, Alfred the Goldsmith watched the street from his street-level shop, its window already open although hours would pass before his apprentices and journeymen were tapping at their precious wares. Josce recognized the smith from his meeting yesterday with the town aldermen. Alfred smiled and came to his feet as he saw his visitor.

"Sir, I hope this morn finds you well come to my house," the merchant said in polite greeting as Josce dismounted. "Your gentle comrades await you in my hall, the chamber just above us. The stairs within yon door"—he pointed in the direction of the portal that stood alongside the shop window—"will lead you there. My daughter will be pleased to serve you as you break your fast."

"You are too kind, master smith." Josce managed a sketchy bow, finding the part of courtly knight cumbersome when exhaustion lay so heavily upon him.

Leaving Perrin to watch their mounts, Josce entered the goldsmith's house. As Alfred promised, the steeply angled stairs within the door led up to the house's second floor. What couldn't be seen from outside was the fact that the steps were open to the tradesman's shop. Alfred watched his progress almost until Josce reached the second-storey landing.

Leaving the stairs to twist back and climb on upward to the third storey, Josce stepped into the hall. And what a chamber it was. Not only did the goldsmith's house extend outward over the street but it also stretched back from the shop until it was three times the size of the lower-level work space. Here, the interior walls were painted a bright blue and stenciled with red cross-hatching.

A line of windows cut into the street side wall, their shutters thrown wide to admit what they could of the day.

Although she held a pitcher like a servant, there was no doubting that the plump, dark-haired lass near the door was the householder's daughter. Rich brown fur trimmed the neckline of her blue overgown, while golden threads glinted in her green undergown. These were surely her best garments, donned in the hopes of piquing the marital interests of her father's gentlemen-guests. Still, her best was far better than anything Josce could afford. Or rather, anything he could have afforded before he'd become warden to his stepmother and sister.

"Josce!" Rafe Godsol's welcoming cry echoed around the room.

Josce's gaze went to the high table at the hall's end and the five men who waited there to break their fasts. Gratitude rolled over him just as it had when Perrin first told him who had come. Here was the rest of his family, his brothers, made so not by blood but by their joint fostering and upbringing at King John's court. For love of him these men had set aside their own doings and duties to come here.

Wearing a leather hauberk atop his brown tunic and a blue cap upon his curling, black hair, Rafe, Josce's dearest friend, rose from his bench at the table's end, a worried look upon his handsome face. Beside Rafe sat Stephen de St. Valery, an earl's youngest son. Beneath his thatch of dark brown hair, Stephen's usual merry expression was banished for the moment. The arms of his sire's house were tooled into the fine leather hauberk he wore atop his blue-and-red tunic.

Simon de Kenifer, dressed in sturdy tan the same pale brown shade as his hair, shared a bench with the dark-haired Hugh de Aincourt, who wore a fine red tunic. The thick scar cutting across Hugh's cheek, a token of their Welsh battles, lent his otherwise dour face a rakish air.

At the table's opposite end sat Alan FitzOsbert, his tunic the same pale gray color as his eyes. With his handsome face and fair coloring Alan was the unwilling darling of ladies addicted to tales of courtly love, paradoxical, indeed, when Alan's own personal standards of behavior were so high that he'd won the pet name "Priest" from his less abstemious companions.

Rafe strode across the room to catch Josce by the shoulders. Another man would have asked after the business of this trip, the whys and wherefores. Not Rafe. "It's pain I see on your face. How fares your heart, my friend?" he asked, his voice gentle.

The corner of Josce's mouth tightened. "As well as can be expected after bidding an earthly farewell to my father and two sisters all at once," he replied, his voice ragged as the gaping emptiness left by those he'd lost opened anew in him.

Rafe reared back from him, his dark eyes wide.

"Clarice and Adelaide are gone as well?!" His shock was echoed by the men yet at the table.

" 'Twas that awful band of thieves who did it," offered Alfred's daughter, speaking in carefully cultivated French. "The brigands slit the throats of those wee noble lasses and left them to die," she continued, inappropriate excitement filling her voice as she spilled the lurid details. "Papa says this is what comes of having a sluggard for a sheriff. Evil men do as they please whilst Reiner du Hommet spends all his time wrenching pennies from the purses of hardworking folk in order to enrich our greedy king."

Josce whirled on her. Too tired to contain his emotions, much less understand them, he let what ached in him explode. "How dare you demean my lord sire's death by making it into a complaint against our king!" he roared.

The girl whitened. The pitcher slipped from her hands to shatter at her feet, watered wine splattering the expensive embroidery at her hemline. Her lip quivering, she backed away from Josce, tears leaking from her eyes.

Footsteps thundered up the stairs, then Alfred appeared upon the landing. The smith's eyes widened as he looked at Josce. Only then did Josce feel Rafe's hand on his arm. His friend was striving to keep Josce's sword in its sheathe when Josce hadn't even realized he'd reached for his weapon.

What ached in Josce collapsed. In confusion

and regret he shoved his sword back where it belonged. God help him, but these last days he'd been a ship tossed on a stormy sea, each new wave leaving him more lost than the last until he no longer knew where he was or what he felt about anything.

"Pardon master smith," Josce managed, his voice quiet, his apology sincere. "My grief leaves me overwrought. I mean neither you nor your daughter any harm. Shall I leave your house?"

Alfred's face relaxed. He bowed slightly, granting Josce the forgiveness he needed. "You're no more overwrought than any other man would be in your position, sir. Stay, if it pleases you. Iva, you must go to your mother now and leave these men to their conversation," he commanded his daughter. His tone left no doubt that his daughter would be hearing a lecture on immodest female behavior at some future hour.

Gibbering now, the lass whirled and dashed toward the safety of her sire's voice. Her shoes clattered upon the stairs as she raced to the upper floor.

"Call for her when you're ready for your meal, sirs," the smith said, then closed the hall door behind him. His footsteps were a steady thud as he retreated to his shop.

At the table, all Josce's friends were now afoot. Hugh had paled beneath his olive coloring. Simon's and Alan's heads were bowed as if in prayer. Stephen crossed himself.

Rafe's eyes glittered in new anger. "Lady Clarice and Lady Adelaide were but children. What sort of rat-kissers kill babes?" he demanded of the room at large.

"We didn't know," Stephen cried, naught but sadness and shock on his face. "We'd only heard what the man who came to fetch you from Glevering said, that there'd been a battle and your sire was gone."

"Lady Beatrice can but be beside herself," Hugh said softly, "the way she values her daughters."

"You have no idea," Josce replied with a sigh. "Her grief nigh on killed her while I stood blindly by and let it happen."

"Come, sit and tell us all," Rafe urged, his arm now across his friend's shoulders. "And, when you've spilled it, tell us if there's aught we can do for you."

As Josce and Rafe started across the room, Alan eyed his grieving friend from his stance at the table's far end. "You speak of your lady stepmother ailing, but what of you? You look gaunt and worn."

Josce's laugh was a bitter breath. If he was worn, it was because he'd spent last night futtering his enemy's daughter and liking it all too well. "Each day I'm better than the last as every dawn brings me closer to unraveling the mystery surrounding my kinsmen's deaths and wreaking my vengeance."

"What mystery?" Rafe demanded. "What do you know?"

"Come and listen as I remind you how this shire has been plagued by thieves for too long," Josce replied, settling onto the edge of the bench Alan used, as he glanced across his friends' faces. Alan joined him on the seat while Rafe stayed where he stopped. The other three men yet stood, each positioned so they might watch him as he spoke.

"As my sire and sisters made their way here they came upon this very band attacking a spice merchant. Not only did these thieves outnumber the total of my sire's men combined with those of the merchant, these bandits were so well trained they bested a battle-canny knight and all his soldiers." There was no little sarcasm in Josce's voice as he spewed this bit of information. "When my sire was dead these foul men murdered my sisters just as the goldsmith's daughter described."

While the others muttered anew against such an outrage, quiet Alan shook his head. "Thieves with such skills? Men that well-trained would have no need of banditry, not with the north of England arming for rebellion just now." Led by several disgruntled nobles, the always fractious north country was alive with talk of deposing John, who insisted on forcing his rule and, more to the point, collecting his taxes in those distant shires.

Josce sent his benchmate a sidelong look. "You'll think it all the stranger, Priest, when I tell you that my sire was left in his armor with his sword and shield at his side. Not even his signet was removed." His left hand curled until he felt the band of his sire's ring. "So, too, was his purse, and those of his men, yet filled to their brims."

"What?" In his surprise, Hugh dropped back to sit on his bench, his brow clenched. "But this makes no sense. Are these marauders thieves or not?"

"What if they were downtrodden knights who yet cling to some shred of honor?" Simon offered, intelligence bright in his blue eyes. "They didn't wish to kill your sire, but he forced their hands by defending the set-upon merchant."

Josce nodded. "So I think as well. However, if these downtrodden knights of yours had any honor at all they'd be working for some great house as Priest says. Moreover, where are they? There's no uncharted forest in this shire, offering hidden grove or leafy shield in which to hide. Knights have horses to feed and armor to maintain. Yet for seven years has Reiner du Hommet sought these men and been unable to run them to ground."

Stephen leaned forward to see around Simon, his fists braced on the table. "Here's your answer. The whole country knows du Hommet couldn't find his ass in a garderobe. Why our gracious majesty keeps him here as sheriff is beyond me."

"What cares John for du Hommet's character?" Alan scoffed. "All our royal master wants is the blanche and taille this shire owes its king, along with du Hommet's payment on his debt. And both those things the man delivers up each and every year."

Startled by Alan's mention of the sheriff's debt, Josce shifted on the bench to look at his friend. "Priest, what do you know of du Hommet's financial state or the profit he gleans from shire management?"

"Me?" Alan shook his head. "Nothing, save that each year my cousin and his fellow clerks wager as to how long du Hommet will moan and complain before he makes his personal payment." Alan's kinsman was a clerk serving the king's treasury. "Apparently, it's a pageant better than any mummery," he added with a shrug. "Why do you care?"

"The man's debt bothers me." Josce frowned against his nagging sense that what the sheriff owed meant more than appeared on its surface. Giving his tongue free rein, he thought out loud in the hope that what he sought might magically tumble past his lips. "He seems strangely impoverished for his position. If what it cost him to buy the position was truly beyond him, then why did he purchase it in the first place? Did something change that drove him into unexpected penury? Who would remain in a position that cost him more to hold than he reaped from it?"

No answer appeared. He sighed. That left only his original theory to share.

"All this leads me to wonder how far the man might go to free himself from such a burden," he said, preparing to tell his friends that he suspected Elianne's sire didn't seek the thieves but shielded them for his own profit.

Across the table from him Rafe caught his breath, his expression startled. "You cannot think the sheriff is your thief."

Josce's mouth opened to deny this, but his words died unspoken. A great light exploded at the back of his brain. "By God, Rafe, you're brilliant," he crowed to his friend, then once more looked at the others. "I ask you all, where better to hide a well-trained band of thieves than in a castle filled with well-trained soldiers?"

If Simon, Stephen and Hugh shook their heads, Alan gave a disgusted huff. "It wouldn't be the first time a sheriff took from his own folk, although most wouldn't expend the effort to hide what they did."

"True enough," Rafe agreed, a sour twist to his lips.

Josce turned to Alan. "Priest, can I beg your aid?"

"Ask, and it's done," his friend replied without hesitation.

Josce couldn't help but smile in gratitude. "I need to know everything and anything you can discover about du Hommet's finances. If he's our thief, has he used his illegal profit to make headway in his debt? Your kinsman would know if the sheriff's payments have changed over these last years. Can you reach him and return to me before ten days' time?"

Alan grinned, his gray eyes alight at the challenge. "If I can't, then my horse isn't worthy of his oats. Why ten days?"

Josce's smile was grim. "Because I've warned the sheriff that if he doesn't present these murdering thieves to me for their justice, I'll meet him instead, sword to sword. It'll be his life I take in their stead."

"Are you mad?" Hugh protested. "If you kill a royal servant our John might well demand your own death in return. If he doesn't hang you, you'll be banished for certain."

"What choice have I?" Josce shot back. "I won't allow my father's murder to go unpunished."

Silence owned the chamber. Josce glanced across his friends' faces. Worry for him filled their expressions.

"I won't be turned from this," he warned them, the needs of vengeance once again roaring through him.

"Well then, if we want you to live past that day, then we'd best find a way to prove du Hommet's complicity in your sire's death," said Rafe. "No man will deny you the right to kill the sheriff if you reveal him as the bandit's leader."

Rafe's words rang in the quiet. Buried deep beneath Josce's grief the need to live on beyond his sire's passing stirred. It persisted, growing even as grief tried to consume it.

"Aye, if I can prove to John that his sheriff killed a peer, no man will refuse me the right to meet him on the field," he said.

Stephen shook his head. "*If* it's du Hommet, something I find hard to believe," he protested. "You've seen him at court. His bluster and blunder hide a craven core. Such a man hasn't the liver to concoct and carry out such a plot."

"Unless he only plays the buffoon to hide what he does," Simon retorted, his expression one of consideration.

Josce's speculation hardened into certainty with Simon's words. A man capable of using his position to take from his own folk lacked any honor. Without honor, and the honesty that accompanied it, du Hommet was free to portray himself as a man he wasn't.

Unlike his daughter, who couldn't hide her scrupulous nature. What did it say of his own character that he made love to Elianne while plotting to kill her sire? Doing his best to banish that thought, Josce plowed on.

"I believe my sire recognized someone in that troop. That's why the thieves fought to the death, when any other band would have retreated in the face of potential losses. And the price they paid was dear. My sire took at least half of the troop before they finished him."

"If these dead men belonged to the sheriff, wouldn't the coroner recognize them?" Alan asked.

"There was nothing left to recognize after the fire finished its work," Josce replied with a lift of his brows.

Stephen caught a breath. "Jesus God! I remember now, don't you, Hugh? Who was it who told us that these foul men burn their own dead?"

"I'd forgotten that," Hugh murmured, stricken at the thought of such an unholy act. Simon's mouth narrowed. Rafe's skin paled a little.

"May God have mercy on their souls," Alan muttered, crossing himself.

"And for that reason were your sweet sisters killed," Simon said in soft sadness. "At the priory they lived within a shout of yon castle and no doubt knew these men by sight."

It hadn't occurred to Josce that his sisters might also have known their attackers, but as Simon spoke the rightness of this settled in him. To be murdered by men they trusted only made his sisters' deaths more heinous. With that, Josce's need for vengeance returned with all its power, burying his lethal softness for Elianne.

His hands in fists, he leaned forward, longing anew to take the sheriff's life. "I think me I'll go to yon castle and count soldiers. When I find twelve missing, I'll demand du Hommet present them to me else I'll cut his heart from his chest," he growled.

"Guilty or innocent, he can't account for his men this time of year," Rafe retorted, his voice harsh. "With Michaelmas looming, men come and go from that castle like ants from their burrow. Best you take your count after du Hommet returns from court."

Too long! Josce's heart screamed for satisfaction. His vow of vengeance would hold him trapped in this emotional purgatory until he shed blood to free himself. To wait a minute longer than the remaining days of his fortnight before swinging his sword and shattering this prison was intolerable.

"I'm still not convinced it was du Hommet," Stephen said, lowering himself to sit on his bench. "Only when I hear some yokel vow he saw the sheriff in the vicinity of that battle, or you can show me a connection between sheriff and the murdered merchants, will I believe he had aught to do with Lord Haydon's death."

The need to live on past his vengeance again stirred in Josce. What Stephen needed was no less than king and court would demand. When Josce found what Stephen wanted he'd also have both life and justice. "Then I must find a way to prove it to you. My first task must be to hie myself to the area of my sire's last battle and speak with those who live nearby." This wouldn't be an easy pilgrimage or a short one, as the battle scene lay almost a full day's ride from Knabwell. He looked at his dearest friend. "Rafe, would you bear me company whilst I do this?"

"You know I will," Rafe replied, offering a brief smile, then his eyes narrowed in consideration. "At the same time we must trace the merchant's trail, following him back to his last market. Someone might have seen something important, or the merchant may have carried some distinctive possession that we can identify were it to be sold in one of this shire's markets."

With Rafe's words the image of the sheriff's bed appeared in Josce's inner eye, resplendent in its richness. Aye, too rich for Coneytrop's means. "Holy Mother," he cried in excited triumph, looking at the men around him. "Rafe's right, we need to know as much as we can about what's been taken in these robberies, then compare that to what the sheriff owns."

"To do that we'd have to win our way into the sheriff's home to survey his belongings," Hugh replied, the shake of his head saying he thought such a thing impossible.

Josce's smile was small and tight. "Lady Beatrice and I already reside in the sheriff's home."

Hugh's jaw dropped. Alan's expression was no less astonished than either Simon's or Stephen's. Rafe's eyes were so wide that Josce could see a full circle of white about their dark irises.

"You're staying in the home of a man you've vowed to battle?!" Rafe cried in disbelief.

"At his invitation, no less. Nay, at his insistence." Josce glanced across their faces. "Do you see now how all this leads me to suspicion? Is it regret over a job poorly done that drives the sheriff, or is he an evildoer trying to keep a potential adversary under his watchful eye?"

He looked at Simon and Hugh. "The coroner will give me the names and cities of residence for those merchants attacked in these past years. When I have them will you two race to the nearest to make a list of what was lost?"

Both men nodded, but Simon eyed him in rising excitement. "So, tell me. What is it you've seen in the sheriff's house that makes you think he has what he shouldn't?"

Josce's lips lifted in triumph. "A bed, one worthy of a king's ransom."

He looked to Alan. "Priest, while at court ask your cousin if he recalls a will some four years past that named du Hommet as a beneficiary. The sheriff's bailiff and daughter claim du Hommet inherited the bed from a distant relative."

Alan nodded.

"Stephen," Josce looked to the man at the table's end, "I have a chore for you if you don't mind riding with Priest, here, to court."

Stephen's familiar merry smile flashed across his face, then disappeared under a put-upon expression. "A hardship, indeed. You know the sort of surly company he makes."

The corner of Alan's mouth lifted just a little.

"As you are for me, you great fool. With you, it's naught but incessant jests and the chasing of hems at every stop."

"But without a wench in my arms and a laugh on my lips there's nothing worthy about me at all," Stephen protested. "Such is the duty of a younger son, to make his sire regret his birth."

That made his companions laugh. Despite all that troubled him, Josce couldn't stop his own grin. These taunts and pokes were a comfortable habit, a reminder of how long they'd all known each other.

"So what is it you'd have me do at court?" Stephen asked.

"You'll join Haydon's steward as my representative. Martin presently seeks out those noblemen attached to my lord sire, hoping to muster support enough to force our dear monarch to accept my sire's will as written. It's your gilded tongue I'd employ in this cause."

"And what shall I say to my lord father's peers?" Stephen asked, a hint of the sober and intense man who hid behind the carefree mask appearing in his voice.

"Why, you'll convince all who listen that I'm the king's man. You'll say that come what may, even in the face of rebellion, I'll support my sovereign. That is, as long as our royal master honors my lord sire's will and makes me warden of my stepmother and my youngest sister." The newborn possibility that he might survive past the sheriff's death that brought these words to Josce's lips.

More than one of the men around him caught his breath as they heard this. It was Josce's certainty that the king would never honor the Baldwin's will that made him ignore them to continue.

"You'll also hint that should our gracious monarch refuse me and take half of Haydon for himself I may be driven into the rebels' arms. Indeed, I may be so upset that I'll take my new brother-by-marriage with me, putting half of Haydon's wealth and all of Haydon's army at our backs."

"Brilliant!" Stephen hooted as the rest of the men added their own votes that this would win Josce the agreement he needed.

Their confidence lifted some of what sat so heavily on Josce. Once again, he looked at his friends. "By God, but I don't know what I'd do without all of you. Did I forget to tell you that I'm glad to see your homely faces?"

"As we are yours," Alan replied, landing a friendly buffet on Josce's back. "Stephen, go you and charm the goldsmith's lass back down here so we might break our fast and be on to these chores our Josce sets us."

Chapter 17

So thin he was nigh on skeletal, one shoulder humped higher than the other, Thomas Attegate, the porter who tended the door of Knabwell's royal castle, grinned at Elianne. "Well now, aren't you just a sight for these old eyes, mistress."

"Thank you kindly, Thomas," Elianne said. With her free hand she gave a matronly pat to her headgear, a modest linen scarf held in place by a ring of braided fabric, then offered him a prim bob. The skirt of her better green overgown, worn atop a fine white undergown, touched the landing's surface.

As she moved, the makeshift pack slung over her shoulder shifted. Elianne straightened with a start to keep it in place. Thomas shook his head at the sheriff's daughter and her unwieldy burden.

"What brings you to us this day, looking the part of a lady but with a peddler's pack upon your back?"

"If you have to ask that, Tom, then you're more addled than usual," Elianne teased. "What ever brings me to this drafty heap of stones except my sire and some chore he sets me? Today, he craves linens for his bed and a fresh tunic," she said, shifting her bundle off her shoulder and into her arms. Rolled into the fullness of one sheet were the bed linens and her father's clothing.

"As for my attire"—she sent him an arch look—"didn't I just shock this town to its toes by racing through the marketplace two days past in my workaday fare? I thought I might repair the damage by actually looking the part of a sheriff's daughter for once."

Thomas only laughed. "That's it, mistress. Keep the gossips guessing. One day a hoyden, the next a gentlewoman."

The cheeky grin Elianne shot him died into a sigh once she was inside the castle's hall. She had a far better reason for what she wore than appeasing the town gossips. Once she gave her father what he wanted she intended to attempt a visit with Prioress Gertha.

Elianne prayed the prioress would see her. Nay, she prayed the other nuns could convince the prioress to rescind her ban on the du Hommets and take her in as a lay sister. Awakening in the garden with the memory of Josce in her arms had left Elianne no doubt that she needed the convent's sanctuary, and swiftly so. Nay, it was heavenly intervention she needed, an angel with a blazing sword to keep her away from Josce. After the pleasure of last night she knew without doubt that she'd sin again with him at the first opportunity.

As always at this time of year the hall was crowded and noisy, what with so many men waiting to see her father. Threading her way around clutches of folk, Elianne made her way to her sire's office. Sir Gilbert stood before her father's closed door, his stance saying he'd see to it no one pestered his employer this morn. All the better for her, since she had no desire to meet her sire, especially not today. There would be hell to pay if even a hint of what had passed between her and Josce reached her father. An hour had elapsed since Pippa and Aggie had found her in that garden and Elianne yet shook over what might have happened if Josce had yet been with her.

"Mistress du Hommet." Sir Gilbert's greeting was brusque. He had little liking for her. At more than a head shorter than her, he hated looking up into her face.

"Here." Elianne shoved her bundle at him. "My sire called for these. You may give them to him when he has a free moment."

Sir Gilbert shoved the bundle of linen right back into her arms. "Take them yourself. He waits for you and none too patiently, either. He expected you at prime."

"Sir Adelm told me to arrive an hour before

terce," Elianne snapped back, liking the deputy as little as he did her.

Gilbert's lip curled. "That's what our lord sheriff gets for sending a bastard to do a true man's work."

Anger for the sake of the two bastards she loved raced through Elianne. She drew herself up to her tallest and leaned toward him, her superior height forcing him to crane his neck. Face black, Gilbert glared up at her, his neck stiff and his shoulders so tense they looked ready to shatter.

"Little knight," Elianne said, her voice harsh, "has anyone ever told you how small a man you really are? Small, smaller, smallest," she said, holding up a hand and closing her thumb and forefinger until they met. Leaving him sputtering at her insult, Elianne pushed past him and opened her sire's door.

Inside, Reiner paced. Not yet three hours old, the sun streamed into the room through the office's narrow window, offering up a vibrant slice of an autumn's golden day. It was bright enough for Elianne to see the stain that marked her father's new gown. She stifled a groan. How could he be so careless? Then again, why should this gown be any different than the myriad other things he'd ruined?

Almost slamming the door to announce herself, she started toward his worktable. He whirled to face her. "Here," she said, dropping her pack upon its surface. "Your linens and your fresh gown, as you commanded. Now, remove that tunic." She held out her hand. "With any luck that stain hasn't yet set."

"Where have you been!" her father shouted, bracing his hands on his table as he leaned toward her. "You were to be here at prime."

"I was not," Elianne retorted, crossing her arms. "Sir Adelm said an hour before terce. That means I'm right on time."

He frowned, then grimaced, chagrin dancing across his face. "I thought I told him prime."

"Well, you didn't. Now, strip," she commanded her sire, "and I'll be on my way. In case you've forgotten I'm entertaining a noblewoman in our house."

Hot color leaked into Elianne's cheeks; it wasn't the lady she entertained. As proof of her guilt burned on her skin she cursed herself and her long habit of goading her sire. If she was to shield herself and the wrong she did, it was foolish to irritate him when she needed him calm.

Rather than snap at her, panic once more set to whirling in her father's gaze. He gnawed at a thumbnail. "It's good that you dress well to honor the lady," he said, sounding more nervous than approving as he acknowledged his daughter's attire. "So, how does she?"

Elianne frowned. Where was his warning to watch her tongue? God knew her comment had been sharp enough to warrant it. Something was very wrong here.

"She's well enough to forbid me any access to your bedchamber, leaving me to sleep in the kitchen with Aggie and her girls." As the frustration of dealing with the noblewoman overwhelmed Elianne, her heart opened and words flowed from her mouth before she knew they were there. "Father, when next you invite guests, can it please be someone who truly wishes to visit?"

Elianne's hand almost flew to her mouth as she stifled a groan at what she'd said. What was wrong with her! Here she was goading him yet again. Tensing, she waited for her sire to scold or even reach across the table and strike her for her boldness.

Instead, he spat out his thumbnail and asked, "And the noble bastard? What of him?"

A bubble of almost hysterical laughter rose to fill her throat. What did her sire want to know? That his daughter had nearly cried when she'd awakened to find Josce already gone this morn? Or that the very thought of his eventual departure from Coneytrop made her ache? Perhaps her father wanted to know that Josce had called her Lianne last night, taking her name and changing it into something that belonged solely to him.

Aye, Reiner du Hommet might want to know all this, but there wasn't any chance his daughter would tell him a word of it. "What of Sir Josce?" she asked.

Her father started on his other thumbnail.

"Does he ask after me and my doings, or talk to you about the thieves?" he asked as he gnawed.

Comprehension hit Elianne like a stunning blow. All caution dissolved. "You traded my hope of a future with the nuns so that I might bear tales to you about what Lady Haydon and her stepson do in our home? Oh Papa, how could you!"

Her sire flinched at her cry, but rather than the decent shame or a hint of guilt her charge should have wrung from him, annoyance filled his face. "You'll keep a civil tongue in your head when you speak to me," he snapped, sounding like himself at last, then his irritation collapsed.

"Have pity, Elianne. You must know I did my best to corner these thieves. Yet here comes Lord Haydon's son, promising to take my life for what I cannot change. Help me just a little," he wheedled. "Tell me what he says to you."

Elianne's jaw tightened until her teeth gritted. Her father didn't deserve to know anything about what Lord Haydon's party did or said. "What if all I can tell you is that Sir Josce says nothing to me because I am your daughter and he hates you?"

"Don't think you can fool me," her sire threw back, his brows dropping over his eyes as his jaw tensed. "I know what goes forward at Coneytrop."

Guilt and dread exploded in her. God save her, he knew about the pool and last night! Elianne nearly lifted her arms to ward off blows. Rather than dash around the table to punish her, Reiner remained where he was, his face twisted in pleading.

"Come, Elianne, I know you spent time alone with him in your garden yesterday afternoon. He must have said something to you," he cried, and a piteous sound it was.

Relief was swift and heady. Her secret, Josce's secret, was yet safe. And so it must forever stay. Elianne forced her body to relax and prayed her expression was flat.

"Aye, we spent time in the garden. He entered without my permission and I didn't realize he was there. When I found him I was so startled that I collided with my arbor and caused it to collapse." She congratulated herself, for not a word was false.

"You can imagine the sort of conversation we had after that." If her father chose to interpret this to mean something other than what had actually happened, or didn't ask for an explanation, it wouldn't be her fault.

Just as she expected, her sire assumed the worst. His face fell, his shoulders slumping apace. Panic returned to whirl in his gaze. Pulling off his cap, he dragged a hand through his hair as he stared at the top of his table.

"More fool me. Of course she'd shout and drive him away from her until he couldn't bear to use her, not even as an ear," he muttered to himself, his tone distant, as if he'd forgotten she were in this chamber with him. "Why couldn't she have been a real woman, one that a man might desire to use?"

Shock tore through Elianne. Her father had hoped, nay he'd planned, that for vengeance's sake his enemy might abuse his innocent daughter. What little loyalty she yet retained for him shattered. As it died it took with it even the respect that God commanded a child give to the one who made her.

"Perhaps if I'd had a true father, one who loved and cared for his children rather than making tools of them for his own profit, my character might have been better molded," she retorted, her tone mimicking his distraction.

Her father's attention returned to her with a snap. Two red spots took life upon his cheeks, the only color in his face. Dropping his cap upon the table, he lifted his hand and started toward her, ready to strike.

Outside the door, the thundering rumble of so many people talking all at once changed, the sound ebbing into one of quiet curiosity. Reiner's gaze flew to the door. His hand faltered.

"Stand aside, man." Josce's voice was loud enough to penetrate thick wood as if it were no barrier at all. "I have business with the sheriff."

Stunned, Elianne whirled to look at the door. God help her, she couldn't meet Josce in here, not right now. What if she looked upon her lover and her father read more in her face than he had a right to know?

Elianne knew exactly what her sire would think, that her secret could be of some use to him. Reiner would be relentless, even brutal, as he sought to discover what it was she hid. The need to protect Josce and their relationship spurred her into motion. Although there was no place in this office to truly conceal her, she sidled into the chamber's farthest corner as swiftly as she could, taking refuge in the meager shadows there.

"Business?" Even through wood Sir Gilbert's scorn was clear. "The lord high sheriff didn't mention a meeting with you this morn. That means you'll stand and wait like all the rest if you wish to see him, sir." The knight spat out the honorific; apparently, Gilbert's feelings about bastards extended even to those who were the sons of peers.

This time, Gilbert's prejudice piqued no reaction in Elianne. Instead, she prayed the knight's rudeness would drive away Josce at least long enough for her to escape. Or that her father's panic would spike until he refused to see Josce. Her gaze shot to her sire. Across the room, Reiner danced in indecision, stepping for the door, then retreating, then once more moving toward the door.

"You'll stand aside or draw your sword." There was deadly menace in Josce's voice now.

Rather than deter her sire, who claimed to fear Josce, the threat made Reiner spring for the portal. Elianne's heart dropped. Only now did she realize she'd chosen the wrong corner. It was the opposite corner that would be shielded by the door as it opened.

The tenons and mortises screeched, so violently did her sire yank open the door. As if already driven to it by a sword's point Sir Gilbert backed into the new opening, stopping when Elianne could see the back half of him. Although the knight's stance was protective, Elianne doubted he meant to shield his employer. It was far more likely that Gilbert didn't wish to cede ground to Josce. Doing so would mean admitting he wasn't as powerful as the bastard he despised.

"For God's sake, Gilbert," Reiner snarled, catching his deputy by the shoulder and shoving him back through the portal and into the hall, "stand aside and let Lord Haydon's son enter."

With Gilbert out of the way, Josce stepped into the room, stopping at about the same place the deputy had occupied. Elianne pressed herself as far as she could into her corner. Hiding from Josce did nothing to stop her reaction to his presence. Oh, but she loved how he looked.

Caught in day's new light, his golden hair gleamed. He wore the same knee-length yellow tunic that he'd worn last night, only today he sported a sleeveless leather hauberk atop it. Green chausses covered his legs, the crossgarters that held them to his calves the same color as his tunic.

As Elianne savored the way his clothing clung to his form, revealing the breadth of his shoulders, the strong landscape of his arms, and the curve of his calves, desire reawakened. Her need to touch him was no less now than last night. She almost took a step toward him, before she caught herself and realized what she'd nearly revealed.

Frantic to protect herself and Josce, she looked to her sire and sighed in relief. For the first time in her life she was grateful for her sire's disregard of his daughters. As near as Elianne could tell, her father's attention hadn't strayed from his visitor. Nor had Josce's gaze left the sheriff.

"Do come in, Sir Josce," Reiner invited, far more pleasantly than his guest's hostile words to Gilbert warranted. As he spoke, Reiner stepped to the side so his visitor might pass. "Pray, take your ease as you tell me what I can do to assist you this morn."

The only movement Josce made was to plant his fists upon his hips. "You may assist me by saying you now have in your custody the thieves who murdered my lord sire."

His deep voice echoed out of the doorway into the now quiet hall. A muted rumbling rose from those who listened. There was something in that sound that said a number of the listeners were only now recognizing just who this knight was.

"Would that I could give you such welcome

news," Reiner replied, a touch of a whine infecting his words. "Unfortunately, there is nothing to tell you. As I said, this is a canny troop as accustomed to hiding as they are to thievery."

The upward jerk of Josce's chin suggested that her sire's answer didn't surprise him. "In that case I'd best remind you how urgent it is that you scrounge up a bit of luck and succeed in this task."

As Josce spoke his hand fell to his sword's hilt in blatant threat. There wasn't so much as a sigh from those listening in the hall. A shudder raced up Elianne's spine at the unnatural quiet. In that breathless moment, the only sounds were the cries of horses and grooms from the nearby stables and the distant ring of hammers as Knabwell's smiths worked at their forges.

"Of course I know how important this is to you and your family—" her father began, his whine more prevalent now.

"Enough excuses," Josce interrupted, taking an aggressive step toward her father. Reiner reared back, eyes wide and face white. The corner of Josce's mouth lifted at this, his smile harsh.

"So, at last you remember how your own continued health and well-being rest upon satisfying my need. Hear me again, du Hommet, for it seems you've forgotten from our first meeting. This morn makes it a fortnight less three. Eleven days. That's how long you now have in which to produce those marauders. Fail me, and it'll be you I send to our Maker in their stead on that eleventh day, calling it just payment for your incompetence."

Noise exploded from the hall. Some listeners laughed, others groaned, while still other men cheered in approval of Josce's challenge. Elianne stared at her lover's profile in shock. When had she forgotten that Josce craved her sire's blood to soothe his own grief?

"You dare to threaten the lord high sheriff?" Gilbert howled, his voice cracking as it rose into an outraged falsetto. He thrust into the room to stand between Josce and Reiner.

"I dare," Josce retorted, his voice lifted but calm as he spoke over the rising and renewed din in the hall. "For the love I bear my murdered lord sire and my lady sisters, I dare." With that, he turned on his heel and strode back out into the hall.

"My lord, give me leave to arrest him," Gilbert shouted, pivoting to face his master.

"Nay!" Reiner screeched. "You'll touch him not. Now, leave me be!"

He shoved his deputy from the chamber, then slammed the door behind Gilbert. With his shoulder braced against the thick panel as if to hold it closed against attack, Reiner faced his daughter. So great was his fear that he panted.

Elianne studied the man who'd made her. Four and twenty years as his daughter meant she knew his every mood and expression. What she saw now made her heart quail. It was printed upon both his face and body for her to read: the greed, the knowledge of wrongdoing and the cowardice. All of it whirled together in his gaze until it looked like panic and guilt, the same guilt he should have felt for misusing her but hadn't.

Holy Mother, her father not only knew who these thieves were but he protected them for reasons of his own.

Elianne's eyes narrowed in rising outrage. Nay, it wasn't for just any reason that he might shield the thieves. Only for profit's sake would her father risk his own life. These thieves paid their sheriff for his protection.

Outrage grew. Here was why her father worried over what Josce did. Here was why he'd destroyed his daughter's future and sent her to live with his enemy, hoping she'd inadvertently learn something about Josce's plans. Noblefolk had been murdered. As the consequences of his greed loomed before Reiner, he grew ever more desperate to find some way to escape his just fate.

Only then did the whole of what this meant register with Elianne. It wasn't just any nobleman her father's greed had slaughtered but Josce's father. Her stomach bucked. She clapped a hand to her mouth to hold back her meager breakfast.

God help her, but when Josce discovered what her father had done whatever feeling he had for her would be destroyed. He could never care for the daughter of the man responsible for his father's death. Not only had Reiner du Hommet stolen his daughter's future but he'd also destroyed her only love.

With that, Elianne's heart took fire in righteous wrath. She straightened to boldly face her sire. By God, but this time he would pay the full price for what he did. She would see to it that he did.

"Tell me," she demanded of her sire. "It's time to bare your breast and confess to all of what you've done."

He whitened with her words and huddled closer to the door. "I didn't do anything," he muttered. "It wasn't me."

If she wanted proof of his involvement, here it was. Her father only denied when he wallowed in wrongdoing. Elianne's anger grew, this time aimed at herself. She, of all people, should have recognized that he was once more scheming. The very gown he wore should have told her as much. He only spent coins they didn't have, as he had for his new tunic, when he believed one of his plots was about to return a profit.

"Oh, you did something, of that I'm certain. In fact, I think I know exactly what you've done. You've been protecting these thieves for your own profit." With every word, Elianne's indignation grew. So did the volume of her voice. "May God take you, you let them do as they pleased, knowing those debased bandits would kill folk." She slammed her fists upon his table. "It's the blood of innocent children that stains your hands!"

Eyes ablaze, Reiner snapped out of his cower. "I'm not responsible for anyone's death, not man or child," he roared, more in panic than in rage.

"Oh, but you are," she retorted, so hot she could barely see. "You can't escape your sin because you looked the other way, and you know it, else why would you be shaking in your boots now? By God, Father, you're terrified that you won't escape blame this time."

She paused to draw breath, then crossed her arms and glared at him. "And die you will, although not by the hangman's noose as you deserve. Instead, it will be Sir Josce's sword that takes you. He should kill you for what you've done!" she charged, feeling for that moment like heaven's most vengeful angel.

With her tirade, the anger died from her father's face, leaving only worry in its place. "How dare you speak so to me, accusing when I did nothing. I am your father, the man to whom you owe life and loyalty." It was a thready protest, weak as water.

"Owe you loyalty?" Elianne threw back, too far gone in her own contempt and anger to pay heed to what she said. "I owe you nothing, not after all you've stolen from me. Without thought or concern for my fate, you took my future and hoped that your enemy might misuse me for your benefit. Nay, after what I've learned this day you'll be fortunate if I so much as shed a tear over your coffin when you're gone."

Her sire's head snapped back as if she'd struck him. The pathetic man dissolved, leaving behind the bully Elianne knew so well. His lips drew back from his teeth as rage took light in his face. With his hand held high in the promise of violence, he surged out of his corner toward her.

Elianne held her ground, angry beyond all fear. Let him beat her. Better that he killed her than that she should endure Josce's hatred. Better that she die than be revealed to the world as the daughter of the man who betrayed his position to steal and slay the innocent.

As if he read her thoughts upon her face, Reiner came to an abrupt halt less than an arm's reach from her, his hand still high. The rage drained from his face. His eyes closed as he released a slow stream of air. His hand sagged back to his side. When his eyes again opened, both anger and panic were gone.

"You're right, daughter," he said, his tone remorseful, his voice soft. "You owe me nothing, not even sorrow at my passing. I have badly used you. For that I must beg God's forgiveness."

The hair on the back of Elianne's neck rose. "What is this?" she demanded, preferring his violence to the ploy he now tried on her.

"An apology," her father snapped, fiery lights

flickering in his hazel eyes, only to die away in the next instant. "You're right to chastise me for all my past wrongs. I've been a poor father, giving thought to no one's concerns but mine own. I was wrong to try to use you as an ear against the noble bastard. Know that if I thought the prioress would listen I'd go to her this very hour and beg on bended knee that she forgive me and give you sanctuary."

Elianne eyed him in disgust. What sort of fool did he think her? She wasn't her mother or her sisters, who had all been easily coaxed, cowed or befuddled by his words. Nor was what he'd done this time a simple indiscretion, as most of his past schemes had been. It was murder that now stained his soul.

"Try to understand, Elianne," her father continued, beseeching. "I'm an old man, old and frightened. I vow to you that despite what you think of me there's no blood upon my hands, no fault for which I need seek penance. Yet, in eleven days' time, Sir Josce, who is young and strong, will challenge me, sword to sword. I can't defend myself against one as powerful as he."

"Do tell, Father," Elianne said in harsh reply, her arms crossed before her. "I want to know how you can defend yourself at all after what you've allowed to happen."

"I haven't done anything," he almost shouted, then caught himself. He extended a hand toward her, imploring, as moisture gleamed in his eyes. "You must believe me. Against that, how can you let me die this way? Help me."

Help him?! Not if she'd loved him with all her heart would she have aided him, not after this. It wasn't just Lord Haydon and his daughters who were gone but seven merchants and their men, as well. Of those her father had allowed to die, how many had younger daughters like herself, without provision or dowry, who now starved or went homeless because of him?

"Would you make me God? Only He may allow or disallow your death," she replied. "Nay, Father, your fate doesn't rest upon my shoulders, but your own. If you are truly innocent"—Elianne's voice thickened with scorn at how impossible she thought this—"then it's truly God you must seek out as your refuge. Kneel before Him and make your vows of innocence, knowing He will see into your heart and judge accordingly. After that, you can go boldly onto the field to meet Sir Josce, knowing our heavenly Father will guide your blade and destroy your opponent so you might live. Thus will all mankind know that no sin taints your soul."

"Such faith." Her father sighed, a sound not of despair but impatience. "Would that I had as rich a store as you. Don't turn your back on me because my belief is weak, Elianne," he begged again, his plea now edged with a hint of anger. "For the sake of the shared blood that flows in our veins help me prove to Sir Josce that I'm not responsible for what he believes I've done."

He caught her by the arms, drawing her closer to him. "Elianne, you're my child, my own daughter," he said, an affection he'd never known for her now filling his softened voice. "It's only a little thing you need do to prove my innocence, both to him and you. It's a chore barely worthy of your notice, one that will take only a little time. Why, you hardly need to leave Coneytrop to do it. I'll understand if you cannot do it for me because of how I've misused you in the past. In that case do it to save our name. Do it to keep Sir Josce's false charge from blackening your own repute."

Even with the fabric of her gowns between his flesh and hers, Elianne's skin crawled where her father touched her. Aye, but that reaction wasn't as bad as the way her heart recoiled as she understood what he wanted from her. Whatever she was to do it meant that he would escape all blame for his actions.

Aye, but onto whose shoulders would that blame shift? Horror tore through Elianne. Jesus save her, but either her father wanted to make a scapegoat of his daughter so she was hanged in his stead, or once she did this task for him he'd finish her himself to protect himself!

Terrified, Elianne planted her hands on his chest and shoved with all her might. He yelped in surprise and stumbled back, his hands opening. She whirled for the door and freedom.

"Nay!" her father roared, grabbing her hand where it lay upon the latch.

With a wordless shout Elianne drove her elbow into his chest. Gagging, he slammed against the wall behind the door. She threw open the panel.

On the other side of the portal, Sir Gilbert whirled to face his employer's office. His eyes were wide, his mouth agape. Elianne careened through the opening, sending the smaller man tumbling.

"I need you," her father screamed from right behind her.

Aye, he needed her to die for him. She lifted her hems. Her sire's hand alit upon her shoulder. Elianne shrieked and sprang into the folk crowded around the door.

Men shouted as she tore blindly through their midst. They scattered and fell before her. Leaping over a portly burgher, she glanced over her shoulder.

Her father bulled his way into the disordered crowd. His fists flew as he tried to carve a path. Despite that, the petitioners closed in on him from every side, each one crying out that the sheriff should hear him.

Trapped, Reiner du Hommet bellowed his frustration to the rafters. "You'll not abandon me, you stupid bitch!" His words rang against the hall's stone walls. "Come back, or I vow I'll kill you."

The threat followed Elianne out the door as she

passed a startled Thomas. Her father meant it. He'd kill her for abandoning him to the fate he'd justly earned, just as he'd kill her if she aided him. Either way, her father planned that she would die.

Tears stung at her eyes. She streaked down the stairs and across the castle's inner yard. Perhaps she should let him kill her. There was nothing left of her life, not now that she was the daughter of a murderer and the lover of a man doomed to hate her for the blood that coursed in her veins.

Chapter 18

Outside Knabwell Castle's two defensive walls, Josce paid the lad who'd held his horse, then swung into his saddle. He turned the big mare, intent on making his way back to the smith's house, where his friends now prepared for their departure from Knabwell. As the horse moved Josce caught sight of a tall woman dressed in pretty green as she raced through the castle's gate. The woman deftly dodged and darted through the lane's heavy foot traffic, her neat golden brown plaits swinging beneath the edge of her prim white head covering. Despite her dress he knew her. It was Elianne in a proper headcloth.

Damn him, but if that was Elianne, then she must have been in her father's office a moment ago. That meant she'd heard his threat. A part of him screamed that he couldn't afford to care what she'd heard; he had to let her go. To chase her down and explain meant encouraging her affection when there was no hope for an honest relationship between them. All she could ever be to him was his paramour, and Elianne deserved better.

Unfortunately, the rest of Josce's body paid no heed to this logic. His hands moved on the reins. His heels struck his mount's sides. The horse leapt into its stride, moving far more swiftly than was safe in so crowded a lane. Men cursed and women cried out. Aye, but they fell back and let him pass.

Ahead of Elianne a lumbering, ox-drawn wagon blocked the lane, the vehicle nearly as wide as the street itself. Josce watched her shift to the left, only to find no passage in that direction. It was the opportunity he needed. As Elianne wheeled to the right, he urged his horse forward to stand between her and the wagon's side.

She nearly collided with his mount before she saw it. Crying out, she staggered back from the beast. Josce vaulted from the saddle to grab her by the arm before she had a chance to catch her stride.

"Lianne," he said, catching her other arm in case she thought to fight him.

"Josce?" She stared at him in tearful surprise. Beneath the fine embroidery that edged her headcloth, the pain filling her pretty green eyes said it all. She'd heard his threat, and it had destroyed her.

Everything in Josce demanded that he convince her that his need to destroy her sire was righteous. Impossible, when her father's death meant her own ruin. At just that moment a group of rowdy apprentices came out of the alley behind them, the lads all dancing and jabbing at each other in mock attack. One of them bounced into Josce's shoulder, only to rebound into his mates with a shouted, "Pardon." It was a reminder of just how public this meeting of theirs was. Too public.

"Come," Josce commanded Elianne, retaining his grip on one arm in case she decided to escape him.

Instead, she followed almost meekly as he led her and his horse a few steps farther down the lane. At the end of a cloth merchant's establishment he put her back against the shop's wall so the drape of the merchant's wares concealed her from one side. Positioning his horse so the bulk of the beast's body stood between them and the street, he shifted, using his own body to block glances coming from the final direction. Now that he had the privacy he craved, Josce didn't know what to say. She watched him, her lower lip quivering. Fresh tears started from her eyes.

"Ach, Lianne." Hopeless as it was, he wanted her to understand how his vow of vengeance bound him. It wasn't as if he capriciously chose to destroy her sire and her life. His father's death demanded retribution.

"Help me, Josce," she murmured softly. With a shaken breath, she scrubbed the back of her free hand across a cheek to wipe away the wetness. "I pray you kill me now."

Horror tore through Josce at the thought of Elianne dead. "What! I will not," he cried. "Why would you even ask such a thing of me?"

More tears tracked down her cheeks. She turned her head to the side as if to hide them from him. "I cannot bear to live on knowing the foul blood that flows in my veins. Or, that you will soon despise me for who I am." This was a bare whisper.

Josce frowned at her. "What care I for whose blood you own? I could never despise you."

It was true. He didn't care that Reiner du Hommet had begotten her, or that she was the daughter of the man responsible for his sire's death. Not since the pool had Elianne belonged to her father. Hadn't Josce made her well and truly his own last night?

Elianne pressed a hand to her lips. "You'll regret those words when you learn the truth," she whispered through her fingers. The pain in her gaze overflowed again. "Oh, Josce, I think my father knows who the thieves are. Worse, I think he protects them for his own profit."

A warmth not unlike that he'd known in the presence of his friends flooded Josce. Another woman would have done her best to camouflage the truth until she could weave a web of words to shield herself from harm. Not his honest Elianne. She spilled all without hesitation, then begged to die because her father's actions caused her lover pain.

Reaching out, he brushed a tear from her cheek. "I know that," he said softly. "I knew it, or at least suspected it, from the moment I encountered your sire at the priory."

Shock widened her eyes. She leaned back from him. "You did? But, if you thought that, how could you not have hated me as well?"

Pretty pink color came to life in her cheeks. It wasn't fear of hatred that put that sort of color into a woman's face but the memory of lovemaking. That Elianne might think about the joy they made together pleased Josce well indeed.

Dear God, but she was lovely, even in distress. Reaching out, he traced his fingers down the curve of her cheek. As she'd done before, she leaned her head toward his hand so he might cup his palm to her face. The gesture said she yet trusted and cared for him despite the threat he'd made against her sire.

"I told you from the first that it was never you I meant to harm," he said. "Whatever your father has done, I know you had no part in it. Your innocence fair glows from you."

"You don't hate me," she whispered in trembling awe, then fell against him, her arms wrapped about his waist. Josce swallowed. Lord, but it was heaven to feel her head upon his shoulder. Then she began to shake, a sure sign that she cried once more.

"Nay, now. No more tears," Josce murmured, stroking a hand down her back. "It wouldn't do to have you spoil your pretty face when you look quite the fine lady this day."

Still sniffling, she straightened. If crying had reddened her nose a little, tears clung to her eyelashes to make her eyes sparkle. "You think me fine looking?"

Josce bit back a pleased laugh. No ploys or subtlety for his Lianne. "I do, indeed. I like it all the more because only I know what you look like when your hair is loose about you and you've naught but a blanket to shield you from the night."

It didn't matter that they stood upon one of Knabwell's lanes. His craving for her from last night flickered back to life in no way abated by his previous satisfaction. In an instant banked desire blazed into an inferno. God help him, but he needed to feel her mouth on his this very moment. His head lowered.

Elianne shied back from him, touching her fingers to his lips to forestall his kiss. "We cannot," she whispered, then shot a worried glance about them. She sighed in open relief when she found no one could see her. "We dare not."

It took great effort for Josce to release his need

for her even as he gave thanks that Elianne had sense enough for both of them. "Would that you weren't right," he murmured, his hand coming to rest upon the curve of her waist. "Just know that I want more than anything to feel your mouth on mine right now."

A tiny, pleased smile touched her lips, then it was gone, leaving her expression far too sober for Josce's tastes. "But I do know how much you want it," she said, "for I want it no less. It's because we cannot control what happens between us that I planned to go to the priory today. I mean to beg Mother Gertha to reconsider her ban upon my family and the sanctuary her folk have so often asked her to offer me."

"Nay!" The word came from his lips with such violence that Elianne stared at him in surprise.

Josce was no less startled. What did he think he was doing, commanding her? Only fathers and brothers had that right. Or, husbands. This rationale did nothing to change the way he felt.

"Nay," he repeated more quietly this time, "not yet."

"You would have me wait?" she asked, hopelessness and confusion tangling in her gaze. "To what end, save that of my own destruction?"

Josce caught her free hand in his, twining his fingers with hers, then laid their joined hands against his chest. "What if the prioress accepts your plea this very day? Once you're within the convent's walls, we'll never again see each other."

The ache that rose with this idea was intolerable. "I'm not yet ready to let you go," he finished.

The pain and hopelessness drained from Elianne's face. Her expression softened until her beauty fair ate up Josce's breath. "You care for me," she whispered.

"I do," he agreed, then sighed. "And more deeply than is proper or even sensible, considering how long we've known each other and who we are." A part of him screamed that admitting this only bound them all the more tightly one to the other when what he needed to do was destroy that connection.

"Wait but a little," he went on, the words coming from his heart rather than his common sense. "Do so knowing that we'll have no more opportunity for—" His tongue knotted, refusing to spill the word *sin* in describing their lovemaking. "I leave Knabwell and Coneytrop this morn and will be gone for a time. Wait until I return so I might offer you a proper farewell."

Who did he think he fooled? There was no farewell save one he couldn't offer her on this street right now. Josce swallowed. That one included grassy gardens, bared flesh and moonlight.

Sorrow filled Elianne's eyes. Was it over their parting, both this temporary one and the more permanent one that they both knew must follow? That she should miss him even before he left her sent a strange wave of pleasure through Josce.

Oh, to have a wife who would count the hours

between his departure and his return. Such was not usually the case, at least in most of the marriages he knew. Nay, most unions were the sort of armed and often icy truce that Beatrice and his sire had shared. Nor could Josce expect anything else. It was the price of marrying for the sake of property and wealth, rather than the liking of the individuals involved.

"How long will you be gone?" she asked, a forlorn quaver in her voice.

"I cannot say," Josce replied. "Perhaps four or five days." Absolutely no longer than ten days, since he meant to slay her father on the eleventh.

Elianne's face clouded with fear. "What am I thinking? I cannot wait even a few days for you, Josce. May God take me and my tongue! You cannot know the things I said to my sire. Against that the only place I'll be safe is in the priory and under Mother Gertha's protection. Oh, Josce!" She pressed a hand to her brow. "What if Mother Gertha won't have me? I've nowhere else to go that my father cannot reach me."

Worry for Elianne exploded in Josce. He had no doubt that du Hommet would kill his daughter, especially if Elianne's death could in any way shield the sheriff from harm. Rage followed. Elianne was his. No man threatened his woman, not unless he wanted to be torn limb from limb. Josce started to turn, ready to rush back to the castle and confront du Hommet once again, this time with more deadly consequences.

Logic screamed so loudly that it drowned out all else. If he confronted du Hommet now, without the rules of a duel to guide their meeting, the sheriff's deputies would surely interrupt. That would leave Elianne vulnerable. She didn't need a champion; she needed solid sanctuary. Aye, but it must be one where she remained within his reach. That he could provide.

"If you want safety, Lianne, go home," Josce told her. "At Coneytrop, Lady Haydon and my lord's men will stand between you and your sire."

"Hardly so," Elianne protested. "Lady Haydon cannot bear my presence now. If my father comes demanding me, she'll happily throw me out the gate and slam the doors behind me."

It was a harsh laugh that escaped Josce's lips. "Hear me now. Save for when Lady Beatrice was mad with grief I've never known her to let her emotions get the better of her, not when she has a goal in mind. If you want her protection, you need only convince her that you'll aid her in achieving her vengeance."

"You're not listening," Elianne cried, her expression somewhere between disbelief and hopelessness. "How can I convince her of anything when she won't let me near enough to even speak?"

Josce pressed a finger to her lips to stop her complaint. "Approach her humbly. Tell her what you told me about your sire."

Elianne blanched at his words. Josce smiled a little and lifted his finger from her mouth. "It's what she wants to hear, I promise you," he told his lover. "You may sweeten your plea by offering to open Coneytrop to her, allowing her to search for proof of a connection between your sire and the thieves. Trust me, against that she'll keep you safe until my return."

As Josce fell silent he congratulated himself upon devising the perfect task for his stepmother. It would keep Beatrice occupied and under Nick's protective eye. Moreover, Josce was certain there was nothing at Coneytrop for his stepmother to discover that might point to du Hommet's guilt. That meant there was no chance Beatrice might force a confrontation with the sheriff prior to his own return.

"God help me," Elianne cried softly, shame's bright color filling her face. "I cannot bear to confess to anyone the sort of sire I have."

"You told me," Josce reminded her.

She dismissed his words with a wave of her hand. "That's different."

Josce's heart warmed in the most wondrous of ways at this. "How so?" he asked. Even though he knew very well what her answer would be, he wanted to hear her speak the words aloud.

It was a startled look she sent his way. He saw the instant she understood herself. As the awareness filled her gaze, her cheeks took fire.

"I told you because I knew, despite my fear and doubts, that you wouldn't hate me for what I said. Shame on me for ever thinking you would. How could I do so when you care for me the way I care for you?" she whispered.

Here it was, spoken where the world might witness. She trusted him above all others. It was bittersweet knowledge, for it left Josce longing to be the only man who ever held this place in her heart, not the one doomed to abandon her.

Again his vow of vengeance and its consequences loomed before him. The possibility that he might die and leave Lianne without a protector didn't sit well on him. It was as much for his own sake as for hers that he needed to be certain she would be safe forever after.

"Tell me that you'll do as I say. Remember that in aiding Lady Haydon you may well win the sanctuary you so covet. A word from her to the prioress and the convent's doors will open without hesitation for you."

Josce choked on his words. Somehow, he had to accept that Elianne would be a nun. After all, she had to live somewhere, and no matter how much he wanted it, it wouldn't be in his arms.

She sighed none too happily. All resistance drained from her. "Because you ask it of me I will try," she promised him, then shook her head. "I fear you underestimate how deeply your lady stepmother despises me."

That only made Josce smile. "I am the last one to ever underestimate Lady Beatrice's scorn, having lived so long with her dislike."

"She dislikes you?" Elianne cried, her brow creased as if the thought of anyone disliking him was impossible.

Josce winked at her. "You speak without thinking, Lianne. Remember that I'm my sire's bastard, the boy-child Beatrice failed to provide for his line."

To his surprise, all the worry and fear fled Elianne's face. Her eyes narrowed as she drew herself up in new outrage. "How dare she despise you for your birth! As if you had any choice in it. Better that she hate your sire for the adultery he must have committed to get you than blame you for something over which you had no control."

Only his Lianne would think it wrong that a bastard be blamed for his birth. Her defense of his existence stirred a strange sensation within Josce. He swore he felt his heart open. Then, before he knew what was happening, he felt the sheriff's daughter step inside that organ. It snapped shut upon her heels as if it meant to keep her there forever after.

Another surge of desire followed, this wave so strong it shook him. There was nothing at all of lust to this emotion. Instead, what he craved was to wake up each and every morning to find Lianne at his side. He wanted to know she pined for him when his knightly duties took him from her. He wanted to watch her belly swell as she gave life to his children. It was permanence and lifelong commitment he desired of the sheriff's daughter.

Unnerved, Josce released her hand and stepped back from her. She gave a quiet cry and reached for him, as if to draw him back to her, only to think better of it an instant later. As her hands fell to her sides, Elianne's chin tightened. The sorrow returned to her face.

Once more awed by the depth of her honesty, Josce sighed. It was painted on her face for him to read; she'd let him leave her without complaint, both now and later, when he'd depart Knabwell for the final time after exposing her father and ruining her life. Aye, and she'd thank him for what he'd done, because that was the sort of woman Lianne was.

She tried to smile. "You cannot know how grateful I am for all the care you've shown me. May I repay your gift with one of my own? Let me serve you as you prepare for your trip."

Of a sudden Josce gave thanks for Perrin's presence. To extend this moment with Elianne was dangerous indeed, especially in his increasingly muddled emotional state. "There's no need. My servant has already retrieved my belongings from Coneytrop and now waits for me here in Knabwell. Better that you go home and keep yourself safe so I need not worry over you as I depart the town."

"If that's what you'd have me do," Elianne said, disappointment laying heavily in her words.

That meant the time for parting had come. Neither one of them moved. A moment passed.

The need to kiss her grew until it overwhelmed his sense. He leaned toward her. She sighed, her hands coming to rest against his chest. Her head lifted toward his.

"For God's sake and mine, man, move your horse before he does damage to my goods!" the cloth merchant shouted, leaning out of his shop window to shake a fist in their direction.

Josce jerked upright. Elianne offered him a quick, sad smile, then darted around his mount and onto the street. He followed, leading his horse. As Josce threaded his way through the city's daily traffic after her, he watched Elianne.

Her no-nonsense pace gave a capable twitch to her skirts. Her plaits gleamed a honey brown against her green-clad back. Green was a good color for her, for it made her eyes seem greener still. Aye, but that gown was too plain, the fabric being only wool with nary a stitch of embroidery to decorate it. After they were married he'd see to it she had another, better gown made in just that shade.

After they were married? The thought brought him up short. His horse snorted at the abrupt halt, then nudged Josce's back with her nose as if to prod her master into motion. Like a man trapped in a dream, Josce came around the mare to mount, turning the creature toward Alfred's shop.

How easily Josce planned for a future he would never own. It was time to end this now, before he weakened his vow and thus betrayed his sire.

In another half hour he'd leave Knabwell, its sheriff and his daughter. If Josce's journey provided the proof he needed to demand justice, there was no reason for him to ever return here, certainly not to fulfill his vengeance.

In all truth if Josce found what he needed the best place for him was in Westminster at court. By law, du Hommet had to appear there by Michaelmas, the twenty-ninth day of September. As Josce stood before the king's justices and the nobles of this land, if not John himself, Josce could present what evidence he'd discovered. If his proof served, no man would refuse Josce the chance to challenge du Hommet on the field, and serve justice with his sword.

Not even on his stepmother's behalf did Josce need to return to Knabwell. If Beatrice still ailed by September's end, then she could move to the priory. If she recovered, then Nick could escort her home to Haydon.

Josce's heart protested against this plan. He paid it no heed. It would be better for both him and Elianne if he never returned.

Chapter 19

Dressed in only the woolen garments he wore beneath his mail with his surcoat belted atop them, Adelm strode up Baker's Walk toward the priory. He should have already donned his chain mail and broadsword, and been an hour outside of Knabwell on his way to Westminster to rent Reiner's housing for the Michaelmas court.

Years ago, his sire had appointed Andelm the task of finding a temporary court residence. And a good thing it was that Reiner had done so. Because of Reiner's accidental foresight no one at Knabwell had yet questioned why Adelm's missing twelve hadn't returned from the chores that had supposedly kept them busy in the shire's south. Why should they, when waiting to join their captain as he rode toward London made far better sense?

Now all Adelm need do was meet his phantom troop on his way to Westminster and London. Once he and their ghosts reached that filthy city, Adelm would release his already dead men to visit London's stews. There, these hapless souls would fall victim to some whore's disease and make their second and final departure from this earth.

Of the men who had survived the battle with Lord Haydon, most had used the morn's unexpected delay to say another farewell to any loved ones they had in Knabwell. None of them planned to return from London. Instead, they'd take leave of the sheriff's service, dispersing for new and safer pastures.

Adelm, himself, wasn't so sanguine over another hour spent in here. All the extra time did was give him longer to fret over the possibility of Reiner's betrayal.

Once Adelm took leave of his sire, there was no hope of controlling Reiner. Without his son to monitor him, would Reiner's panic worsen until he revealed all to Haydon's bastard? Adelm rejected this with a shake of his head. No matter how anxious Reiner got he'd never willingly implicate himself, as long as those spices remained hidden, Reiner couldn't escape blame.

Would Reiner recruit another to retrieve and destroy the spices for him? Again, Adelm rejected the idea. Who could Reiner trust with such a secret? No one, not when it doubled Reiner's risk of exposure and betrayal.

The possibility that his father might recruit someone to do the task, then end that unfortunate's life, woke, only to ebb into the realm of impossibility in the next instant. At any other time of the year Reiner might have tried it, but not just before a court appearance. Autumn and Easter a sheriff was in such great demand that he owned no privacy, and that made secret murder difficult.

Nay, it all came back to one thing. As long as Reiner remained physically incapable of retrieving what Adelm had hidden for him, then Adelm was safe.

He glanced up at the road ahead of him. Riding down to the fork of Baker's Walk and Priory Lane came a nun mounted on a donkey. One of the priory's menservants walked at the wee beastie's side, serving as the sister's escort.

Even at a distance and with a wide-brim straw hat to disguise her face Adelm recognized his mother. It was the way Amabella sat upon her little mount, her spine lance-straight, her body held aggressively forward in the saddle, that identified her. Adelm wondered if the other nuns ever saw the carefully controlled rage his mother ever wore like a cloak.

Although Adelm had no doubt that beneath Amabella's hat brim she watched him as closely as he did her, she gave him no sign that she recognized him. Nor would she. As always they'd play the parts she'd scripted for them in her message. He strode on until they were nearly abreast of one another, then lifted his hand as if to hail her.

"Sister Cellaress," he called. "Good morrow to you."

"Why, Sir Adelm," Amabella cried as if surprised to find him on the lane, drawing her donkey to a halt in preparation for a bit of dialogue.

As she stopped Adelm threw the convent's manservant a sharp, swift glance. There was nothing to read in the man's face regarding this "chance" encounter save boredom. It was a testimony to Amabella's caution that no one connected to the priory yet realized that none of her supposedly happenstance meetings were ever what they seemed.

"I hope you weren't coming to the priory expecting to see me this morn," Amabella said, her tone sober, even chiding. "Mother Gertha has made it clear she'll have none of the lord sheriff's men upon our grounds."

"So I'm told, although I'd hoped otherwise," Adelm replied. Having seen the prioress's explosion and edict for himself, that was an understatement. "How angry is she, Sister? So much so that I couldn't trade upon my familiarity with your house and Mother Gertha for a religious purpose? I'd hoped she'd allow me the use of her church." Here he deviated from his mother's script. "Before I leave for Westminster and court I'd like to light candles and pray on behalf of the sweet Ladies Haydon."

With Amabella not but two yards from him he couldn't miss the frown that flashed across her face. She didn't like it when he surprised her. Not that she could complain about what he'd said. It served her need well enough.

Amabella shook her head. "You may ask, but I doubt she'll allow it, even though she herself says prayer is to be encouraged in all men." With that, she gasped and looked at her escort.

"God in His heaven, how could I have forgotten?" she cried prettily to the servant. Reaching to her belt, she unwound a rosary.

"Sister Margery left her beads at matins service this morn. I tucked them in my belt for her, then forgot to return them before departing. This is the third time I've done that. I vow I'm becoming as addlepated as she."

Amusement shot through Adelm. Three times had his mother pilfered the old nun's prayer beads as a ruse to be alone with her son. Of course, it helped that Sister Margery was always losing the strand, along with everything else she owned. The entire convent, from the prioress to the lowliest of scullery lads, watched for Margery's belongings, often finding them in the most surprising of places.

Shifting in her saddle, Amabella thrust the strand at the servant. "Hamo, while Sir Adelm is here to bear me company run them back for me. There's no need to find Sister Margery. Just leave them with Sister Portress."

The whole while Amabella addressed the man her gaze never came to rest upon the servant's face. Adelm glanced at Hamo. The blankness of the man's expression said he didn't appreciate the cellaress's attitude, just as it also said he knew better than to expect anything else, at least from this nun. Perhaps it was because of Adelm's own isolation from those around him, but his mother's arrogance troubled him. She, who'd been humbled by both her family and her lover, ought to be more compassionate toward those beneath her, more like Elianne.

As Hamo took the strand and turned to trot back toward the priory, Adelm caught the stolid little donkey's bridle. Amabella's seat in the creature's saddle brought them almost eye to eye. There was no mistaking his mother's need to vent what stewed in her. It glowed like sin in her dark gaze. Against that Adelm led the small creature to the side of the lane, where they would be out of traffic's way, as well as out of earshot. When they stopped he looked at his mother.

"So, let it spill. What boils so hotly in you that you'd call me to you this morn when you know I should be gone from here for both our sakes?"

"I cannot believe what's happened," his dam hissed in return. "All is ruined! We're finished."

Her words sent a shaft of fear through Adelm.

Once again, death panted behind him, eager to steal the breath from his lungs. Not yet! He wasn't ready.

The sensation ebbed almost as swiftly as it had come. That was a lie. He was ready to die; he'd been ready from the moment he'd turned his back on Sir Josce and left Coneytrop's hall last night.

Adelm relaxed in acceptance of his own ending. As that happened, he sorted through what his mother had said. It wouldn't be a threat of exposure that had her so upset, otherwise Amabella would never have arranged this meeting. Instead, she'd have swiftly and brutally cut her only child from her life to save herself. So it was some other kink in her plan that tormented her.

"What's happened?" Adelm prodded.

"I only received the message yesterday after vespers. That bitch's son who was my uncle had the nerve to die three weeks past," she fair snarled. "How could he do this to me before I could transfer your wealth as we planned? Now, instead of getting what you need through his will all you receive is the ten virgates of farmland and the mill my dam purchased for you upon your birth."

Adelm blinked. He had an inheritance, one he hadn't needed to steal? For reasons he couldn't begin to name this pleased him well, indeed. Ten virgates was a good-sized plot, more than enough to support a peasant family, while a mill meant consistent income. A sense of sadness followed. They were his but he would never own them, for his life was finished.

But Elianne's wasn't. Adelm nearly smiled. When he died what was his would pass to Elianne. Better yet, what he gave her would be as honest and clean as she, untainted by any of the wrong he'd done in his life. It was perfect. With this little bit of land and income Elianne could buy herself a home within some other convent's walls if Mother Gertha wouldn't have her.

"How dare that old numbskull leave this earth before he served me as he should?" his mother was ranting, her tirade delivered at a whisper. "By God, but those paltry fields wouldn't even lift you above Reiner's pig-kissing sons-by-marriage."

Adelm ignored her complaint. "Why does this vex you? We still have what you sent to London, unless it's gone astray."

"Have it?" This would have been a screech had she not been whispering. "We no longer have anything."

That caught Adelm's attention. "My uncle would steal from his own kin?" he demanded. Was there no family in the world that didn't turn on itself, parents eating their own young, the young battling between themselves over what belonged to the other?

Amabella sent him an impatient look. "Not steal it, but he'll keep it for his life's time. Ach, this is my own fault. In my hurry to see your wealth transferred and my certainty that my uncle might yet serve me, I didn't think to consider other ways to pass it to you. With my uncle now dead, only Gerard's estate can serve us, his wealth vast enough that no one might comment when a goodly portion goes to his bastard nephew. And therein lies the problem."

Amabella paused to scrub a hand over her brow. "Gerard is only a few years my elder. He could live far too long for our purposes."

She grimaced. "May God take him! But, while he lives, he'll have the use of what should be yours. As the years pass he'll turn himself a right pretty profit. Your profit. Damn, damn. I know what he'll do with it. He'll use what should have been your wealth to advance not one but both his daughters into elevated marriages."

It was pure hatred that took fire in Amabella's dark eyes. Her hands tightened into fists. "I came so close. I won't be cheated now of what I want," she muttered, her voice held to a bare whisper.

This was another stark reminder to Adelm that Amabella's son wasn't her first concern. She didn't care that her child might be cheated. All that mattered was that her long-savored plan to avenge herself on her sire had been thwarted.

Bitterness twisted in the pit of Adelm's stomach. As it was with his father, so it was with his mother. Each put their own needs ahead of their child, each finding in their son just the tool they needed to help them achieve their own aims.

When Amabella's head again lifted, her gaze was intense. "Nay, I won't let this happen. You will marry upward before either of those bitches of his do. Here's how you'll wrench your wealth out of his control." She leaned toward him to keep her next words private. "When you reach Westminster you'll travel to London and visit my brother."

That took Adelm by surprise. Until this moment Amabella had adamantly insisted that he not visit her relatives. She claimed caution as the reason. The farther apart all those involved in this scheme remained, the less chance there was to connect them should any one portion of what they did be revealed.

"Tell him you've come to settle your portion of my uncle's estate," Amabella instructed. "Inform my foul sibling that I said those acres and that mill are to be immediately sold. To my brother's amazement the sale will turn him and you an unexpected profit. In fact, the profit will be the exact value of all I sent him, less his own fee, of course. You may tell him he can have double my uncle's usual percentage."

Adelm shook his head at her words. He didn't want to sell his inheritance. He couldn't, not if Elianne was to have it.

At the movement of his head, his mother's confidence slipped. "Ach, you're right. It's too easy to discern in a sale that he's transferring untoward profit. Were he another man Gerard might risk it, but my brother is too great a worm."

Again, surprise shot through Adelm. He'd always believed his uncle a willing and greedy partner, not unlike Reiner. "Are you saying now that your sibling might betray us?"

"Are you mad?" She spat out a harsh laugh. "Betraying us would mean betraying what has passed through his coffers. No one will believe he didn't know the full scope of all my uncle did whilst under his roof. With what vast sums he gives to the Church, it'll look as though he tried to buy his way out of sin." She sneered.

Amabella leaned back in her saddle to loose a scornful breath. "There's no place for religion in business. Does he truly think he can bargain with the Almighty? A few prayers and a smattering of good works won't erase the wrong we do. Nay, we're all doomed for it, all of us headed straight for hell." She laughed at this, not an iota of fear in the sound.

Adelm sighed. She was right. They were damned. That was, if an afterlife truly existed. Adelm was no longer as certain as he'd once been that death ended all. The weeks since the murder of those two innocents had felt much like the hell he'd always imagined. He cleared the thought from his throat.

"Against what you say how can you be certain he won't give all of what's ours to God and His church, and be rid of us at last?"

Amabella straightened with a strong enough jerk that the donkey huffed in protest and sidled.

Surprise flushed all trace of anger from her face. "What, and cheat his own kin?! Never! You may as well say he won't change his will to include you the moment he receives what I've sent to him."

Her protest was so honest that Adelm almost laughed. So, his uncle was but half a thief, refusing to steal from his own blood even as he profited from the wrongdoing of others.

As Amabella relaxed in her saddle, astonishment filled her face. "What a fool I am. But here's how you'll get your wealth!"

Her eyes narrowed and her mouth tightened to a grim line. "As I said, in London go you to meet with my brother. He's Gerard, Robert's son, a mercer, his home standing in the shadow of St. Paul's. Do more than make his acquaintance as you meet him. Work to cultivate his trust. This way, if he hasn't already received what I sent, he'll make a point of informing you when our wealth arrives. Once he has it in his hands and in his will you must slay him in secret."

Her words tore through Adelm like a sword strike. Once again, one of his parents planned that he'd do murder. Roaring from the depths of his memories came the way Clarice had trembled in his arms as her life ended.

Adelm's stomach wrenched. His hands burned where her innocent blood had stained his skin. He rubbed his palms against the body of his tunic. Frigid emptiness opened up within him, growing until it stole his will and ate up all his energy. From some abstract corner of his mind came the thought that this must be what death felt like.

Desperate to escape both his mother and the awful sensation, Adelm released the donkey's bridle. He stepped back from the beast. With his movement his mother cast a wary glance behind her. Hamo had just appeared at the bottom of Priory Lane. When Amabella looked back at Adelm, her face was clear, her eyes fair guileless.

"Godspeed you on your journey," she cheerily bid him.

Adelm nearly laughed. That his mother could spill those words as she sent him off to do murder was beyond irony. He turned without a response and strode away from the woman who had given him life.

Less than an hour after winning her sire's promise to end her life, Elianne paced before his closed bedchamber door. The hall behind her was dark and empty, wood being too dear to waste in lighting an empty chamber.

This morn everyone was out and about. Haydon's master-at-arms was working his men in the yard, or so said the muted clang of swords against shields that rang in through the hall's open doorway. As was his duty, Richard supervised the hamlet's harvest to see that his master wasn't cheated. With the breakfast tables cleaned and disassembled, Aggie and her girls were in the kitchen, hard at their many autumn chores.

Sister Ada had joined them while Lady Haydon rested. When Elianne had put her head into the kitchen a few moments ago, Ada and Aggie were having a friendly argument over exactly what herbs should flavor a brewet. As for Sister Cecilia, she'd returned to the priory this morn. The noble widow was no longer ill enough to warrant both of the priory's most skilled healers.

All in all that made this the perfect moment to enter the bedchamber and convince Lady Haydon that she didn't hate the sheriff's daughter as much as she believed. Elianne grimaced. This was idiocy and Josce was wrong. No matter what she offered the lady, Beatrice wasn't going to shield her. Aye, and the noblewoman certainly wasn't going to recommend her enemy's daughter to the priory.

Behind the bedchamber's door, wood splintered in an explosion of sound. Elianne cried out and leapt back from the door. Fabric rent. Pottery shattered. The lady shrieked, the sound fraught with pain. Terrified for the widow, Elianne wrenched open the door.

The splintered remains of a stool lay against one wall. One of her father's precious bedcurtains was torn in twain. A diamond-shaped gout of plaster was missing from another wall, white crumbs littering the rush matting along with shards of what had been Coneytrop's only crockery pitcher. Light streaming through the window caught on the green bits as they glinted, dark and wet, amidst the shattered plaster.

Her head bowed and shoulders heaving, her fine red hair streaming down her back, Lady Haydon stood at the room's center. The widow wore naught but her chemise and that garment gaped on her, torn as it was from neckline to breast.

Arms crossed tightly before her, the lady lifted her head to look upon this interloper. There was no recognition in her dark eyes. Worry tore through Elianne. Had Lady Haydon once more taken leave of her senses? She took a backward step, meaning to race for the kitchen and Ada.

Beatrice rocked unsteadily upon her naked feet. "They were just children," she cried, "hardly more than babes."

There was such pain in her voice that Elianne's feet froze to the floor. Tears jumped to her eyes. She nodded, as much to show that she recognized what tortured Beatrice as to acknowledge the remark.

"Someone put a knife to their sweet flesh and cut them." This was a hoarse statement, as flat and as dead as the lady's children.

What those poor babes must have suffered before God claimed their souls. Elianne's tears spilled from her eyes to trace warm tracks down her cheeks. Again, she nodded to Josce's stepmother, this time to show she shared her ache.

Lady Beatrice's brow creased. The pain spread from her gaze to her face until her features twisted against it. "How could anyone kill innocent children?" she pleaded.

There was no answer to this question, at least none that Elianne knew. She could only shake her head against the unthinkable. Beatrice lifted her face toward the ceiling.

"Lord, You let someone murder my babies," the noblewoman howled to heaven, her shout so loud that Elianne started. "How could You take my darlings from me like that?" she demanded. "You didn't even give me a chance to bid them a final farewell," she added, the words a harsh breath.

Silence reclaimed the room, broken only by Beatrice's gasping breath. Then, with a sound like unto a dog's bark, the lady's face crumpled. She dropped to her knees. A sob exploded from her. As if the sound drove her to it, Beatrice fell forward to lay prostrate upon the matting.

Another sob wracked her, then another and another. Each seemed to tear up from the depths of her being before it exploded from her. At last, Beatrice's whole body spasmed against her pain as her fist pounded a terrible tattoo upon the braided rushes.

Elianne's heart shattered. Here, before her, cloaked in naught but raw emotion, was her father's legacy. How many other widows and mothers sobbed because their husbands or sons had died at the hands of this shire's thieves? All because her sire had devised a new way to line his own purse.

Against Beatrice's need and her father's wrong, Elianne's fear for herself died. She hurried across the room to kneel beside Josce's noble stepmother. "Oh, my lady, I'm so sorry," she said softly, again and again, all the while stroking a gentle hand down the woman's back as the lady cried.

It was a long while before Beatrice's sobs became but quiet, pain-filled hiccups. As the lady lay limp and spent upon the matting, Elianne's nervousness returned. She couldn't do it, coward that she was, not when Beatrice's heart broke so over her lost children. She couldn't beg for herself, not after what her father had done.

"It isn't fitting that you should lie upon the floor, my lady," she said at last.

Drawing a shattered breath, Beatrice shifted an arm to pillow her head. "I suppose not." With her face aimed toward the floor her voice was barely audible.

"You must rise and return to bed," Elianne told her.

"I cannot." This time, Beatrice's words owned an aching edge as if she feared she might never again be able to move.

Elianne made a comforting, soothing sound, then once more stroked the lady's back. "You can with my help, but you must turn over. I can aid you from there."

With a broken sigh Beatrice did as she was bid, rolling onto her back. Her cheeks and brow wore an imprint of the matt's weave. Her face was red, her eyes puffy, their dark irises dull against what the outpouring of her heart had cost her.

"Mary save me," the noblewoman breathed as she eyed her companion, "but it's you."

"I fear it is," Elianne replied in hopelessness, waiting for Lady Beatrice to smite her or shout out that she should leave.

Instead, the lady only freed another aching sigh. That the noblewoman's grief might be so deep that it could eat up even hatred woke Elianne's shame. This was all her fault. She should have seen what her father had been plotting. Instead, she'd blinded herself to his doings all because what he did hadn't been troubling her. It was rising guilt that spurred words from Elianne's tongue.

"Oh my lady, know that if there were any way I could give your daughters back to you, I'd do it. As God is my witness, I didn't know what he was doing."

Confusion flickered through Lady Beatrice's dull gaze. "What? Who?"

Elianne bowed her head. "My lady, I believe my sire protects the thieves who stole the lives of your daughters and your husband."

That brought new light raging into the lady's eyes. Beatrice's mouth twisted into a harsh line. Her jaw tightened. Reaching out, she caught Elianne's hand in a grip so tight that Elianne nearly cried out.

"Which is this?" Lady Haydon demanded, her voice hoarse from sobbing. There was no kindness in her tone. "A selfish sham of penitence to ease your own soul's aching or an offer to aid me in my vengeance? If it's the first, then go beat your breast elsewhere and leave me to my honest grief. If it's the second, say it now and plainly so, so we'll have no mistakes between us. For the sake of my darlings and their stolen lives, will you help me avenge myself against your sire?"

It was a terrible question, a sin against God, who commanded His people to respect their sires and dams. Could she turn her back on all that she knew was right and aid her father's enemies in destroying him? Elianne swallowed. A daughter who betrayed her sire would be a pariah. No man or woman would ever again trust her.

Even as fear for herself and her future held her tongue, the voices of all those her sire had betrayed in one way or another echoed in her. She heard her mother, her sisters, Mother Gertha, poor sweet Isabelle, his second wife, and Isabelle's stillborn son. And what of the dead merchants and their men? What of Clarice and Adelaide, and Lord Haydon? To a one, they also cried out that Reiner du Hommet must pay.

Against that, Elianne had no choice. Even still, she couldn't speak the words aloud. All she offered Beatrice was a single, slow nod.

Vicious excitement took fire in the noblewoman's eyes. "Help me up, then. We have work to do."

Chapter 20

Hunger gnawed a hole in Adelm's stomach. He tried to spit out the road dust, only to discover there was no moisture in his mouth. He touched his tongue to his lips. They were so dry he wondered if they bled.

It was yet another day too hot for the season. Although it was only morning, the woolen garments he wore beneath his chain mail were already sodden with sweat. This when he had hours of travel remaining before he reached Knabwell.

At least his mount and the one he led were fresh and moving at a sprightly pace. Two horses guaranteed he'd reach the city before late afternoon. A flicker of regret shot through him.

To get these two he'd had to trade his own horse, a friend of long duration. Adelm shook away the emotion. If he had to ride a horse to its death, better that it not be that sweet-natured, thickheaded creature. No horse had the stamina to make the trip from London to Knabwell in two days, and Adelm had to be in Knabwell today. The morrow marked a fortnight since Haydon's arrival at Coneytrop, the date on which Sir Josce had demanded that Reiner produce the thieves.

It was what Adelm had found in London that now chased him back to Knabwell only four days after he and his decimated troop had reached Westminster. Yesterday, he'd gone to meet with his uncle as his mother had commanded, only to discover in Gerard another soul like Elianne, good-hearted and direct, a man who valued his family over his own profit. In that Amabella was right. Her brother lacked the usual temperament of a man of business.

Gerard had tearfully begged his nephew to sin no more, not because what Adelm did threatened Gerard but because the man truly feared for his nephew's soul. Then, rather than send Adelm from his house because of his wrongdoing, Gerard invited his sister's bastard to dine with him. Much to Adelm's surprise, at that meal his uncle had introduced him to his household as a kinsman, doing so without hesitation and despite Adelm's birth or what Gerard knew of his nephew's sins.

It was there that Adelm had met his nieces. Black of hair as he'd been in his youth and with eyes as dark as his, the lasses were happy children. Adelm had judged them to be the same ages as the Ladies Haydon.

Once again, sickness overtook him. His stomach lurched and twisted. Clutching the reins too tightly, Adelm closed his eyes to fight the sensation.

It was a mistake. His nieces' images formed behind his eyelids. Then, as had happened time and again since their introduction, the image changed until Adelm saw himself holding them as he had Clarice and Adelaide. Even as he fought to prevent it, his imagination moved that knife across their throats until their blood flowed.

The voices followed, not those of his nieces but of the two sweet little lasses he'd killed. Clarice only ever wept, her wordless sobs heart wrenching in their terror. Adelaide spoke to him as she'd done that day, her words wispy and trembling: *But I thought you were fond of me, Sir Adelm.*

Adelm shook his head until both the images and sounds disappeared, then he lifted his gaze to the road in front of him. His purpose lay ahead of him. Aye, and he saw it now as clearly as he saw the dirt and grass of the roadway. He would stop at the priory first, then find his sire.

Seated on a stool in her father's bedchamber, Elianne lifted her head. With her needle poised for the next stitch in the shirt she made for Dickon, part of his yearly pay, she concentrated. Aye, there it was again.

"Mistress! Mistress!"

Mabil's distant cry put the girl perhaps halfway up the house's exterior stair. That Mabil shouted meant her news was of some import. Aye, but was it important enough to free her from this prison?

Elianne looked at Lady Beatrice, who dozed in Coneytrop's only chair. They'd moved the seat from the hall into this chamber for the lady's use because Beatrice refused to enter the hall save for meals. Haydon's lady declared it inappropriate for her to mingle with the servants and soldiers. Beatrice also used this chair to raise her above anyone else seated in her presence. It wasn't that Beatrice was pompous by nature, she was only very aware of her rank.

The lady was also very much improved since her arrival at Coneytrop. While it was true that Beatrice still struggled to rise above the blow dealt her by her daughters' deaths, dark rings no longer marked her eyes. There was a more natural roundness to her face. Indeed, Ada had returned to the convent a few days ago, after having told the noblewoman not to travel for another fortnight.

Two more weeks. The very thought of that much more time spent in Beatrice's company exhausted Elianne. She'd never survive it, not when the lady demanded her hostess share her self-imposed exile. Beatrice needed her. Now that Ada was gone, only Elianne was allowed to soothe the lady during her daily bouts with grief.

Beneath Elianne's exhaustion, worry rode her like a brutal horseman. Her autumn chores now stacked up faster than the wood brought to Coneytrop for winter fuel by those peasants bound to her sire. If she didn't soon break free, her household would starve for certain in the coming season.

That was, if she survived as long as that. Her father remained relentless in his effort to regain custody of her. Each and every day found Reiner at Coneytrop's gate, demanding Beatrice give up his daughter.

Just as Lady Haydon had promised on the day of their pact, Beatrice steadfastly refused him. That simple refusal had worked well enough until yesterday, when Reiner had appeared with four men at his back and tried to ride past Haydon's soldiers guarding the gate. Only when Master Nicholas, the commoner who led Haydon's men in Josce's absence, commanded his men to bare their swords did he retreat.

Elianne sighed as hopelessness and fear tightened their embrace about her. She knew all too well what drove her father to such recklessness. Josce's promised day of reckoning was at hand. Reiner was frantic to save himself.

Mabil came to a panting halt in the bedchamber door, her skirts swinging about her legs. Elianne held a finger to her lips, warning the girl to quiet. Too late.

"Mistress, you really must come see this," the lass cried out.

The shout startled Lady Beatrice from her dreams. Coming upright in the chair, the noblewoman looked toward the doorway. When she saw who was there, she vented an irritable sigh. "Mary save me, must you always shriek so?"

Elianne cringed. The two women struck sparks off each other. Had Elianne not been so heartsore over her own problems she might have stirred herself to do more than merely watch as they rubbed each other raw. Unfortunately, these days her tongue seemed weighted with lead while her progress through the hours felt like walking through a thick, gray fog.

"I didn't shriek," the pretty lass retorted, her jaw taking a stubborn jut. "I called to my mistress."

"A servant doesn't argue with her betters," Beatrice scolded. "Nor does she shout out her message without first waiting to be recognized and asked to speak. You're a child no longer. It's past time you learned to control yourself."

Pressing one hand to her aching head, Elianne closed her other into a fist. She stared down at the half-constructed garment in her lap and silently willed Lady Beatrice to hear how grief lent her voice an almost vicious edge.

Mabil sniffed. It was as haughty a dismissal as any Elianne had ever offered. "My message wasn't for you, my lady, but for my own mistress."

Beatrice shot to her feet. Her fingers whitened, so tightly did she grip the chair's arms. "How dare you! I'll see you driven from these walls for your cheek."

Mabil blanched, then answering anger flared in her pretty face. "You don't have the right to send me away from Coneytrop," she shouted. "This is my home! You don't live here." Her message forgotten, Mabil whirled and disappeared from the doorway.

"Why, that impertinent, disrespectful little brat," Beatrice cried, her eyes wide in shock. "If this were my house she'd have been turned out years ago with her back well striped to remind her of her manners. By God, it shouldn't surprise me that your foul, murdering sire keeps so discourteous a servant."

Her hand yet cupped over her brow, Elianne recognized all too well what the new tremor in Beatrice's voice meant. So it began, the pattern made familiar after days of repetition. First, the lady would indulge herself in a round of recriminations against her host, then, once Beatrice worked herself past outrage, she'd lose herself in another spate of grief-stricken sobbing.

"Well, it won't be long before that insolent creature is repaid for her disrespect," Haydon's lady ranted on, spilling what tortured her into the only ear she deemed acceptable. "Once her master is destroyed that bit of baggage will find herself without home or hope of livelihood."

The words hammered Elianne. Her shoulders sagged. Beatrice never remembered that Reiner du Hommet wasn't the only one who named this house his home, that it was also the place of Elianne's birth and the source of her comfort.

How could her life have been so completely destroyed in so short a time? Tears welled as Elianne once again faced the loss of all she held dear. She scrubbed at her eyes. It seemed that all she did with any competence these days was weep.

If only she'd found a single hint to tie her father to the death of Haydon's lord. Instead, not a shred of proof existed here at Coneytrop. She and Aggie had combed the bins, cellars and barns, then Elianne had scoured the accounting books, seeking unexpected wealth. The estate was just as poor as it had ever been, not a single pence where it shouldn't be. If her father was enriching himself through thievery, he wasn't hiding his new wealth in his home.

Again, tears stung at Elianne's eyes. What if, blinded by lust for his enemy, she'd wrongly accused her own sire of evil? So it went, day after day, her thoughts ever circling 'round to Josce.

Four days, he'd said, mayhap five. Instead, it had been ten. Ten horrible, hateful days without so much as a word from him. She was abandoned, and rightly so. What man would value a woman who made herself a whore to him?

"It won't be long now before Reiner du Hommet is dead. On the morrow, when my stepson returns," Beatrice ranted on, her hand waving as if she intended to conjure Josce out of the heavens, "he'll see that the sheriff meets his Maker and receives heavenly justice for what he's done."

As the lady's words collided with Elianne's own painful thoughts, all the heartsickness, dissension and hopelessness of the past days congealed into an emotion too great to contain. She threw back her head.

"I cannot bear this another moment!" Her sharp, shrill cry exploded in the room.

Beatrice dropped back into the chair to stare at her hostess in stark and silent surprise. What boiled in Elianne brought her to her feet. A ruthless kick sent her stool tumbling across the room. Dickon's shirt flew, the precious needle and ball of thread going with it. Her hands fisted, while her heart pounded as if it meant to burst.

"What's wrong with you?" Beatrice asked, her voice stunned and small. "What are you doing?"

Elianne turned on her. What she could no longer contain vented from her. "How can you sit at my side and openly plot a vengeance that will destroy me, as well as my sire?"

Beatrice blinked as if she only now realized that's what she was doing, then her brow creased in irritation. "How can you say that you'll be destroyed? Haven't I vowed to protect you in trade for the aid you offer me? Do you question my word?"

What Elianne had worked so hard to ignore surged up from its hiding place to drive words from her lips. "You cannot protect me. I am already destroyed."

As surprise dimmed, new irritation darkened the lady's face. "You babble, girl. Be clear."

Beatrice's peremptory manner sent another wave of anger crashing over Elianne. Caution died beneath its onslaught. "You want clarity? Listen closely then. A month ago I was the sheriff's impoverished and useless daughter, but at least I owned my pride and my repute. Now, I am the daughter who betrays her sire to his enemies. Who can respect me after that, no matter what my sire has done or not done? On the morrow I will be the child who turns her back as her father battles a younger, stronger knight, knowing as I do that he faces certain death in that meeting. Who can ever trust me after that, especially when my betrayal is based on nothing more than the speculation that he participated in the deaths of your kin?"

Elianne meant to stop there. What she'd said was all the lady had a right to know. Instead, the words kept falling, shoved past her lips by the part of herself that needed to hear the truth spoken aloud to believe it.

"I am also the woman of loose morals who turned her back on God's law to twice bed a man I barely knew. I am the strumpet who bears your stepson's child."

When the last word was out Elianne pressed a hand to her lips. Her knees shook. God help her, but it couldn't be true, it just couldn't be.

Yet not once since her courses had begun in her eleventh year had they been late by even a day, not until this month. Seven full days had passed since the day her bleeding should have begun without so much as a hint to suggest a belated arrival. Too long had Elianne lived with Aggie to doubt what this meant.

Beatrice's face whitened to the pasty shade it had been on the day of her arrival at Coneytrop. Her dark eyes widened as if in shock. "He bedded you? You carry his child?" Her voice was hushed and breathless.

It was Lady Haydon's reaction that drove home to Elianne just how completely she'd ruined herself. There was no place in the world left for her, not now that she bore a bastard for a bastard. As the enormity of it all overwhelmed her, she snatched up her skirts and whirled. Out of the bedchamber she raced, then out of the hall and down the stairs.

In Coneytrop's yard Haydon's men shouted, some donning their armor, others racing in the direction of the main gateway. Her father's daily appearance was at hand. Good. That meant no one would be watching the postern gate.

Craving the freedom she'd been denied these past days, Elianne veered to the back of the compound and that narrow opening. As she raced through the smaller gateway, the need to run until she couldn't take another step filled her. Aye, she'd race from Coneytrop until everything that had happened here, all the wrongs she'd done over these last two weeks, was but a distant memory.

Chapter 21

Seated atop his plodding horse, Josce stared blindly at the gentle roll of the hills before him. All he could see was his own death looming before him. Days of searching had turned up nothing to directly and conclusively connect Reiner du Hommet to the thieves. Thus did Josce return to Coneytrop and his avowed duel with the sheriff, the same duel that would later cost him his life.

The same duel he no longer craved.

Although the pain of his sire's passing was still a raw gash in Josce's soul, the need to spill his own blood to ease that ache was gone. It was too late for regrets, just as it was too late to save himself. He'd given Beatrice his vow to avenge her daughters, and he wouldn't be forsworn. A man who broke his word might as well be dead.

As he'd done time and again on this journey,

Josce reviewed all he now knew, seeking the missing piece that would connect du Hommet to the thieves. On the day before Baldwin of Haydon's death, the sheriff had indeed met with the spice merchant. Witnesses said that du Hommet's arrival had caught the merchant preparing to depart from the abbey and fair with the others of his ilk. Ultimately, the meeting had delayed him by a single day. That was the scenario Josce expected, but what had happened after didn't aid his cause at all. For all of the day of the battle, witnesses marked the sheriff's progress away from the merchant and the place of Lord Baldwin's death.

While nothing put the sheriff at the site of that battle, Sir Adelm had been within ten miles of the scene earlier that same day. Only hours before the battle must have been joined, the sheriff's captain had stopped to collect tolls from a nearby bridge. The bridgekeeper confirmed not only the knight's appearance but also that Sir Adelm had arrived sooner in the month than expected. However, this man added that such a thing wasn't unusual for the knight. It seemed Sir Adelm made a collection whenever his duties brought him through the area.

Josce grimaced. There was little enough to suggest that du Hommet was in league with the thieves. That left even less to connect Sir Adelm to those brigands.

Nor had Simon and Hugh had any better luck in their search. None of the merchant widows they'd interviewed said their husbands carted a rich bed. Even though Josce's friends now took their quest to widows of the farther-flung merchants, Josce had given up any hope they'd find something to justify what he had to do. Not unless Alan, who should have returned to Knabwell by now, had incontrovertible proof of the sheriff's thievery, something Josce highly doubted, would his life path be altered.

The need to live on past what he planned for the morrow once again set to howling within Josce. It brought with it Elianne's image. He no longer questioned how he could feel so bound to a woman he barely knew. Instead, as he had for every day of their separation, Josce cherished his memories of her. There was the way she held her head, and the sweet way her lips lifted when she smiled. Following that came the recall of how she'd tossed her hair over her shoulders to brazenly reveal all of herself to him.

Then, there were her fingers curled around his shaft. Even remembered, that sensation was strong enough to startle a visceral reaction from Josce and wake him from his dark musings. He lifted his head, his lungs filling with the scents of warm leather and horse sweat.

The hills before him wore a cloak of verdant velvet despite the season, grazing sheep distant white dots. Beyond sheep, nothing moved across the landscape, not surprising given that the harvest was hard upon them. It was the season itself that Josce counted on to protect him and his men as they returned to Coneytrop.

He shot a glance over his shoulder. With a steady squeak of saddle leather and jingle of harness rings, Perrin and three of Haydon's soldiers rode in silence along the track behind him. Like him, they were without armor. At Josce's command, they'd rolled their weaponry into their cloaks and tied the bundles behind their saddles, leaving their shields at the home of their previous night's host, a well-to-do peasant.

The possibility that du Hommet might ambush Haydon a second time had spawned Josce's ruse, such as it was. If the sheriff's men watched the roads, it was an armed, mailed knight accompanied by four soldiers they sought. Thus did Josce and his men become careful, casual travelers along the shire's quieter byways, or, in this case, stock trails. Although they hadn't met a soul in hours, the closer they came to Coneytrop the greater the risk grew. Only once they'd crossed the next two miles and finally shut that farmstead's gate behind them would Josce know if his plan was bold brilliance or sheer idiocy.

"Sir," Perrin called from his place at the end of this small troop, "someone moves upon the hill behind us."

Josce's heart shot from his chest. Every muscle tense, he roweled the big mare into a turn. As Josce rode back up the hill toward Perrin, Haydon's soldiers scrabbled their weapons out of hiding.

Stopping just below the hill's crest, Josce looked in the direction Perrin pointed. A figure moved swiftly up the face of the hill behind them in the direction of Knabwell, and its sheriff. There was something odd about the runner. Josce squinted. The blue of the figure's clothing stretched from shoulder height to the ground. Skirts. Relief almost made him dizzy.

"It's a woman," he called back to his men, then gave vent to a short, sharp laugh. "What do you think? Is du Hommet so low that he'd set a woman to spying upon us?"

Only as the words left him did Josce realize who he watched. Elianne! "Jesus God, but what does she think she's doing?" he shouted.

Alone and unprotected, Elianne was vulnerable to all sorts of threat, but mostly to her father. The very thought of his Lianne cold and dead cut Josce in twain. He drummed his heels into the mare's sides. She grunted in surprise and picked up her heels.

"Where are you going?" Perrin shouted after him.

Josce jerked the startled animal back around and into an abrupt halt. What in God's name *was* he doing? Abandoning his father's men to save the sheriff's daughter, that's what.

He might as well abandon his vow of vengeance.

Which was exactly what he wanted to do—nay, it was exactly what he *had* to do.

Only then did Josce finally recognize the insanity of what he contemplated. If Baldwin of Haydon had wanted such a sacrifice from his beloved son, then he wouldn't have willed that it be Josce and no other who was to care for his family after his final departure. It was Josce's mule-headed determination to give up his own life for vengeance's sake, not any affection he might have for Elianne, that betrayed his sire.

Frustration tore through him. It didn't matter what he wanted or needed to do. He couldn't be forsworn.

From deep inside him came a tiny voice. The oath he'd given Beatrice hadn't included anything regarding the sheriff's death; that had been his own plan. All he'd ever promised his stepmother was to aid her in wreaking vengeance on those responsible for her daughters' deaths.

A smile tugged at Josce's lips. Aye, and now that his thoughts were at last clear, he knew just how to wreak a fate worse than death on Reiner du Hommet. All he need do was let the sheriff live on past their battle.

Vicious satisfaction stirred, warm and deep. On the morrow Josce would stand before all of Knabwell and shout out his challenge to du Hommet. In it, he'd include his suspicion that the sheriff colluded with the thieves, then publicly beg

God to guide his sword to prove the sheriff's guilt. After that Josce need only defeat the man, something he had no doubt he'd do. Every witness to the battle would see this victory as holy proof of the sheriff's culpability. The taint would permanently befoul du Hommet in the eyes of the shire. John would have to replace his sheriff, leaving Reiner to die broken, impoverished and debased.

That was vengeance enough to satisfy Josce, but it wouldn't satisfy Beatrice, not now that she was certain the sheriff had caused her daughters' deaths. She'd never forgive her stepson if du Hommet lived past the morrow. In retribution she might well fight his appointment as her warden in order to sever his connection to Haydon.

Josce shrugged away the thought. She could try, but she would fail. Shifting in his saddle, he once more found Elianne's distant figure.

She turned away from the hill's crest, then raced back down the hillside. All his life, the men Josce respected had lectured him to do what his heart told him was right. Although Josce knew full well this wasn't one of the instances they'd meant, his heart insisted that taking Elianne as his own was right.

"Sir Josce?" one of the soldiers called to him.

Josce looked back at his men. They watched him, concern for him on their faces. He grinned. They were right to worry about him. Without vengeance to cloud his mind and bind his heart, the freedom that welled up in him was heady stuff.

"Ride on to Coneytrop without me. I'll find my own way back," he commanded them.

"But what of the sheriff and ambush?" one of the men called to him.

"Should du Hommet attack you between here and Coneytrop, call out that I'm not with you. He only has interest in me, so he should leave you be. As for me, I'll take my chances."

With that Josce put his heels to his horse and set off to catch Lianne.

Heart pounding, her breath gasping from her lungs, Elianne slowed. From this vantage point she could see the top of Knabwell's tallest church towers. Rather than offer her the sanctuary she so craved, it was a terrible reminder of all she'd done wrong and all she'd soon lose.

With what ached in her to drive her feet, Elianne turned her back on the city and ran blindly until she could barely lift her legs. When she finally staggered to a breathless halt, she almost cried out in surprise. In her pain she'd come to the very place she needed. Here she could hide from all the world, at least for a time.

Not but a few feet from her, the stream that fed Coneytrop's summer bathtub tumbled over the earth's ragged lip to splash into the pool some twenty feet below her. Elianne peered over the rocky ledge, sensing more than seeing the place where the long fissure split the wall's face. In the cave behind that crack, where she and her sisters had woven better, gentler worlds for themselves, would she find the sanctuary she needed.

All she need do was climb down the wall to reach it. Elianne considered the moisture-slickened rocks. Lacy ferns, thick moss and the occasional star-bright daisy marked the tiny crags she'd have to use as handholds. The last time she'd climbed to the cave this way she'd been eleven. Somehow, she didn't remember it looking as daunting as it did now.

Yet, with each breath, her need for this sanctuary grew by leaps and bounds. What choice had she save to climb? The only other route to the cave was from Coneytrop, and she had no intention of returning to her home any time soon.

Kicking off her shoes, Elianne tucked her hems into her belt, then again stepped to the earth's edge. The falling water boiled as it hit the pond. What if she slipped? Would her sodden clothing drag her under to drown? Not even the depth of the ruin facing her was enough to make Elianne long for death. That surprised her. However broken, she yet held her own life precious.

Against her need to survive to the morrow's dawn she stepped back to strip off all but her chemise. Bundling her other garments together, she tied them with her belt. With her clothing tossed over her shoulder, she started down the slippery rocks to her childhood refuge.

* * *

Elianne had been nearly a quarter mile ahead of Josce when she'd jogged over the rippling union where this hill crashed into yet another massive roll of earth. Once over the crest, she'd disappeared as if swallowed whole. Now, as Josce's horse neared the same crest, the mare lifted her head, her nostrils wide. Only then did Josce taste the moisture in the air and catch the distant sound of tumbling water.

Dropping over the rise he found himself in a wee dale caught between the two hills. No more than ten yards long, this cup of land was deep enough to conceal his horse should anyone look up from the base of the hill. A substantial stream sprang out of the hillside itself to course along a mossy furrow to where the dale ended. There, the water arched ever so slightly out into open air, sparkling in the sun, only to fall, writhing and twisting, out of sight behind misty folds of grassy earth.

It still took Josce a moment to recognize that he stood above Coneytrop's pool. But where was Elianne? Leaving his horse to drink her fill from the stream and nibble at the lush grass, he strode to the wall's edge and peered down toward the water below him.

Terror stole his breath. Dressed in naught but her chemise, the bundle of her clothing hanging from one arm, Elianne inched her way down the slick wall, using her fingers and toes. Before Josce could muster his tongue to call to her, she thrust through the sheet of water and disappeared into the hillside itself.

He blinked. The image of a long crack on the hill's face woke from his memory. The tumbling water must hide a cave.

Sensations rushed up from within him, none of them having to do with concern for Elianne's safety. It was the recall of what they'd once done at the pool that fed his imagination. A cave was a place of seductive privacy. The need to once more hold Elianne in his arms and lose himself in the glory of her body tumbled over him.

Josce caught himself. Now that he meant to live beyond the satisfaction of his vengeance he wanted more than secret trysts with his Lianne. But even as thoughts of marriage rose, his father's legacy haunted him. To wed the woman he wanted was to betray his sire's plan for him.

Setting aside these thoughts for now, he returned to his mount. After he'd seen to his horse's comfort, offering an oatcake in reward for all her effort on his behalf, Josce retrieved his sword from behind his saddle, then stripped off his clothing for the climb down, bundling it as Elianne had done. With that pack and his weapon slung across his back, he started down the slick wall.

Chapter 22

Drawing in a deep breath, Elianne thrust herself into the falling water. She let the cascade pummel her for a moment, washing away dirt and sweat, then pushed into the cave's entrance. Now that she was no longer a slender child the opening was almost too narrow for her, the rocks that jutted out from either side nearly touching her back and belly.

The cave's threshold was a thick line of moss. Stepping past it, Elianne brushed spider silk and water from her arms, then shivered. As always, a steady chill breeze wended its way through this place, drawing from the doorway to move past the area she and her sisters had used for play. Where it went after that Elianne didn't know, having never ventured farther inside than where light reached.

A few steps beyond the doorway the path took

a sharp upward turn to the right. That corner stymied the water spraying in from the falls, leaving the floor in the next chamber drier. She stepped into the tiny chamber she and her sisters had made their own. Enough pallid light penetrated to this point to reveal three seats of carefully piled stones.

Elianne smiled. How they'd worked, diving into the pool to find the right rocks, then carrying them back here to make their thrones. If the seats now seemed impossibly small, the lacy droplets of water that ever oozed from the cave's ceiling had burnished them to a richness worthy of any queen.

Something lay across the stack of rocks she'd once claimed. Reaching out, she picked up a crude sword made of crossed branches bound by a willow withe. It shouldn't surprise her that Will and his brothers might make her playground theirs, despite the fact that their mother had told them that the devil himself dwelt in here; Aggie worried that her bold boys would push past the darkness that edged this room and be lost in the earth's bowels. Aggie's warning must have daunted her lads, for, if this toy told the tale, Will and his brothers hadn't been here in the recent past. The weapon was spongy from the wet.

Setting her bundled clothing on the slick stones, Elianne sighed, then frowned. A hint of a smell tickled at her nose. Turning, she drew a deep breath and found it again. Faintly sweet, the aroma came from the thick darkness that cloaked this chamber's far end.

As she took a step toward the fragrance, something changed in the steady thrum of the falling water. An instant later, the light in this room died to near blackness. Her heart in her throat, Elianne whirled toward the opening. Someone was in the doorway, someone far larger than Will or his brothers.

There was a man's quiet grunt. Metal scraped on stone. Torn between her fear of the darkness at the cave's end and the impossibility of anyone else entering this place at the same time she did, Elianne froze. An instant later, the interloper stopped in the entrance to her erstwhile throne room.

"Josce." She breathed his name in disbelief.

Like a saint's halo, light from the opening streamed around him. It found gold in his dampened hair and sparked on the metal of his sword's hilt where the weapon's handle thrust up over his shoulder. His wet skin gleamed. Elianne blinked. He wore nothing but the loincloth men affected to cover their most private parts.

She shook her head. This had to be some sort of a dream. It wasn't possible that Josce might find her here. Outside of Coneytrop, no one knew of this cave's existence.

"What are you doing here when you should be hiding safely behind walls?" the father of her child demanded, his tone proprietary. "I chased you across the hills for at least a mile. What if I'd been your sire?"

As he spoke, Josce joined her in this tiny chamber. Dumbstruck, Elianne could only stare at him. They were so close that his arm brushed hers as he shrugged his sword from his shoulder. Clad in its leather sheath, the weapon thudded dully against stone as he set it on the floor.

He dropped his bundled clothing atop her own, then turned to face her. Her dream put his arms around her. She caught her breath. There was nothing insubstantial about him. His skin was warm and damp where he touched her. Elianne's hands came to rest against the powerful planes of his chest. He lowered his head to lay his mouth atop hers. It was a gentle, quiet kiss.

Then his mouth moved atop hers just a little. Seductive heat flickered to life within her. Yet too stunned to stage any sort of resistance, she relaxed against him. The need to feel more of him overwhelmed her. She stroked her palms against his chest. The very feel of his skin against hers woke that wondrous pleasure he made in her. It stirred with enough strength that she shivered.

Her reaction was his. With a gasp he tore his lips from hers, then pressed kisses to her cheek, her brow, then the tip of her nose. Releasing her, he caught her face in his hands.

"Oh Lord, but kissing you is far better than I remembered," he said, his voice hushed as if in awe. "You cannot know how badly I've craved you since we parted. Not one day passed that you weren't in my thoughts, Lianne."

His words stabbed through the sensations holding Elianne in thrall. Aye, he craved her, no less than she craved him. And what had this craving of theirs bought her save her ultimate destruction? Nor did it matter to her body that what they'd done between them had ruined her. All she wanted was more of him.

That even her body might betray her just as everyone and everything else had shattered Elianne's control. A sob broke from her. Another followed. She fell against him, trembling as the torment of these past days poured from her.

"Hey now," her lover crooned quietly, pulling her closer still.

He let her cry, rocking her gently in his embrace, his chin resting on her bent head. At last she had no tears left. Utterly empty and shuddering in hopelessness, Elianne could only lay against him.

Once more, he stroked a hand down her back. "Tears weren't quite the greeting I expected from you," he said, a touch of amusement in his low voice.

How could he laugh when she was destroyed? Anger rushed in to fill the new void. She shoved back from him with enough force that breath gusted from him. He released her. Elianne started to push past him. Josce shifted, catching her by the upper arms.

Even in the cave's dimness there was no mistaking the confusion that marked his face. "What are you doing, Lianne?"

"Leaving you," she retorted. Once more she put her hands upon his chest, this time to force him back from her. Although she shoved, he moved not a whit. "Let me go."

"I won't," he said, his eyes narrowed and his jaw tensed, "not until you tell me what upsets you." This was no request, but a command.

Days of Beatrice, her vehemence and demands, fed the flames within Elianne. "What arrogance Haydon breeds," she snapped. There was enough shrillness to her voice to make some part of her wonder if she was as hysterical as her noble guest. "What makes you think you own the right to command me to anything? Why should I be at your beck and call when on the morrow you intend to murder my father, then abandon me to claim your new inheritance? You'll leave me with no home, a ruined name, no future"—she caught a broken breath—"and your bastard growing in my belly."

She'd meant to fling her words at him, but as they left her mouth, anger shattered into panic. "God help me, what am I going to do?" she finished in a horrified whisper, then hung her head.

No sound followed this save that of falling water. In the quiet Josce slipped his hands down on her arms to cup her elbows. His thumbs stroked the bend of her arms. Despite the dark emotions tangled in Elianne his caress sent little sparks of sensation rushing through her.

"Are you certain?" he asked at last.

Elianne's heart crumbled at his flat tone. It was as she feared and just as her father had promised. A man who set his seed in a woman other than his wife didn't offer his whore aid or comfort. Nay, he denied the child and left the woman to bear the scorn she had so rightly earned by giving up her purity.

"I keep hoping I'm mistaken," she managed, her voice trembling, her gaze yet aimed at her folded hands. As if prayer could help her now! "But my time is now seven days overdue when it's never before been late."

Again silence followed her words, the quiet stretching far longer than was comfortable. That panicked part of her screamed that she must hold onto Josce. He couldn't be allowed to desert her and his child. Then Elianne's spine stiffened. Not even to save herself would she beg. If he didn't freely offer her aid, she and their child would die with their pride intact.

Josce made a quiet sound. It grew into a deep, rich laugh. Startled, Elianne raised her head to look at him.

Even in the cave's dimness his smile glowed. He caught his arms around her so tightly that her breath whooshed from her. Her feet left the cave floor.

"Shame on me!" he cried out, his voice fair

thundering in the small room. "My friends always warned me that I put too much trust in my ability to control myself, that one day passion would overwhelm me and I'd forget my caution. And, so I've now done, seducing an innocent maiden and putting a babe in her belly. Against that, I must do as my father taught and accept my responsibility. I fear I'll have to wed the poor, abused lass and make a legitimate heir of my child."

Elianne struggled free of Josce's embrace. When her feet once more touched the ground, she shook her head, certain she'd misheard him. "You can't be serious. I have no dowry. You'll be a laughingstock if you marry me."

"Well now, I should have thought of that before I got a babe on you, shouldn't I?" Josce retorted cheerfully. "I've left myself no choice, no choice at all."

As he grinned at her, Elianne's knees weakened. It was the first time she'd seen his smile untainted by grief. The bend of his mouth was beautiful, just like him. Still, she shied away from all that marriage to Josce meant.

"On the morrow you'll kill my sire. Wed me after that and there's no one who won't believe I betrayed my father to have you. You'll be tainted by what they see as my dishonor." The thought that she might become nothing more to Josce save a hated millstone around his neck made Elianne's heart twist painfully in her chest. Better that he kept her as his mistress.

A frown appeared on Josce's brow as if he were considering her protest. He nodded slowly a moment later. Elianne's spirits sank to her toes as she damned her sense of honor. Why hadn't she simply told him aye? Because she couldn't let him be destroyed for her sake. All that remained to be done now was for him to rescind his proposal.

"Your point is well taken," he said, then again smiled at her. "And just as easily dispatched. To spare your repute and our marriage I won't kill your sire."

Elianne gaped at him. "But you've threatened—" she began.

Josce pressed a finger to her lips to still her protest. "Aye, so I did, but it was only a threat, rising out of my grief and spewed with careless disregard for my own life, as well as the responsibilities my sire's death laid upon my shoulders. To kill your father is to court my own demise, and that I cannot afford to do, not in the face of my father's trust in me, or now that I know I'd leave behind a babe. How can I abandon you after that?"

A whole new panic washed over Elianne. "What if there is no babe? What if next week proves me mistaken?"

Josce's laugh was low and deep. "Too late to back out now, Lianne. You've ruined me for all time. Knowing what it is to be bastard-born, I took great care never to spill my seed where it might take root. Until I met you." His face softened. "Now that I've had a taste of your passion I find I cannot live without it. Wed with me, Lianne. Say the words," he demanded softly. "I need to hear them come from your tongue. I need to know you want to marry me as badly as I want you as my wife."

An emotion so huge that it brought tears to Elianne's eyes filled her. Their potential babe was but an excuse. He wanted her regardless of her poverty, or what her father may have done, or the fact that he ought to despise her for giving herself before their vows were said.

"I will marry you," she whispered.

"Perfect," he murmured, then lowered his mouth to take hers.

This time his lips moved across hers with all the passion Elianne's wayward body craved. Whatever resistance remained now collapsed as swiftly as her desire for him grew. Her arms slipped around him as she pulled herself closer. As her breasts flattened against his chest he groaned against her mouth, then his lips slashed across hers. His hands came to rest against her hips. His fingers moved. Elianne gasped as she realized he was gathering up the fabric of her chemise, steadily lifting its hem.

"What are you doing?" she whispered against

his mouth, even though she knew very well what he intended.

She felt his smile against her mouth. "Making certain that I really have planted a babe in your womb," he whispered in reply.

A moment later and he'd stripped her garment from her. Once again his hands came to rest at her hips, his fingers wondrous warm against her bare skin. Elianne melted, heat and wetness seeping from her. One of his hands slid downward, seeking out her nether lips. When he found what he sought, Elianne gasped, her hips shifting with his caress.

Josce made a noise, the sound raw with want for her. His desire was no less than hers. Elianne lowered her hand to the cord that belted his loincloth, following it to the knot that closed it. As her fingers traced across the flat of his abdomen Josce laughed against her mouth, the sound of his amusement as heady and wild as Elianne felt.

After his loincloth dropped away she trailed her fingers across his belly once again, winning a shudder from him. In retribution for her taunt, he moved his finger. The sensation was so wondrous that Elianne cried out. At the same instant she closed a hand about his shaft.

His kiss deepened until Elianne's head spun. No thought remained save her need for his passion. Yet twined together, he lowered her to the cave's floor. In some distant place in her mind

Elianne knew surprise when her shoulders and head came to rest against something other than stone.

Before she could consider this, Josce's mouth closed atop her breast. He suckled. Pleasure crashed over her. She cried out and writhed against it.

He persisted in this glorious torment until need was a fire in Elianne's belly and holding him within her all that mattered. Clasping her arms about him, she lifted her hips to his in invitation. With a quiet gasp he accepted, shifting so his shaft slipped between her thighs. Elianne gave him no chance to retreat. She thrust upward and took all of him into her. He groaned.

A moment later and he raised himself above her, his forearms braced at either side of her. Although they were stretched into the darker portion of the cave, enough light remained for her to see his face. His expression was impossibly soft.

"Dear God, but you drive me mad with wanting you." His voice was hoarse.

Elianne smiled, cherishing everything about him. If moving beneath him pleased him, then she would please him well indeed. Again, she arched beneath him, craving more of the sensation that ever shot through her with this.

With a gasp he collapsed atop her, then began to move in earnest. His mouth took hers. A magnificent pressure built in Elianne's womb, the sensation promising the explosion of joy she'd known in the garden.

His breathing grew ragged. He drove into her. She shook, her body arching up into his at the same time her hands came to force his hips against hers. His movements quickened.

Starting as a tiny ripple, pleasure grew until it washed over her in great, shivering waves. Elianne cried out against it, her voice echoing about them, then lost herself in joy. It could have been hours, days, or even years, before pleasure ebbed enough that she could think again.

Panting, Josce relaxed atop her. His breathing slowed, but his heartbeat was a rapid pound against her breast. He shifted against her, then touched his mouth to hers.

"Lianne, you have said you'll marry me, but can you love me?" He breathed his question against her cheek.

Elianne smiled, her hands stroking his back. "I cannot help myself. I think I already love you, and not just because you drive me mad with pleasure."

Josce's chuckle was warm and deep. "You'll love me better after we're wed and finally have a bed beneath us. Not that I haven't immensely enjoyed the strange venues we've made use of."

As he spoke he rolled to the side, taking her with him as he went. Elianne frowned as what lay beneath them crackled and crunched with his movement. Scents, sweet, spiced and sharp filled her next breath.

"I smell pepper," Josce said in surprise. "What are we laying on?"

"I don't know," Elianne replied, sitting up beside him.

More scents flowed into the room with her movement. She placed a hand on what covered the floor beneath them. The material owned the texture and feel of fabric that had been oiled for waterproofing.

Shifting to sit tailor fashion beside her, Josce reached out to pull back the end of the greased cloth. A dozen smaller, darker bundles lay beneath it. He lifted one, a tiny sack. As he brought it closer to them, the air came to life with a rich, dark aroma strong enough to make Elianne catch her breath.

"Mary save me," Josce said, new excitement in his voice as he cradled the scented sack in his hand, "but that's a smell I know. It's cinnamon. These are the dead spice merchant's wares! Here at last is the proof I need. Your sire leads these thieves."

Chapter 23

Josce heard Elianne gag at his words. In concern he shifted toward her. She doubled over, her shoulders shaking.

"God help me, but he did worse than simply shield the bandits," she cried in a tight and tiny voice.

Pitying her, Josce wrapped an arm about her and drew her into his lap. Her head came to rest against his shoulder, her pain hot against his bare skin. He stroked her hair.

"Do you cry for him?" he asked gently, only now considering that du Hommet's child might well have some affection for the man who'd sired her, despite the wrongs he did to her and others.

"How can I, after what he's done?" she replied, sounding heartsore and broken. "Yet how can I not? It's his blood that runs in my veins. For all my years, his life has twined with mine."

Catching herself, she straightened, then lifted her head to meet his gaze. Josce recognized the grief that marked her features as akin to his own. And why not? There were many sorts of deaths. For a child to realize her parent was a murderer was certainly one of them. He pushed a stray strand of her hair behind her ear.

"I see that you ache, but there's no surprise in your face. Did you suspect he might have done more than simply protect the brigands?" he asked. As she'd done when she'd comforted him, Josce made his words a quiet statement, lacking all judgement.

"Aye," she sighed. "I think I knew it was worse than I cared to confront when my sire did all but kneel before me at our last meeting." Her lips tightened, then twisted in pain.

"It was a small chore he begged me to do for him. He claimed it was easily done, that it wouldn't take me far from Coneytrop. He told me that by doing it for him I would help him expose those who had murdered your kin. Yet, how could he know where this proof was unless he'd participated in that murder?" The sweep of her hand indicated the spices. "And here we are in the middle of that very chore."

Then, her expression hardened. "Seeing this, I understand why he panicked when I refused him. If these were discovered here, in this hidden place, he would be surely and completely damned. The existence of this cave isn't known outside of Coneytrop."

She drew a shaken breath. "Aye, and there was no one better than me for him to ask to remove these. Nor would I have lived long after doing his little chore. He couldn't risk my continued existence. He knows I'm not the sort to hold my tongue when I see injustice done. You see, to save himself from the fate you promised him, he planned to publicly betray the man who put these here for him."

Josce frowned at this. "What makes you think anyone but your sire put this here?"

A brief and scornful laugh escaped her. "My father can't swim. Even if he could, or manage the climb down the wall, he's too fat by far to come inside."

At her words Josce leaned a little until he caught a glimpse of the entrance. She was right. He'd had to shove himself through the doorway, and he owned none of du Hommet's bulk.

As Josce considered that, he realized what he'd overlooked by keeping all his thoughts and suspicions focused on Reiner du Hommet. What the sheriff had done he hadn't done alone. Now as Josce pondered who might have aided du Hommet in his thievery, all the fragments of what he'd learned in the past week congealed into a whole. In that instant, and as if it had lain there waiting for him to finally turn his gaze upon it, the identity of one of du Hommet's cohorts rose before his inner eye.

Sir Adelm was a slender man. The captain was also the man who'd accompanied du Hommet to the priory to greet Lady Haydon when by all rights it should have been one of the deputy sheriffs. Why would du Hommet choose his captain over more highly placed men unless something bound them, one to another? Josce's mouth tightened. There were two things that could tie men so closely: trust and distrust.

Out of the recesses of his memory came the way the sheriff's captain had twice eyed him the way one might assess a potential adversary. And in Coneytrop's hall Sir Adelm had confronted him. Then the captain had used his words like weapons, seeking out any advantage he could find. Ah, but the keystone to all this was the fact that Sir Adelm had been seen near the battle site that day.

A fierce joy took light in Josce. He would have it all—Lianne, his vengeance and his life. All he need do was carry these spices to court and lay them, along with the tale of their discovery, before the king's justices.

Aye, but before he reached London, he'd have to reach Coneytrop and Haydon's men. Because what he'd found was so vital, reaching that farmstead seemed the more difficult journey. Josce came to his feet, his arms around Elianne, urging her to stand with him.

"Come, my heart, it's time we left this place."

* * *

Only a quarter hour later Josce was once again dressed, his sword now fastened on over his tunic, and leading his horse and Elianne down the hill. Hanging from his saddle was his precious proof, the oiled cloth making a stiff sack when tied shut with his tunic's belt. They walked in silence, Elianne a few feet away from him, their paces matching, as it had at the priory.

Once again savoring that strange intimacy, Josce glanced at the woman he meant to wed. Elianne's expression was hollow, her arms crossed tightly across her midsection. Hoping to ease a little of what ached in her, he stretched out a hand in invitation. She glanced from his fingers to his face, then, with a small smile, put her hand in his. As Josce closed his fingers around hers he smiled at the sensation. By God, but there was nothing about this woman that he didn't value.

Against that thought he pulled her close to his side. With a sigh, Elianne leaned against him, winding one arm around his waist. Josce draped his arm across her back to keep her close to him. So she would stay for all the rest of their lives.

Returning to Coneytrop was a simple matter of following the base of this hill. They circled it until they met with the rutted path that led from Knabwell's road to the sheriff's home. From there they wended their way to the hamlet.

Dust rose from their footsteps as they walked

along the road. The raucous call of a crow was the only sound. Josce frowned and glanced out at the hamlet's fields. Scythes and sickles lay discarded in the nearest stand of wheat, while none but the geese worked their way through the recently harvested plots. The open doors of the hovels lining the road stared back at Josce like empty eyes, even as chickens and pigs milled in peaceful domesticity before them.

It had the look of a battle scene, the folk all gone into hiding. He glanced ahead of him. The farmstead's wall rose up, the curve of that expanse hiding Coneytrop's gate although the opening lay a quarter mile farther down this path.

"Where is everyone?" Josce asked Elianne.

She roused herself from her painful thoughts to look about her. "I don't know," she replied in surprise.

"By God, you'll open these gates this moment!" Even though it came from Coneytrop's distant gate, Reiner du Hommet's burly shout was loud enough to shatter the day's quiet.

Elianne's head snapped up, her eyes wide. She stopped stock-still. "Mary save me, but I forgot that he had come."

His hand at his sword's hilt, Josce halted, tense, his ears straining. The clank of shields hanging from saddles rose above the sounds of stamping, snorting horses. Du Hommet hadn't come to his home alone or unarmed to demand entry.

"What are you doing back here? Didn't you hear me when you came the first time this day? I will not open this gate to you."

Josce relaxed. That scorn should fill Nick of Kent's sharp reply meant his father's master-at-arms didn't believe du Hommet any threat.

"I think me you'll change your mind," du Hommet shouted back, sly triumph filling his voice. "See what I managed to chase down?" Horses nickered and snorted, as if the mounted men around the wall's bend shifted. The rumbling of masculine shock followed.

"Are you mad?" Nick shouted out, no longer sneering. "What cause have you to hold our men as your prisoners? Free them now, unless you want war with Haydon on your hands."

As Josce understood who it was that du Hommet held, he released Elianne's hand. Turning to his horse, he opened the knots on his saddle pack. His rolled cloak opened enough to reveal the chain mail wrapped within it. There wasn't time to arm. The best he could do was prepare to swing his sword. He pulled his steel-sewn gloves from his pack.

"If you want your men, then open the gate and give me my daughter. Only then will I release them to you. Defy me and I vow I'll spill their blood," the sheriff shouted back.

Cold rage curled its hand around Josce's heart. He shoved his hands into his gloves. At Coneytrop's gate Haydon's men howled in protest. Beneath it ran another chord of masculine voices, the tones of concern filling the sound.

Elianne leapt to his side and clutched his arm. "What are you doing?" Her voice was barely louder than a whisper.

"What I must," Josce retorted, wishing he had his shield. Without its protection he would be vulnerable indeed. Gloves on, he turned to look upon the wall's curve ahead of him, his thoughts beginning to narrow into battle readiness.

"You would defy me?" Although outrage and surprise filled the sheriff's voice, the volume of his words suggested that it wasn't at Nick that he threw them.

A grim smile twisted Josce's lips as he understood. Du Hommet's own men were counseling their better to caution. Josce lifted himself into the saddle. As the sheriff's stolen spices bounced against his leg, myriad scents escaping it to perfume the air, he glanced at Elianne. Her face was white with fear as she looked at him, her hands now clasped as if in prayer.

"Oh Lord help me. You mean to face them alone," she cried at a whisper.

"Lianne," Josce started, only to fall silent as Nick once again raised his voice.

"Du Hommet, listen to your men," Haydon's master-at-arms shouted out. "You cannot be so foolish as to threaten Haydon. Now release our soldiers and leave before you do aught that you'll later regret."

Again Josce looked at the woman he'd hoped to wed. The possibility that he might not survive to give her his vow woke, only to be crushed under the demands of duty. "Lianne, I am the one who sent Haydon's own into the arms of my enemy," he told her gently. "Against that, I have no choice. I must free them."

"It's all of you who'll regret this," the sheriff shouted to the troop who held his home from him. "I am the lord high sheriff of the shire." Arrogance, outrage and desperation all tangled in his tone. "Now, you'll do as you're told and open the godforsaken gate. Give me my daughter, or I vow before you and God that I'll do as I said and kill these men."

With a gasp, Elianne whirled in the direction of Coneytrop's gate. "Oh, please God, don't," she said in a low voice.

Du Hommet's second demand for his daughter was all the reminder Josce needed. Not even to rescue men he'd put in harm's way could he let the woman he loved out of his protection, not when her life would be the forfeit. Aye, but saving Elianne from her sire greatly complicated matters. Du Hommet stood between them and Coneytrop's front gate. Reaching the postern meant making a far too time-consuming circle around the farm. Unacceptable, when his men remained captive. Yet Josce meant to expose himself to du Hommet in order to win their freedom. He couldn't do that and keep Elianne at his side.

Or could he? The answer to this puzzle meant an even more foolish gamble than riding disarmed across the shire. What Josce intended was a mad dash with a naked back and only the hope that Haydon's army would catch him in time. But, what choice had he?

Shifting in his saddle, he untied his pack. He threw the cloak and the expensive armor contained within it into the verge alongside the path. However costly, the armor weighed four stone. If Josce survived what he planned, he could retrieve it. If he didn't, he wouldn't need it.

Elianne whirled on him. "He means to kill your men. What he does to them he'll do to you. He's not alone, nor is he an honorable man. If you challenge him he'll set his men on you rather than meet you sword to sword." Panic sparked in her eyes. "God help me, I must hide. Should he see me with you, he'll believe, rightly so, that I've betrayed him. He'll be beyond enraged; he'll seek your complete destruction."

Josce's laugh was harsh and low. Now there was a defense he could use. Blind rage in a warrior could do as much damage as another man's sword. He thrust out a hand to the woman he loved.

"Mount astride behind me, Lianne," he commanded.

"Are you mad?" she cried.

At Coneytrop's gateway, a man's furious shout rang out. The cry rose into a screech of pain, then dropped into abrupt silence. Raging screams followed as Haydon's men cursed the sheriff for doing murder.

Dark fury woke in Josce. With that, the state he sought before battles took hold of him. Josce's world constricted until all he saw was the work that lay ahead of him and the blood that must be shed. As always, it brought with it an icy emptiness that consumed all emotions.

He snatched Elianne's hand, meaning to pull her into the saddle. She resisted.

"Mount." To his own ears the word sounded distant, as if he were far from himself. Her eyes widened, but she did as he told her. Even before she was settled, he urged his horse toward the bend in the wall.

"Fasten yourself as tightly to me as you can," he warned her as they rode, "and don't release me, no matter what."

Without hesitation Elianne did as he bid and pressed herself against his back, her arms clutched about his waist. Josce walked his horse around the wall's curve, then drew the mare to a halt. From here, it was about a furlong to the farmstead's doorway. Josce could see rising above the wall at either side of Coneytrop's gateway the heads of a dozen of Haydon's men, the shafts of the ladders on which they perched jutting up above the last line of stone.

The sheriff sat upon his horse before that same gate, a dagger in his hand. Du Hommet was dressed for war, wearing his mail, although he'd forgone his helmet and coif on this hot day, baring his white hair to the sun. Twelve soldiers rode with him, the men dressed in vests of steel-sewn leather, helmets on their heads and their shields dangling on their arms. To a one, their swords were yet sheathed.

Josce's gaze dropped to the body sprawled upon the roadbed, one of Haydon's soldiers. Perrin and the other two knelt beside him as blood drained from the man's slashed throat, soaking into the earth as he died.

At this gruesome reminder of what had been done to his sisters Josce once again lost himself to the needs of vengeance. Ah, but this time he did so knowing he could swing his sword with impunity. It was war the sheriff had just declared on his father's house.

Josce loosed a piercing whistle to call all attention onto him. Defender and attacker alike turned their heads in his direction. Josce lifted the bundle of cloth that contained the spice merchant's wares, then kicked his horse into a turn so the sheriff was sure to see that his daughter rode with his enemy.

"Du Hommet," he bellowed, "look upon me and see what I found in that cave behind your waterfall." Even at this distance Josce could see du Hommet's face whiten.

"What are you doing?" Elianne hissed in terrified complaint, then clutched him all the more tightly.

Josce ignored her. "What say you? Can you catch me and retrieve what you so need before I reach the priory?" He threw the dare at a shout so Nick was certain to hear his destination and follow.

With that, Josce drove his heels into his horse's side, grateful that the big mare had rested and fed. She had a huge heart and even more spirit, his brawny lass. Aye, and she'd need every bit of her heart if she was to carry two riders and remain ahead of the sheriff all the way through Knabwell to the priory.

Chapter 24

Elianne lost all hope of living on past this day. It wasn't the Josce of the cave who called out these words. Nay, this was the ruthless knight who'd coldly commanded her to mount behind him, a madman who had just doomed them to death by revealing that he'd been in the cave.

Josce didn't realize that he'd just freed her father from his panic. Without panic to bind Reiner and with nothing left to lose, there would be no stopping him now except death, either his or theirs.

Just as she expected, her father's frenzied shriek was almost triumphal. At the same instant Josce's mount sprang into motion. In front of her, the man who would be her husband leaned low over his horse's neck.

"It's your fastest I want, lass," he told the creature, his tone yet harsh. Despite his cold words, his mare did his bidding, stretching into a steady gallop.

Just as Josce had commanded her, Elianne clung to him with all her might. She needed all her strength. Each meeting of hoof to the ground tried to jar her out of the saddle. The dirt the mare kicked up stung Elianne's thighs where her flying skirts bared them. Air tore past her, stealing the breath from her mouth, even as dust clogged her nose.

They were halfway to the place where this rutted path met Knabwell's road before she heard it. Over the thunderous tattoo of this horse's hooves on the earth came a steady rumbling. That sound grew until it was all Elianne could hear.

She turned her head to look behind her and forgot to breathe. A smoking cloud of dirt put her sire and troop no more than four hundred yards behind them and gaining. This, when any hope of survival lay in the more distant cloud that said Haydon's troop pursued. Ach, but Josce's soldiers were only now leaving the hamlet behind them.

Even as Elianne told herself not to look at him, her gaze moved to her sire. Riding at the head of his troop, her father's silver hair streamed back from his face. Rage twisted his features, his teeth were bared, his eyes narrowed. To look upon him was to look upon her death.

With a fearful cry, she turned her gaze forward, to the hope of sanctuary. Knabwell's walls seemed impossibly distant. Despair closed its awful hand about her. They weren't even going to breach the city gates ahead of her sire, much less reach the priory.

"Faster, my brawny lass. It's only a little farther." The rush of the wind tossed Josce's flat, harsh words back at her as he urged his horse to greater effort.

Again, Elianne glanced over her shoulder. Eyes wide and foam staining its mouth, her father's horse was now but a few bare yards behind them. With a scream she buried her head against Josce's back so she didn't have to see.

Josce's horse raced off of Coneytrop's trail onto the wider strip of dirt that was Knabwell's road. Her heart in her throat, Elianne peered up over his shoulder, willing the walls to move closer to them. At least there were no wagons on the road. Pedestrians scattered, shouting as they flew for the verge. Men pushing handcarts trundled out of the way as swiftly as they could.

From the corner of her eye Elianne caught movement from beside her. The nose of her sire's horse was almost even with her leg. She opened her mouth to scream, but no sound left her throat.

"I have you!" Reiner howled, his voice sounding so close that Elianne was certain he already reached for her.

"Lianne, hold tight," Josce roared.

And then they were aloft, flying over a handcart filled with apples. Even before Elianne had time to be frightened, Josce's mount once more found the earth beneath her feet. Elianne's head nearly snapped off the stem of her neck as they landed.

Without hesitation, Josce's horse leapt back into her gallop, racing on toward Knabwell's gate. The thunder of their pursuers died into screams and shouts. Elianne dared a backward look.

In the distance, Haydon's troop had just started up Knabwell's road toward them. Far too close at hand, Reiner brutally beat his heels into his horse's sides. It heaved and stumbled as it struggled to regain its stride.

Bloody and broken, the driver of the handcart lay upon the roadbed. All order lost in their ranks, the dozen soldiers who followed her father had come to a near standstill behind their sheriff, as if they needed him to lead them to the man her father wanted to catch. Hope woke as a tiny flicker inside her, even as Elianne sent a prayer winging to the heavens for the fallen man. This tragedy may well have bought her and Josce the time they needed to reach safety.

Iron shoes rang on the cobbled apron before Knabwell's gate. Without slowing, Josce drove his horse into the wide opening. Hope died. The gatekeeper was certain to step in front of them as he called them to a halt. Whether he was trampled or they slowed to avoid him, they'd lose all they'd just gained.

To her utter astonishment the gatekeeper stayed in the shadow of the portal he guarded. "Hey now, slow down, sir," the man shouted as the knight's sweat-flecked horse shot past him. His words faded almost as swiftly as Elianne heard them.

"Which way?" Josce demanded well before they reached the fork in the lane ahead of them.

"Right," Elianne cried, not daring to point. He'd said she mustn't release him. Not that she could have unlocked her hands from around him. Nay, terror had permanently fused them, one to another.

Down one lane, then another, they flew toward the center of town. Elianne stared about her in disbelief. Rather than the usual crowds, there was barely a soul out and about.

At last they exploded out into the city's center. The wide field used for the weekly market should have been empty; the morrow was the day for selling. Instead, the expanse writhed with humanity. Rather than the regular lines of merchant stalls, tents of brightly colored cloth, each marking a temporary festival hall, stood haphazardly about the field. Strolling hawkers raised their voices as they shouted out the value of their wares. Musicians played, folk danced in rings to their tunes. The scent of roasting sausages and fresh ale filled the air.

"Nay," Elianne groaned. Held prisoner by both

Beatrice and her own melancholy, she'd forgotten the annual celebration of Knabwell's patron saint.

"Damn, we have to slow," Josce said and pulled his mount into a canter as the mare started into the crowd.

A woman squealed and shied away from the sweat-stained horse. Her husband lifted his fist. "That's my wife's best you're ruining, man," he shouted. "You can't ride through here! Get down and walk that beast as custom dictates."

At the man's complaint Elianne leaned forward, her heart in her throat. "He's right. We can't ride through here. If we try they'll surround us and pull us from the saddle."

As she spoke, the sounds of racing horses echoed out of the lanes they'd just left. Hopelessness ate her alive. If they couldn't ride through the festival, her father could, even if it meant deaths. Indeed, if her sire thought to raise the hue and cry, demanding that the townsfolk stop them, then every man here had an obligation to do just that: pursue and capture them for his sheriff. They were finished.

Josce yanked his horse to a halt. "Dismount." It was yet another ruthless command. She fair leapt from the saddle. He was afoot in the following instant, the bag containing the spice merchant's wares in his hand.

"We run from here," he said, grabbing her hand.

For the second time in two weeks Elianne found herself dashing through Knabwell's marketplace. Josce aimed for the most direct route across the expanse. It was also where the press was the thickest.

"Nay, this way," she cried, wrenching up her skirts with her free hand. With his hand yet in hers, for she'd die before she let him go, she led him to the edge of the field. The distance to Baker's Walk was longer from here, but with fewer people, passage would be easier. Shifting and dodging, they dashed through the folk along the edge of the crowd. They were about halfway to the Walk when she caught the sound of her father's voice.

"Where are they?! Make way. Move aside, you damn fools! The lord sheriff's business!" His shout tore through the day's gaiety. Ah, but he didn't raise the hue and cry.

Minutes—or was it days?—later she and Josce burst from the crowd's far edge. Terror made Elianne's legs ache as she raced up Baker's Walk with Josce beside her. The fork onto Priory Lane loomed.

She threw a glance over her shoulder, and triumph exploded in her. They would reach the priory! Her father hadn't yet entered the Walk.

Their panting breath the only sound on the lane, they raced past the pensioners' cottages, then the guest house. Never had Elianne been so grateful to see the convent's great, arching gateway. Mathilde appeared out of the wee gate chamber that was the portress's domain. The nun gaped at her former student as Elianne and Josce came to a gasping halt before her.

"Elianne?" the portly sister asked, filling the single word with a thousand questions, most of them having to do with the fact that it was Josce's hand Elianne held.

"In the name of Beatrice of Haydon," Josce called out, fighting to calm his breathing, "I beg sanctuary in your holy house for Elianne du Hommet. Her father intends to do her mortal harm."

Mathilde's eyes grew round in shock. Elianne shrieked at what Josce said. Wrapping her fingers as tightly as she could over his, she started into the portal, trying to drag him with her. "Not just me, but you, too."

"Nay, Lianne," he told her.

In that instant the knight who'd coldly commanded her obedience at Coneytrop dissolved. In his place stood the man who'd spoken to her of love and meant to wed with her to make their child legitimate. Tears started to her eyes. He was going to abandon her, when she couldn't bear to lose him now.

"You said I mustn't release you," she protested, pressing his trapped hand against her chest. "I won't let you go. The sisters must save you as well as me."

It was love for her she saw fill the wondrous

blue of his eyes. He shook his head and gently disengaged her fingers from his. "My heart, there's no safety for either you or me here, not as long as your sire lives. Think on it. Your father is a man who did murder for his own profit. His soul is already damned. These walls and their holiness won't deter him from pursuing us."

All hope of surviving collapsed. Josce was right. Her father was beyond stopping.

"However, if I enter these walls," Josce continued, "I won't be able to draw my sword on pain of damnation. Nor will Haydon's men be able to come to my rescue. Nay, if we're to survive I must hold him outside the walls until my sire's men can reach me.

"Take this for me." He passed the bag he carried to her.

Destroyed by the truth of what he said, Elianne clutched the bag to her chest in place of his hand. Scents, rich and lush, rose up to taunt her. From the bottom of Priory Lane came the drum of horses' hooves, the thundering ringing out like the call for the world's end. And it was, at least for her world.

Josce couldn't hold her father and a whole troop at bay by himself. Nay, he'd die. Once again, Reiner du Hommet would escape paying his rightful price for his wrongdoings. Instead, and just as he'd managed all his life, her father would see to it that his kin paid that price for him.

Josce shot a glance over his shoulder, then once

more faced her. Leaning forward, he touched his lips to hers. His kiss was brief, but he managed to fill the caress with every bit of the affection he felt for her.

"Have faith, my love," he whispered, then turned to face the men who came.

Josce took a stance about a foot in front of the gateway's center. His sword sang as it left its sheath. He juggled the blade in his gloved hand as if he enjoyed the feel of it, as if he looked forward to battle and death.

"Elianne, what's happening?" Mathilde demanded, her voice raised in fear and confusion.

Elianne couldn't answer her, not when grief pinned her tongue to the floor of her mouth. Haydon's men would never reach the priory in time, not when they couldn't ride through the marketplace like the sheriff had. Oh God, Josce was going to die right here before her.

Frozen in fear, she listened to the rumble of racing horses grow to a roar. Her father's heaving mount staggered to a halt only a few feet from Josce. Iron shoes clanging on stone, the sheriff's men rode to a halt behind their sheriff and dismounted.

Eyes wild, his face streaked with dirt, Reiner almost fell out of the saddle so swift was his dismount. He snatched his shield and drew his sword. Bitterness stirred within Elianne, sharp and foul. As always, her father would hide behind a wall as he attacked the innocent.

Mathilde cried out. Veil flying, she sprang for the open gate door. Hands braced on its back, she gave a great heave. Elianne gasped as the door began to swing shut. If Mathilde closed it, Josce would be trapped with nowhere to retreat.

"You cannot," Elianne shouted, racing to wrench Mathilde away from what was the nun's duty.

Pulling away from her former student, her eyes awash with terror, Mathilde stumbled back from the door, wringing her hands. Elianne took a stance before the opening, her arms spread. On the other side of the portal, metal hissed from leather as the sheriff's troop all drew their swords. Mathilde's eyes widened. The portly sister whirled.

"Mother!" she shrieked and raced for the prioress's office.

Elianne pivoted. The sheriff's men now formed an uneven semicircle behind their master. All of their swords were bare, their shields in place as they faced her lone knight, who lacked the least bit of protection. Grinning like death and bellowing, her father threw himself at the man she loved.

Chapter 25

Josce raised his sword as the sheriff barreled toward him. So this was why men didn't take their wives with them on campaigns of war. Reassuring Lianne had cost him the emotionless state he donned to do battle. Its absence left him feeling more vulnerable than the lack of either chain mail or a shield.

Their swords clanged as they met. It was a wild attack on du Hommet's part, his blow without plan or purpose. Once, twice, thrice, the sheriff swung. Josce stopped each strike. Then, as his opponent drew back his arm for an overhand blow, Josce hammered his sword into the center of du Hommet's shield.

Gasping, the sheriff staggered back from him. In that instant Josce studied his opponent. There was nothing left of the panicked coward he'd met at Knabwell's castle. Instead, rage and the determination to destroy his enemy glowed like a fire in du Hommet's gaze.

Again, the sheriff threw himself at Josce. This time as their swords met, du Hommet tried to force his stroke downward. Scorn and arrogance flooded over Josce. Here was a man accustomed to battering his way to victory. The sheriff would need to do better than that if he wanted to succeed today. With a powerful shove Josce sent du Hommet reeling back from him.

The sheriff stumbled on the uneven cobbles to collide with several of his men. Josce's arrogance deflated. It was a timely reminder that it didn't matter how skilled du Hommet was. Sheer numbers guaranteed him his victory.

His sword at the ready, Josce waited for the others to rush him as one. The soldiers remained where they stood, every one of them wearing uneasiness like a cloak. Confidence rose. Their hearts weren't in this.

The echoes of distant screams and shouts reached him. It was noise enough to suggest that Nick had reached either the gate or the marketplace. It wouldn't be long now. Aye, but it wouldn't take him long to die if these men chose to fight.

Josce scanned the force. That one held his shield too high. Yon beardless boy trembled. The ugly one wore his arrogance in his sneer. Exploitable weaknesses all of them.

Panting, du Hommet caught his footing only to find his soldiers standing uselessly behind him.

"What's wrong with you benighted fools? Don't stand there. Take him," he shouted. "Kill him."

Rather than rush Josce, the men shifted, glancing from one to another. That they would cling to honor when their master did not was another exploitable weakness.

"They dare not," Josce called out. "They know you unjustly attacked Haydon. Against that the man who kills me may well hang for my murder."

"Murder?" Sly intelligence flashed in du Hommet's gaze.

Josce watched as the sheriff's rage disappeared, leaving nothing behind it but his determination to see Haydon's son as dead as his father. A pity, that. Now du Hommet was a far more lethal adversary.

"It's not murder I do here, but justice," the sheriff protested, his mien as convincing as any mummer's. "I invited you to use my home and you ruined my daughter. You'll pay with your life for that outrage."

It was sheer happenstance that the sheriff's charge was the truth. All du Hommet wanted was the right excuse, the words that would free his men to attack with impunity. It worked. The hesitation drained from the sheriff's men. They would come for him this time. Du Hommet again raised his sword, grinning in the certainty of victory.

It was that smile that sent Josce tumbling back into welcome coldness. In relief, he let it own him. Time slowed in its icy grip. He saw the movement of the sheriff's sword as a slow arc, a rash and unfocused circle. Du Hommet's shield drooped.

Dodging the sword, Josce brought his own weapon down on the upper edge of the sheriff's shield with all the power he owned. A screaming du Hommet crashed to one knee. He flailed as he fell, knocking into the men beside him. Josce drove his sword into another man's unprotected thigh. Howling, the hapless soldier staggered to the side.

Feinting to his right, Josce whirled. His blade rang against the shield of the soldier trying to slip behind him. As his sword rebounded, he gave the weapon a twist, then smashed the flat of the blade against another man's helmeted head. The soldier's eyes rolled back and he collapsed.

The man's shield, the item Josce so needed, dropped from his arm. With his eye on that precious piece of weaponry, Josce brought his sword down on another man's arm. It was a poorly executed blow. Rather than remove the limb, he but broke bones.

As his arm snapped, the soldier shrieked and reeled into two of his mates. All three tumbled together to the ground.

A flick of Josce's wrist relieved the youth of his weapon. The lad fainted as his sword flew from his fingers and fell to the side. The man beside him tripped over him.

In the confusion, Josce lunged for the shield. He missed. From the corner of his eye he caught a glint. He jerked to the side. Not far enough.

The blow, meant to sever his arm from his shoulder, landed on the outer edge of his left arm. There was no pain, that would come later, but there was damage. His fingers numbed, and he could feel the trickle of blood down his arm. There'd be no picking up that shield now. Josce retreated into the safety of the gateway.

"He's mine," du Hommet screamed, following Josce, his sword at the ready. At their sheriff's command his disordered troop fell back a step, leaving their master to battle his foe on his own.

Josce and du Hommet's swords met, then met again until the clash of metal was a steady rhythm. Hoarding his energy, Josce worked only to deflect the sheriff's attack. Not so du Hommet. Each stroke was made with all his strength. Weight, age and the day's heat all took their toll. Sweat rolled down the sheriff's brow. His cheeks darkened in exertion. His mouth gaped as he sucked in great breaths of air. When the lift of his arm began to slow, Josce recognized the time to exploit another weakness.

With a grin, he said, "Your daughter brought me the spices that damn you."

It worked. Du Hommet's eyes widened. Determination died under rage's rebirth.

"That betraying bitch!" the sheriff trumpeted, then swung wildly.

Josce stepped back out of the weapon's reach. When du Hommet didn't find the resistance he expected, the sheriff staggered into an awkward circle, following the trajectory of his blow. It was the opportunity Josce craved.

Before du Hommet caught his footing, Josce hammered his sword against the man's shield, again and again. He kept his blows rapid, giving du Hommet no opportunity to use his sword. Each blow drove the heavy sheet of metal against du Hommet's arm with bruising impact. Josce knew from experience how each thrust tore at the shoulder's sinews. When du Hommet could take no more, he cried out and reeled to the side, out of Josce's reach.

Even as Josce sprang back to reclaim the safety of the gateway, the soldier to his right attacked. Josce dodged the blow. At the same time he slammed his blade into another man's exposed side. The man fell.

Then the others closed in on him. Beneath the brims of their helmets their faces were hard. They lifted their weapons for attack. Where in God's hell was Nick?

Adelm threw open the door to the prioress's office. Above the blithering of the portress, who shrieked on about unarmed knights, Elianne's death and the sheriff, he heard the sounds of battle. His father roared in rage.

He almost smiled. The prioress was right. God was going to grant him a chance to redeem himself before he died. Aye, and he wouldn't have to prostrate himself before some sham of a holy man and spew their ritual words to do it.

Down the stairs Adelm went. When he reached the hard-packed earth of the courtyard, he lifted his heels to run. His legs refused him. He hadn't eaten enough this day to sustain him, and his body was overworn by his travels. The best he could manage was a slow jog.

The clatter of feminine footsteps rose from the steps behind him. "Stop, Sir Adelm," the prioress shouted after him. "You have sinned enough. Don't do this."

Adelm ignored her. Their business, hers and his, was finished. She had more than she'd expected out of it, while he'd gotten exactly what he needed. Amusement tugged at the edges of his thoughts. Despite the prioress's vow to have no more to do with du Hommet or his men, all it had taken to open her door to him had been the mention of his mother's name.

As he neared the gateway, Adelm reached for his sword's hilt and missed. Cursing himself and what this meant for his purpose, he tried again. This time, the weapon left its sheath.

A few yards ahead of him stood Elianne. She was half turned away from the gateway, as if she meant to run farther into the convent. Terror held court upon her features. The angle of her body let him see the fold of dark brown fabric that she clutched close to her.

Adelm recognized what it was. To his surprise,

relief washed over him. That she held what he'd hidden meant nothing would be left undone when all this was finished.

Again swords clashed on the other side of the priory's walls. A moment later and the noble bastard retreated into the convent's doorway. He was unarmed, save for gloves and sword. The left shoulder of the big man's tunic was torn, blood seeping from a wound. Aye, but what stained the rest of his attire hadn't come from his own body.

Adelm looked past the knight. Seven soldiers ringed Haydon's son. Another five lay upon the cobbles. Aye, the bastard was every inch his noble sire's equal, if not his better.

Reiner, his sides heaving, his face red with exertion, staggered into view, taking a stance before Haydon's son. Satisfaction stirred in Adelm. His sire was as worn as he. Somehow, that they should meet while equally exhausted made what he intended feel just.

Elianne's concentration was wholly on the gate. Adelm lay his fingers on her arm. She jerked in surprise and took a backward step, then realized it was he. Emotions flashed through her eyes—affection, gratitude, trust, all the wondrous, startling feelings he knew she held for him.

"Help him. He's all alone against them," she pleaded, despite that Adelm, as the sheriff's sworn man, should have aided their sire. So great was her need to save her noble bastard that she didn't question Adelm's presence here, when he should have been far to the south.

There was no need for her to ask, but then she didn't know that. Once again, acceptance of his own death rolled over Adelm. This time there was naught but peace in its embrace. At the onset of this journey he'd planned to spend his life for vengeance's sake. No longer. What he did now he did solely for his sister, the only person in all this world ever to care for him.

He smiled at her. "Take heart, little sister. I'll shield your love from our sire," he told her gently, then strode through the gate.

Once again du Hommet came for him. Josce readied himself. The sheriff could no longer hold his shield high enough to protect his shoulder. Another opportunity to exploit. Josce's blade crashed down onto the sheriff's left shoulder. Iron rings gave. The metal blade bit through the thick padding worn beneath that armor, then into flesh beneath that.

Bellowing in pain, du Hommet's left arm dropped. His shield clattered onto the cobbles. His left hand hung uselessly at his side.

Only then did Josce catch the jangle from behind him. In that sound he heard his own death. However impossible, there was a knight behind him. With a shout, Josce sprang to the side.

Even as he cursed himself for having to do it, Josce put his vulnerable back to the priory's wall.

Leaving the gate meant he no longer had room to maneuver. All the soldiers could now crowd around him and bludgeon him into oblivion.

It was Sir Adelm who jogged out of the convent's gate, his sword lifted for the attack. The dirt of travel streaked the knight's surcoat. Exhaustion lay heavily in the creases of his harsh face. Set deep in their sockets, his dark eyes seemed dull, as if he were tired beyond living.

Josce raised his blade. Tired though the captain might be, he was still a younger, stronger man than the sheriff. Aye, and if the man truly had killed Lord Haydon, far more skilled than any of these soldiers.

Rather than attack Josce, Adelm jogged past him. A startled murmur left the sheriff's soldiers as they recognized their captain. Astonishment owned du Hommet's face.

"What are you doing here?" the sheriff squealed, fear lurking beneath his surprise.

The knight made him no reply, only swung his weapon. Du Hommet had to hurry to lift his own blade to stop the blow. Their swords rang as they met, then both men staggered back from the other. Again, Sir Adelm raised his sword in preparation for attack.

"Stop, I say!" the sheriff commanded, terror now threading in his voice. "Stop him! Help me," he cried to his soldiers.

"Stay where you are," Sir Adelm countermanded. "This is between him and me."

Lost in uncertainty, the sheriff's soldiers lowered their swords. Stopping where they stood, they watched as, thrust by thrust, the younger man drove his superior back toward the guest house. Du Hommet barely managed to fend off each strike. At last the sheriff's back was pressed to the guest house wall. His only defense was to hold his sword above his heart.

Once again, Sir Adelm lifted his sword, this time for a killing blow. Du Hommet's foot shot out. The younger knight toppled, hitting the cobbles with a clash of metal and the thud of flesh. His sword spun from his fingers.

This time it was du Hommet who raised his weapon to deliver death. Before Josce considered what it was he meant to do, he started away from the wall to rescue the captain. The sheriff's sword arced downward.

Sir Adelm rolled. The sheriff's blow caught him across the back. Bones snapped. The knight arched in pain, then sprawled onto the cobbles, his shoulders heaving against the injury. Josce halted, then edged back and to the side, reclaiming his place in the open gateway again. If that hadn't been a deathblow, du Hommet's next one would be. Aye, and when Sir Adelm was dead the sheriff would return to finish him.

Panting, du Hommet stood over the fallen knight. "Worthless bastard," he gasped out. "I wasted my seed when I made you."

On the cobbles Sir Adelm whipped around to

snatch his sire's leg out from beneath him. With a scream, the sheriff fell. His head met the paving stones with a sharp crack.

Dragging his legs, the sheriff's captain rolled atop his sire. The two men grappled a moment, then the captain was on his side, his father's head trapped in the crook of his arm. Half stunned and caught in this lethal embrace, du Hommet shifted weakly, his fingers prying clumsily at his son's metal-clad arm.

Blood trickled from the bastard knight's mouth. A dagger flashed in his hand. "Today you will pay, Father, just as I have," he wheezed out, spitting blood as he spoke. "Let me show you how they died."

Adelm stroked the dagger across his sire's throat. Du Hommet gagged. Blood pulsed from the cut, flooding his neck. Knabwell's sheriff stiffened, fighting death's inexorable approach, only to shudder into stillness. His sire finished, Sir Adelm collapsed to lay upon his back on the cobbles, his father's corpse sprawled across him.

From the bottom of the priory's lane came the thunder of racing horses. Shouts pierced the rumbling as men urged their mounts on to greater speed. To a man, the sheriff's soldiers dropped their swords and shields. They retreated to stand with their backs against the priory's wall, their hands raised to show that they were disarmed.

It was over.

Chapter 26

The icy emptiness that held Josce in thrall parted. His gamble hadn't been mad but calculated. The proof was that he still owned his life. Aye, and proof of his continued existence lay in the searing pain that coursed down his left arm. Then quiet satisfaction overtook him. He had all the answers he'd come to Knabwell to find.

"Josce!" Elianne shrieked.

As Nick and Haydon's men thundered into the yard, Josce turned toward the gateway. Elianne streaked toward him. Dirt stained her face. Wild strands of hair escaped her plaits. Her hems were torn. No woman had ever looked finer.

It didn't matter that he was wet with exertion or foul with blood, his own and others'. He tossed aside his sword and opened his arm to her. She caught him around the waist. Even though her embrace sent another round of pain rushing through him, he pulled her closer still. She smelled of the spices they'd discovered. Her mouth found his, her kiss as greedy for their future as his was. A moment later, he raised his head and laughed.

"I live!" he shouted to the heavens. A fortnight ago he'd never have believed this fact would give him so much pleasure.

Elianne shoved back from him with a start. "Adelm!" she cried.

Whirling, she rushed to the fallen knight's side. Against all Josce had learned these last moments, that his future wife might show such affection for the fallen knight meant nothing. He turned to follow her as Nick sprinted from his horse to halt before Josce. The master soldier's face was black with rage.

"God damn these townsmen. We had to run them down before they'd let us pass through their green," he shouted, then rage gave way to amazement as Nick at last calmed enough to see what lay around him. "Jesus God, but you did your lord sire proud this day. I'd swear my oath to you in a heartbeat."

Josce laughed at that. Aye, his father would have been proud. Not only had his son wreaked the appropriate vengeance but he'd also survived to take up all the duties and responsibilities that Baldwin had expected him to accept. And Josce's first duty was to see to the resolution of this day's work.

"Nick, we have no further quarrel with the shire's soldiers, not now that their sheriff is dead. Send them back to their castle. After that, see if the prioress will allow her healers to tend to the injured."

"Aye, sir," Nick said, and turned to call out orders to his men.

Content to leave all that needed doing in this man's capable hands, Josce turned to where Elianne knelt beside her fallen sire and brother. Her shoulders shook in grief. He joined her, crouching at her side.

Elianne held her brother's hand, while her other hand was pressed to her mouth to stifle her sobs. The injured knight stared up into his sister's face. Adelm's expression was astonishingly gentle, more life filling the man's harsh face than Josce had ever seen.

Josce shoved the sheriff's body off of the knight in an attempt to ease Adelm's pain. As for inspecting the sheriff's captain for injuries, it wasn't necessary. Blood crept out from beneath the fallen man's back, spreading into an ever widening puddle. The damage du Hommet had done his son was fatal; Elianne's half brother didn't have long.

When Josce's gaze shifted back to Adelm's face, he found the knight watching him. The peace that filled the man's dark gaze was awesome. Reaching deep within himself, Josce tried to summon up anger or hatred. Because of this man, his sisters and sire were dead. Aye, but because of this man, he lived to wed Elianne and see the birth of their child.

"It was you," Josce said at last, his voice low, his tone without judgement.

It was all he needed to say. Grief and self-loathing drove away Adelm's peace. A sigh shuddered from the knight.

"Your sisters recognized me. They called my name to your sire," he wheezed, the frothing blood at his mouth saying his lungs were damaged. Sadness replaced all else in his gaze. "I loved them."

Elianne moaned at this. She sagged. Josce slipped an arm around her to support her.

Adelm watched this, then his gaze shifted to Josce. It was a brother's care and affection for a cherished sister that filled his look. Then Adelm's brow creased. In his eyes lurked the same question he'd set to his fellow bastard at Coneytrop. Adelm needed to know Josce's intentions for his sister.

"We will be wed," Josce answered.

With that assurance, peace once more took possession of the knight's gaze. Adelm turned his attention back to Elianne. "Sister, know that if not for you, there'd have been no good at all in this wretched life of mine." It was a bare whisper, then all his breath sighed from him.

Chapter 27

"You cannot be serious! Women don't make these sorts of decisions for themselves," Mother Gertha protested.

The prioress stood behind her table in her office. Gone was any pretense of serenity. Instead, a scowl creased her brow. A single fold of parchment lay upon the table before her. Lady Haydon sat in the churchwoman's chair not far from her.

Gertha had delayed this confrontation until Beatrice's arrival from Coneytrop, no doubt expecting support from her patron. Instead, Beatrice, once more wearing her linen riding attire with a fine veil upon her head, slumped in the massive chair. Her fingers worked at her temples, as if her head ached.

"Nay, such choices are rightly left to a woman's male relatives," Gertha went on, her tone sharp. She whirled to look at Elianne. "In this case, your half brother stated specifically that he wished you to join our house."

Elianne caught a pained breath as Adelm's image rose before her. Her friend was in truth her half brother, her father's bastard. He was also the man who'd stolen and done murder on their sire's behalf, killing Josce's innocent sisters. Aye, but Adelm had valued her so deeply that he'd saved the man she loved for her.

Again emotions roiled in her, tears rising. Elianne struggled to control them. If life had taken root in her womb, she owed that wee babe better. To weep through her pregnancy was to guarantee her child a melancholy temperament. Aye, but God help her, how was she to feel anything but grief and panic when, on top of all else, this churchwoman meant to steal the future and her child from her?

Seated on a stool at the room's center, Josce shifted a little in her direction. Gone were his tunic and shirt. His bare skin gleamed, the blood of battle washed from it. Sister Ada stood at his left, her needle poised above the top of his shoulder as she closed the gash that crossed it.

"Sit still," the healer nun warned him, her tone chiding.

Rather than heed her, Josce lifted his right arm in invitation. Elianne accepted with alacrity, rounding the stool to stand in the circle of his embrace. Although Josce but rested his arm about her waist, there was no doubting that he claimed ownership of her by his touch. It was a promise that he had no intention of letting the churchwoman bully her into leaving him for these nuns.

Mother Gertha's eyes narrowed. "Remove your arm from her, sir. You've already ruined Mistress du Hommet, seducing her with the sins of the flesh. I'll not allow you to ruin her further."

"You cannot allow or disallow," Josce retorted. "I have asked Elianne to wed with me and she has accepted. That makes me her nearest male relative and gives me the right to make decisions for her. Unless she says now that she no longer wants me, I say that my child prefers I marry his mother. God knows that's what I prefer."

Across the room Gertha stiffened as the child that may or may not exist in Elianne's womb was again mentioned. Elianne smiled as she understood. Josce intended to use their potential babe as a tool, a way to bludgeon the prioress into releasing any and all claim to her.

Now Josce cocked his head to look up at her. "Have you come to regret your agreement to wed with me? Would you prefer that our child be raised as an oblate here, if it be a lass, or be given to monks if it is a lad?" The utter certainty of her response filled his blue eyes.

Still, it was the memory of the pain Adelm had refused to speak of in his own upbringing with the monks that brought words rushing to Elianne's lips. "Nay. I want my child. I choose to be a wife and mother," she said, shifting closer to him.

With a huff of annoyance Gertha turned to look upon Beatrice. "Do something," she demanded. "Speak to him. Tell him that it's madness for him to wed a woman whose father has left her without dowry."

"He's no kin of mine," Beatrice said hoarsely without lifting her head. "I have no sway over him."

Confounded, the prioress swung back toward Josce. "For shame, sir! I would have thought you'd hold your father's legacy in higher esteem than this." Her tone was harsh. "To wed a penniless woman denigrates what Lady Haydon says your noble sire left to you."

"Oh leave be, Gertha," Beatrice said with a sigh, her hands dropping into her lap. She straightened in the chair. "Can't you see his honor leaves him no choice in this matter?" Shame flickered across her face. "What can I do but support him in this? It's all my fault. I'm the one who told him to bed her."

Gertha stared at her noble patroness. "Is that true?"

Folding her hands, Beatrice looked across the room at Elianne. Pain filled her gaze. "Yes. I'm so sorry. I vow I was mad with grief. I ached so deeply over the idea of my sweet babes laid in the cold ground that I needed to hurt others as I hurt. When Sir Josce came to me after he arranged for their burial, I told him to do anything and everything he could to turn you against your sire. I even commanded him to bed you."

Startled, Elianne looked at Josce. Beatrice had commanded him to bed her? But how could that be, when Josce had made their first lovemaking her choice?

The answer was in the slow way he smiled at her. Only then did she recall that the day he'd arranged for his sire's and sisters' burial had been the day after he'd found her hiding at the pool.

"Beatrice, you cannot want this marriage." There was a trace of desperation in Mother Gertha's voice now.

"What else can I do?" Beatrice asked in a small voice with a shake of her head. "It's the only way to make right what I set wrong."

Nothing but regret filled the lady's round face as she once again looked upon Elianne. "You are a sweet lass who deserved better than a wild woman raging at you day and night. You've shown me great kindness, and all I did was abuse you. You should have stopped me sooner."

Compassion and gratitude tangled in Elianne. "How could I stop you when I knew how deeply you ached for your daughters? Would that I had been so deeply loved—" Her voice trailed off into silence.

Her mouth quivering, Beatrice smiled, then her gaze shifted to her stepson. "Josce, I think me you must marry this woman so I can make her part of my family. I've come to be fond of her and would miss her dearly were she to be denied to me."

Josce jerked. Astonishment filled his face. "Madam?"

Sister Ada made a frustrated sound. "For God's sake and mine, lad, hold still. That is, unless you prefer a thick scar and lack of mobility in your shield arm."

Josce went very still. Lady Beatrice's expression twisted until it was both sour and amused. "Well, if you're to be my warden, I think it's high time we came to know one another a little better."

"I cannot believe this!" Mother Gertha cried, sounding fair frantic.

Then, as if startled at the strength of emotion she'd revealed, the prioress whirled to stride toward the wall. Her wide sleeve swung with her movement, catching the parchment on the table. The folded skin shot across its surface to drop onto the floor.

Elianne stepped forward to retrieve it for her, only to frown. Although it was naught but a blob of unmarked wax closing the sheepskin, her own name was clearly printed across its face. "This is mine?"

Mother Gertha pivoted with a gasp. "Nay," she protested.

"But it clearly bears my name," Elianne retorted in confusion.

The prioress's shoulders sagged. "Aye, it's yours. It was dictated to me by your natural half brother. At the same time he created this he also gave me his instructions for you. His desire was that you join our family."

"It's a will?" Beatrice asked in surprise.

Her hands shaking, Elianne pried up the wax, then opened the parchment. She read the first line. *To my sweet sister*. Grief again tore at her heart. The words blurred.

Josce held up his right hand. "Shall I read it for you?" he offered quietly.

With a grateful nod, Elianne handed it to him. His brow creased, Josce read, only to smile. "It is a will, Lianne. He leaves you, his only heir, ten virgates of farmland and a mill with a total income of ten pounds a year. It seems you're not penniless after all."

Horrified, Elianne took a backward step. Adelm hadn't had the means to purchase any lands, not unless he'd used what he'd stolen to do it. "I won't take it," she cried.

Josce shook his head. "It's not what you think, Lianne," he said quietly. "See here?"

With only one hand to use, he had to fold the parchment to the place he meant. Taking it from him, Elianne studied the area, using all she'd learned of Latin at the convent to pry the meaning of the words from the skin.

Know that what I pass to you through this vehicle is without taint of the wrong I have done in my life, having come to me through my dam's family, who it seems has known of me for all my life while I have known nothing of them, much to the detriment of my soul.

Scanning now, she read the description of property that followed, then her gaze shifted to the bottom of the document. Rather than a mark, Adelm had signed his name. So he'd learned more than pain from the monks.

Next to his signature were the marks of the witnesses. One of them had been Mother Gertha. Elianne lowered the skin to look at the prioress. "You witnessed this, yet a moment ago you told Josce I was penniless."

The line of the churchwoman's jaw was tight. Her arms were tightly folded over her chest. "I said your *father* left you penniless." Then her face softened. She stretched out a hand, imploring.

"When Sir Adelm came to me earlier, begging me to make him a will, he did so saying that he intended for you to take a position with us. Elianne, you cannot breed. Think on it. Both father and brother were thieves and murderers. Our Lord promises that the sins of the father are passed to his heirs. Come to us," she pleaded. "In our house you will find the peace that you need to save your soul."

"While you get the use of her inheritance," Josce shot back. "Which is this? An attempt to save Elianne from her sire's blood or a chance to further enrich your house?"

Mother Gertha ignored him to start around the table toward Elianne, yet beseeching. "I've seen what miracles you've worked at Coneytrop even as your sire spent all the profit you eked from it. Come to us and you'll take the position of cellaress. Think on it. Only Sister Nilda and I will be your betters."

Elianne frowned at her. "Where has Sister Amabella gone?"

Gertha's expression flattened. Her hand dropped to her side. "Sister Cellaress has chosen to become an anchorite for the good of her soul."

The horror of such a fate drove Elianne back a step. Mary save her, but Amabella wanted to be forever after bricked into a cell with only a slot through which food and wastes were transferred? The thought of never again running, swimming, not even to feel the sun upon her face or the breeze in her hair was beyond all toleration. Aye, but such were the things that nuns did.

Elianne turned to Josce. Again, he extended his arm to her. She accepted, leaning gently against his side. "How soon can we be wed?" she asked him.

His smile was alive with love for her. Desire sparked in his blue eyes. "The morrow cannot be soon enough."